Rebound
Kate Hawthorne

REBOUND

KATE HAWTHORNE

REBOUND

BY KATE HAWTHORNE

They say the best way to get over someone is to get under someone else...

At least that's what Ben is trying to convince himself. Ready to put his ex-boyfriend in the rear view for good, he connects with a handsome older man who's only interested in something quick and casual. Their rules are simple—no strings, no feelings, and absolutely no kissing.

Thomas has never been with a man before, but in the midst of divorcing his estranged wife, he knows it's something he is ready to act on. He's wondered for years if his attraction to men is something real, so hooking up with an experienced and gorgeous younger man seems like a surefire way to find out. Better yet, it'll kill two birds with one stone: exploring the depths of his midlife awakening and moving forward into a brand kind of new life.

One time together turns into two times, and two turns into something regular, but the rules still apply... until they don't.

Late night phone calls lead to early evening dinner dates, and one by one the rules are all out the window.

Ben was supposed to be Thomas's first time, and Thomas was supposed to be Ben's rebound...but what if the best way to get over someone is also the best way to fall in love?

———

CW: Narcissistic abuse that manifests as physical violence (toward inanimate objects) and cheating, none of which is *between* the main characters.

DEDICATION

For EM and the plot bunny that this story used to be.

CHAPTER 1
BEN

BEN TRACED his finger over the rim of his wine glass, eyes heavy with exhaustion and body sore from use. His boyfriend, Cody, sat across from him at the glass-top dining room table, an uneaten plate of food in front of him. It was a Friday night and, as had become their very short-lived tradition, Cody had grabbed Chinese takeout after work and brought it to Ben's apartment. They were going to eat, watch a movie, and fuck until they couldn't get hard.

It was Ben's idea of a perfect Friday night, but Cody's mood had already put a damper on the evening.

"It's like you're not even listening," Cody complained.

Ben *wasn't* listening. He didn't need to because it was a conversation they'd had at least half a dozen times in the past month. Not to mention they'd only been dating for a month to begin with, and the conversation—or, rather, the complaints— were already tired and old.

"I don't know what you want me to say."

"That you won't do it again."

"I didn't do anything," Ben said.

"I saw the way he looked at you when we were coming back upstairs," Cody accused.

"I can't control how other people look at me." Ben raised his wine glass to his lips and swallowed back the remainder of the contents. It was a large swallow, and he cleared his throat, wiping his thumb across the corner of his mouth to catch the stray droplets.

"Of course you're drinking instead of recognizing that you should have at the very least told him to stop looking at you like he wanted to eat you for dessert," Cody griped.

"Maybe if you drank a little more, we wouldn't have these arguments all the time," Ben suggested. "If you were a less high-strung, maybe you'd realize how ridiculous you sound. Like it's my place to monitor everyone's eyes."

"You're not being fun, baby. Come on, this is our thing," Cody coaxed, pushing his untouched plate toward the center of the table. It rucked up the table runner and nearly knocked over a burning candle. Ben wished he had more wine so, if Cody burned the building down, he wouldn't feel it.

"Our thing?"

"Our thing." Cody stood up and walked around the table. Ben slid his chair back and turned his body to meet Cody's approach. Their knees brushed together and where he used to feel a spark of excitement at the promise of Cody's touch, he only found ripples of unease and repulsion roll up his spine.

"What do you mean?" he asked.

"You deliberately do stuff to make me angry, we fight, then we make up."

Ben scrunched his nose, pushing his chair back to put space between them. "That's absurd. I don't do anything to make you angry—"

Cody interrupted him, "You do *a lot* to make me angry."

"I don't do anything to make you angry," he repeated. "Orb at least, nothing I do ever warrants this kind of anger. And yet you always offer it up."

"Our thing," Cody murmured again.

Ben didn't know what had changed over the past month, but he hated it. He'd met Cody at a bar. Out with friends to celebrate a birthday, Cody had been charming and suave, and he'd hooked Ben from the very first look. He'd leaned in a little too close, but not enough to make Ben feel uncomfortable, just enough for him to be sure Cody was really interested in him. Cody had held his hand a little too tight on their first real date, but again, it was a reminder, a promise. The first time they'd gone to bed together, Cody had taken his time. He'd been gracious and generous, and Ben thought that maybe this guy could be the one.

He couldn't have been more wrong.

But it wasn't so bad. There was a lot about Cody that Ben didn't like, and a few things he did, and while the balance wasn't even—it wasn't insurmountable. Even though they were well on their way. He knew there would be a time in the very near future where he no longer had it in him to tolerate Cody's behavior, let alone the ridiculous notion the constant negging and arguing was somehow *their thing*.

"But you know what?" Cody clapped his hands together and closed the space between them, climbing onto Ben's lap. Cody straddled him and ground against him until Ben's cock had no choice to do anything besides get hard.

"What?" he murmured, closing his eyes and letting his head fall backward. Cody took the movement as an invitation, leaning in and pressing a kiss against the column of Ben's throat.

"If you don't like it, we don't have to." Cody shifted his weight and reached between their bodies. His fingers made swift work of Ben's zipper and then the cool touch of Cody's palm wrapped around Ben's cock.

"Don't have to what?"

"Our thing."

Ben wanted to groan at the statement. The two words

together made perfect sense and none at the same time. Cody wasn't wrong that the fighting and the making up had become their thing, and he loved make-up sex as much as the next guy, but he definitely could have done without the vitriol Cody let loose on him in the heat of those moments.

"I like when we make up," he said, only to be rewarded with the curve of Cody's mouth into a smile against the side of his neck.

"Like this?" Cody pressed the edge of his thumb into the slit of Ben's dick, dragging it back and forth until precum beaded at the tip.

"Not so bad," he conceded.

But it was bad.

It was horrible, and he hated it, but then Cody kissed him and touched him, and he made up for the horrible things, and that was good. It was fine. It was plenty.

Until the next time.

It was a cycle he already hated, but he forgot about that when Cody climbed off his lap, fist still curled tightly around his dick. Ben stood, fighting against Cody's hold, and he let Cody lead him down the hallway and into the bedroom. He didn't complain or say no when Cody stripped him naked and pushed him back onto the bed, and he definitely didn't say stop when Cody removed his own clothes and joined him on the bed.

Ben offered no outward hint of discontent when Cody sheathed Ben's shaft with a condom, then opened the lube and poured a healthy amount over both of their dicks. Ben's erection was so hard it hurt, and he closed his eyes and wrapped his fingers around Cody's waist to hold him steady while he sank down around Ben's dick.

He let out a rough breath, letting Cody set the pace because Cody was good at setting the pace. Cody was good at being mean, but he was good at sucking dick, and he was great at getting Ben off. So Ben chose to focus on the heat of Cody's ass radiating through the condom, the tightness of Cody's muscles as he used Ben's cock to offer an apology. He ignored the hurtful accusations Cody had thrown at him over dinner, forgot about the food that had been wasted over the course of their argument, and instead he slipped into the void of pleasure Cody offered him.

Cody came with a strangled whimper. Hot jets of cum streaked out of his cock and across Ben's chest. He opened his eyes in time to see Cody lean forward and lick the salty mess from his chest, then right himself again and pick up the pace. His expression quickly shifted from pleasure to boredom, and Ben's cock softened. Not much, but enough for Cody to notice.

"This again?" Cody stilled, his fingers splayed apart on the lower part of Ben's stomach.

"Just..." He groaned, and shoved Cody off of him. Climbing off the bed, he tore off the condom and tied it in a knot out of habit. He carried it into the bathroom, tossed it in the small wire trash can, and locked the door. Ben opened the glass door of his shower and stepped inside, pulling it shut behind him. He listened to Cody try to follow after him, the sound of the knob meeting resistance at the lock, and then the rough slam of Cody's fist against the door.

Ben startled, pressing his shoulder against the tile wall on the far edge of the shower. He waited for the water to get hotter, waited for his skin to warm the grout work beneath his arm. Cody's pounding fists turned into softer knocks, and by the time the water ran cold, Ben was fairly certain Cody was gone.

He dried off, ignoring the blurry outline of his reflection beneath the steam in the mirror, and he sat on the closed lid of the toilet to gather his thoughts before unlocking the door. He assumed Cody had left, but he didn't know for sure. From the other end of the apartment, he heard a loud crash, and he feared his table had met the end of its life. He didn't want to go out and check. He didn't want to talk to Cody. He didn't want to say the things that now—more than ever—needed to be said.

Thankfully, he didn't have to do either because Cody came back to the bathroom, announcing his arrival with the thud of his fist against the still-locked door.

"I'm sorry, baby," Cody apologized. "Maybe I took it too far this time."

"What did you break?" he asked with a sigh.

"Just the bottle of wine. It was an accident."

Ben scrubbed a hand down the front of his face. He could feel the scratch of his beard growing in because he hadn't shaved since Wednesday. He'd been a swimmer most of his life, making varsity his sophomore year in high school and then swimming all through college. He could have gone to the Olympics, but he'd given sports the back seat his junior year and shifted his focus to something that wouldn't wreak havoc on his body and force him into an early retirement.

But he hadn't dropped the habits. He waxed his body, he ate well, he worked out as much as his schedule would allow, and he shaved his face daily, but Cody had been picking more fights than normal this week and Ben was tired. He wanted to get out of his apartment and go down to the basement pool. He wanted to swim and clear his mind, and forget he'd been dumb enough to get involved with a man like Cody.

The signs had been there from the first week, and he knew it would only get worse. Cody had gotten violent with the walls and the bedding, and now a half-empty bottle of wine, but never with Ben. He'd never worried about being physically in danger, but he watched his mental health slip by the wayside with every word out of Cody's mouth.

"I think you should go," he finally said.

"I put the glass in the trash," Cody answered, sounding as trite as his feigned sadness would allow. "I didn't want you to hurt yourself, baby."

"Please go."

"Can I see you tomorrow?" Cody asked. "I want to make it up to you."

Ben sighed. "Our thing?"

"See?" He could hear the smile in Cody's voice. "I knew you understood what I meant."

"I still think you should go for tonight," he said. "You should go cool down at your place."

"But I worry about you here all alone." Cody tried the door-knob again. "You didn't even come."

"I'll be fine."

"Can I see you tomorrow?"

Ben recognized the patterns. He knew Cody was on the downswing and his anger had subsided. He wasn't interested in fighting more; he wanted to kiss and make up. He wanted to snuggle and apologize and tell Ben that he only got so mad because he cared so much. It was abuse, and Ben knew it.

And yet he unlocked the door anyway.

Cody was there, his face the perfect picture of contrition. With the exception of the splash of red wine that stained the thigh of Cody's khakis, no one would know what the evening had been like for them. Ben wondered if people would believe him even if he said anything about it.

"Hey," Cody said to him, voice low and soft as he leaned in. It was the same gesture of closeness he'd used the night they met. The kind of surety that made it clear to Ben that Cody knew what he wanted and, before the night was through, he'd get it.

So, with that, Ben knew there'd be no breakup in his imme-diate future. He'd coddle Cody's ego and regroup in the morn-ing. Maybe with a clear head, he could decide the best way to end whatever the thing between them had become.

"You can't see me tomorrow," he said, cursing himself inter-nally as he stepped back into the hallway. "Just see me now."

CHAPTER 2
THOMAS

THE PEN in Thomas's hand had warmed under his fingers, and he twirled it in a casual circle while he watched Jennifer sign her side of all their divorce paperwork. His left ring finger bore a tan line from where the gold band had sat for the past twenty-something years and he hated the look of it. He'd hated the ring, but the absence of it hurt him differently.

"I hate when you do that," Jennifer muttered from across the table, clicking the end of the pen in her hand to retract it before tossing it in the broad space between them.

The conference room table at his lawyer's office was far larger than necessary, though he imagined in a contentious divorce having the space between parties would be absolutely necessary. He'd also noticed the pitcher of water and glasses a frazzled-looking secretary had brought in shortly after their arrival was made of plastic. Albeit the kind of plastic that was designed to look like glass, but plastic nonetheless. Thomas wondered if that had been common sense from the start or a hard-learned lesson.

"Do what?" he asked, throwing his pen alongside hers in the now insurmountable gap between them.

"Make that look so easy." She wiggled her fingers at him and leaned back in her chair with a soft sigh. "So, that's it then?"

A paralegal, whose name he'd never been able to remember, reached for the stapled pile of papers that Jennifer had finished signing and after a quick review, answered, "Yes. You're all set."

Thomas rubbed his hand down the length of his sternum, an unexpected frown pulling at the corners of his mouth. "That feels anticlimactic."

"Well, there's a waiting period," the paralegal reminded him.

"I know. Three months."

"I don't get the point of it," Jennifer said.

Thomas didn't either.

He and Jennifer had discussed the end of their relationship at length on more than one occasion. He hadn't needed more than one chance to talk about it, though. The repetition was all her. All of her apologies and backtracking, and Thomas would never admit he'd willingly decided to use her infidelity as an out. He had made up his mind before he'd even talked to her. When he'd found a condom in the trash can in their guest bathroom, even though the two of them hadn't used condoms since long before they'd had kids. When her face blanched at the question, pale as snow, before flooding red like she'd been burned. Thomas remembered with startling clarity the way Jennifer's hands shook when she'd offered him her first apology.

She'd given him so many, they didn't shake anymore.

It wasn't that they had an unhappy marriage, either. They'd grown complacent over the years, familiar maybe. He'd always thought things were comfortable, but Jennifer had apparently been bored. Bored enough to set up a profile on a married-and-cheating app. Bored enough to go suck dick in hotel penthouses. Bored enough to think she could get away with bringing a man into their home and fucking him in their bed.

"Did you want to get caught?" he asked her, frown straightening into a tight line. It was the first time he'd had the thought and it hit him like a freight train right between the eyes.

He'd spent plenty of time over the past decade fantasizing about what a life without Jennifer would look like. There were things he'd come to understand about himself over the course of his life that he wanted to explore, but knew he never could. Because he was married. To a woman. So the thoughts had remained fantasies, nothing more. He'd never once thought to go behind his wife's back and act on them. That would have been careless and brazen, and yet Jennifer had done just that.

"What?"

"Did you want to get caught?" he asked again.

The paralegal who'd reviewed their signatures reached between them and slowly pulled the pens toward her, then the plastic pitcher, and the two glasses.

Jennifer opened her mouth to speak, but no words came out, and Thomas had seen enough of her apologies to know that was answer enough.

"It's fine," he assured her. "You know, I wish we could have talked about how bad things had gotten before you did what you did."

He was a hypocrite, he knew. Because he'd never spoken to her about the ideas in *his* head, and now he would never have to.

"Thomas, I'm sorry," she said gently, her hands still steady, clasped together in front of her. Now instead of having a matching wedding set, they had matching tan lines. The absence of a whole life lived together, and for what?

Nothing.

"I said it's fine." He turned to the paralegal. "Are we done? What happens next?"

"Nothing, honestly." She looked down at the paperwork and used her fingers to do some quick math. "The two of you wait it out and when May 10th rolls around, you're single in the eyes of the court."

"May 10th."

Thomas snorted, pushing his chair back so he could get up and leave. The room was obscenely large to accommodate the table that could have been used to lay out strategic attacks in a world war, but it felt small in that moment, nearly claustrophobic. He needed air. He needed to be away from his wife—his almost ex-wife, rather. He needed to get back to his apartment that would never feel like home and try to decide what the rest of his life looked like.

"That'll be a nice birthday present for you," she said.

He wanted to snap at her, to tell her this wasn't ever what he'd wanted, even though he'd asked for it. Thomas would have gladly gone on blindly, married to the woman he'd built a life with, built a home with, raised kids with. He would have never breathed life to the ideas that rattled around in the back corners of his brain. He would have never thought her capable of the things she'd done. And while part of him felt like he should be mad about it, like he should resent her for what she'd done, he found himself thankful.

Thomas was…relieved.

"Well, since you haven't gotten me one in years, I'll take it." He checked his pockets out of reflex, making sure he had his wallet, his phone, and his keys. He said goodbye to Jennifer, hopefully for the last time, and made quick work of getting to the parking garage.

He supposed it was a blessing that their children were grown and he wouldn't have to deal with custody arrangements and seeing Jennifer every week to trade them off. And it wasn't that he held any animosity toward his wife. He just…didn't want to deal with her anymore. The life they'd shared was no longer his.

Getting to the paperwork had been a long time coming because they'd made the decision long before pulling the actual trigger. They sold the house they'd owned since just after their youngest child was born, separated their finances, and settled into the tedious process of starting over. It was a shock to go from a two-thousand square foot ranch house filled with comfortable furniture and decades of memories into a small apartment with one bedroom and a noticeable lack of windows, but he'd done the best he could.

Thomas tried to find the best in the situation, immediately buying all of the plants he'd always wanted, but Jennifer never had. He painted the bedroom black, another thing she'd been adamantly against. He liked the neutrality of the color and the way it made the room feel small and cool. He appreciated the way his white down comforter—another thing she'd never liked—looked like it glowed on his bed for how bright it was. The separation gave Thomas the chance to make his home *his*.

Jennifer had taken her half of the proceeds from the sale of the house and put it down on a condo in the city, which seemed to suit her just fine. He'd not seen the place, and he didn't think he ever would, but that didn't stop her from telling him about it. He realized Jennifer wanted to stay in his life, wanted to be friends. He didn't blame her for that. He sometimes found himself wanting to tell her about his day or something funny he'd seen on TV. But that wasn't their relationship anymore.

He honestly didn't know if they'd ever have that kind of relationship. Thomas wouldn't close the door on it with no reason, but he knew it was important for them both to embrace the separation in order to learn what it meant to be single again. So much of his identity and his personality had become tangled up with hers that it was hard to unlearn things and re-learn them in a way that felt authentic. But every day that passed, Thomas found himself feeling more comfortable with the path his life had taken.

He picked up some fried chicken at a drive-through on his way home and let out a long breath once he finally stepped back into his apartment. Even though they'd decided to separate months before, and even though the divorce wasn't final for another three months, he already felt an unexpected sense of relief. Tension he didn't realize he'd been holding rippled out like it was being unrolled, shaking from the center of his spine and out, through his bones and nerves and out his fingertips.

Thomas set his dinner on the small dinette table tucked by the window and let his body lean into the shiver, releasing whatever energy his body was trying to part with. Gooseflesh broke out up the length of his arms and he blew air out of his lips so forcefully it made a sound like he was cold. Jennifer hated when he did that. But Jennifer wasn't his wife anymore and Jennifer wasn't there, so he did it again.

And again.

One more time until the hairs on his arms settled, and he was left feeling silly and alone.

"You got this," he told himself.

Thomas didn't bother to get a fork from the kitchen. There was no point in making dirty dishes. He sat down at the table and unwrapped the small plastic spork the restaurant had provided and set to eating. The chicken was good, better than Jennifer's if he was being honest, and he ate until he was full.

While he did everything he could to appreciate the change his life had taken, he still found himself lonely sometimes at night. He threw away the trash from his meal and took a quick shower, washing off all of the complicated and messy ways the appointment at the lawyer's office had made him feel. Thomas grabbed some basketball shorts from his dresser and pulled them on, padding back to the living room barefoot to watch TV until he got tired.

He briefly thought about reaching out to one of his kids, but Dakota and Kenzie had both been moderately icy with him *and* Jennifer about the divorce. Before telling their kids, the two of them had agreed that neither of them would disclose her infidelity. Their divorce didn't require anyone to pick sides and he wasn't interested in turning the kids against her. They were both grown and had their own lives to worry about. To them, the separation came out of left field and, in a way, it had.

They'd spent one last Christmas together before he and Jennifer put the house on the market. His daughter, Kenzie, had dealt with packing up both her things and her brother's, since he couldn't be bothered. He'd taken the separation the hardest, for some reason making the assumption that Thomas was the one who'd been unfaithful, acting like he'd somehow wronged Jennifer in ways so bad they didn't dare speak of it.

Thomas didn't attempt to defend himself because he and Jennifer had agreed to keep her secret. At the time, he hadn't foreseen the blowback they were getting. It wasn't fair for him to bear the brunt of his kids' blame, but he'd manage it. Maybe when more time passed, he and Jennifer would talk about telling the truth.

But until then.

His life was what it was.

Whatever show he had on ended, the characters and plot blurring into the episode that followed, and the one after that. Thomas realized he wasn't even paying attention. Instead, his mind had wandered to the secrets *he* himself kept. The ones he'd never dared speak out loud.

"It's fine," he assured himself, reaching for his phone. His palm slicked clammy and nervous sweat against the back of the casing as he waited for the facial recognition to unlock the home screen. "No one knows, and even if they did, it's not like it was before."

He swiped through his apps until he reached the last page, the last app he'd downloaded. The one that had been sitting there for weeks, ignored.

"It's okay to want this," he whispered, pressing the pad of his finger down against the icon. "It's okay to want to know what it's like to be with another man."

CHAPTER 3
BEN

BEN STARED at the chain lock on his door, watching it rattle against the wood with every thump of Cody's fist against the frame.

"I'm going to call the cops," he said.

Ben sat on the floor in the entryway of his apartment, knees pulled up to his chest and his palm flat against the door. He could feel the vibrations of Cody's incessant pounding travel up through his forearm and into his shoulder.

"Baby, just let me in so we can talk," Cody pleaded.

"I don't want to talk. I'm done talking."

"You know I'd never hit you, right?"

Ben let his hand fall away from the door, his wrist hanging limp over his knee. The denim of his jeans felt like sandpaper against his skin and he dropped his head against the wall with a thud.

"It doesn't matter," he said. "Enough is enough."

"Are you breaking up with me?" Cody sounded mad, and the door rattled as it was hit again from the outside.

"We aren't even really..." Ben sighed, changing his tactic. "Yes."

"It's Valentine's Day," Cody reminded me,

"Okay." He looked up at the dinner he'd made for them, spread across the table and untouched. Two white taper candles sat as the centerpiece, the wax burning down and pooling on the glass top of the table. Ben had always fancied himself to be a romantic person, but Cody was clearly not cut out for that and wasn't deserving of Ben's attentions anyway.

After their fight two weeks before, things had been relatively calm, but that had only lulled Ben into a false sense of security. He thought that, for the first time, Cody had taken him seriously when he'd said he wanted things to change. Ben had fallen for the act all over again. He was the one who'd suggested they stay in for Valentine's Day. He wanted to cook, and he wanted to be away from prying eyes and close to a bed. He didn't want his boyfriend—or whoever Cody was—to show up with a hickey peeking out of the collar of his shirt.

A hickey from someone who definitely wasn't Ben.

"Let me come in so we can talk," Cody begged again.

"There's nothing else to say." Ben closed his eyes. "Whatever this is between us is over. I don't want to do it anymore."

"Baby. What if I do?"

"It honestly doesn't matter. Because I don't. You can go be with whoever left that bruise on your neck for all I care, but if you don't leave, I *will* call the police."

Cody started to argue with him, but Ben was done. He stood up, double-checked the locks and went into the other room. He climbed into bed, fully dressed, and turned on the TV. He made it about ten minutes into a true crime documentary before turning off the TV and attempting to smother himself with a pillow. Thankfully, the noise from the front hallway had quieted down, so he decided to go make sure Cody had left.

A quick look through the peephole didn't reveal anyone in the hall, but Ben wanted to be certain. He undid the locks and stuck his head out, finding the hallway empty, save for the battered roses Cody had brought for him. Upon seeing the hickey, Ben shoved them right into Cody's chest and kept the momentum going to push him right out the door.

Cody had left the roses discarded on the doormat, which almost seemed like a waste. Ben bent down and picked them up, re-locking his doors and taking the bouquet into the kitchen. When all was said and done, he'd been able to save four of the twelve roses, and he trimmed the stems before dropping them into a pint glass filled with water. He didn't have a vase, he realized, which felt weird. He'd have to pick one up the next time he went to the store.

Ben didn't want the dinner he'd made—roasted chicken and twice-baked potatoes—to go to waste, so he poured himself a glass of wine and sat down at his table for the saddest Valentine's Day dinner in the history of Valentine's Day dinners. The chicken was perfect, as he knew it would be because the recipe he used had belonged to his grandmother. He'd grown up loving her roasted chicken, but she only made it the first Sunday of the month so it was like a treat. She'd refused to give Ben's mom the recipe, instead willing it to Ben when she passed with the caveat he wasn't allowed to share it with anyone besides the person he wanted to marry.

Even back then, he realized his sexuality was a giveaway for the people closest to him. He made it through high school with a lot of ideas about what it meant to be gay, and by the time he reached college, he'd recognized he didn't want to have to choose. With one leg on either side of the line, Ben came out to his grandmother as bisexual before he'd confessed to anyone else. He knew she wouldn't care. She'd always been kind and loving, and she scoffed at his admission, asking if he would have felt the need to tell her if he was straight. The answer was, of course, no, and so with that, she waved off his confession and went on from there.

Things hadn't gone as well with his parents, but they'd come around. His mom's biggest concern had always been getting grandchildren, which he assured her could happen regardless of whether he married a man or a woman, or even if he didn't marry at all. She remained unconvinced, especially of the latter, but that was all for another day, she'd told him. Either way, he knew Cody wasn't ever going to get his eyes on the roasted chicken recipe, but Ben hadn't seen the harm in cooking it for him. He liked it himself and had never maintained his grandmother's cooking cadence anyway.

As the night crept on, Ben washed the dishes and scraped the wax off his table. He took out the trash, he drank a bottle of wine, and then he decided to make a very bad decision. He opened One-Night and turned on his location. Ben had never shied away from a casual hookup, and with the wine pumping through his veins, he was just buzzed enough to go for the gold. He knew that anyone online at 10 p.m. on Valentine's Day was going to be in the market for one thing and one thing only—and that was perfect for him. Hell, he'd even host.

Ben carried his phone into the bedroom so he could check his nightstand for condoms and lube, then he sat on the edge of his mattress, and started to scroll. There wasn't really anyone who interested him and he was just about ready to call it a night when a direct message pinged into his chat box.

"Original," he muttered to himself, swiping to the guy's profile and checking the user name. "TM45968. Whatever that stands for."

The man was attractive, even though he definitely didn't know his angles and had no idea how to take a flattering selfie. He looked a little older and he had a definite dad bod with a soft layer of skin that wrapped his stomach and puffed out over the top of his jeans. It was a shirtless picture and the man was tanned, with a sparse patch of salt and pepper hair that covered his chest, matched with a darker happy trail that disappeared into his pants.

You up? the message asked.

Ben frowned down at his flaccid cock between his legs and answered, *Not yet, but I could be.*

He was rewarded with a smile and three flickering dots, indicating the user was typing a longer message. Ben could tell the guy was close, his location showing up less than a mile away on the app tracker, which would prove extremely useful if the rest of the conversation went well.

TM45968: *You're cute. Hot, actually.*
BenO22: *You are too.*
TM45968: *You're close.*
BenO22: *To you, yeah.*
TM45968: *Can I ask your name?*
BenO22: *Ben, obviously :) - what about you?*
TM45968: *Thomas.*
BenO22: *I can host. I'm neg and DDF.*
TM45968: *DDF? Sorry, I'm a little old and don't know all the slang.*
BenO22: *Disease and drug free.*
TM45968: *Oh, God, that's embarrassing, so am I. So am I.*
BenO22: *Good. That's fine. I use condoms anyway. Do you want to come over? I'm not looking for anything serious. Just feeling lonely tonight.*
TM45968: *Do you bottom?*
BenO22: *I can. If you give me half an hour.*
TM45968: *What's your address?*

Ben sent Thomas his address and tossed his phone onto the bed without a second thought. He stripped on his way to the bathroom, turning the water in the shower to room temperature so he could get himself cleaned out. It took two tries for the water to run clear and he knew eating that entire Valentine's meal on his own had been a bad idea. If only he had the foresight...but he rinsed a third time just to be safe, holding the water in until his stomach cramped from the fullness.

After he finished, he switched the water to his normal shower head and gave himself a quick wash, paying extra attention, of course, to his ass and balls. He had the feeling whatever Thomas was after would be very wham bam, thank you, ma'am, for lack of a better term, but he still wanted to make sure he was clean and ready.

Ben's cock began to harden while he dried off, thinking about how long it had been since he'd bottomed. Cody preferred to bottom, and by prefer, it was the only thing he ever did. It didn't bother Ben, even though he did appreciate the variety of a versatile relationship when it presented itself. He thought back and realized it must have been at least six months since he'd been with a partner willing to top.

A spark of fear-laced anticipation ran up the length of his spine. There was always a little worry before he bottomed. For as long as he'd been active with men, the way Ben loved and loathed the stretching burn of penetration had never quite worn off. His dick leaked against his hand, and he stepped into a pair of black shorts that did nothing to hide the way his erection tented the fabric. Ben pulled on a clean white undershirt, tore a condom off the strip in his nightstand and tossed it on the pillow. Then… he waited.

Half an hour on the dot after their last message, someone knocked at his door. Ben found himself faced with a brief fight-or-flight moment when he thought it might be Cody there, but a look through the peephole showed it was Thomas. At least, he assumed it was Thomas. The man didn't have any pictures on the profile that showed his face, but the body type looked right.

He pulled open the door, dragging in a strong whiff of Thomas's cedar-smelling cologne as he did.

"Are you Thomas?" he asked.

"You're Ben." Thomas's voice was a rumbling baritone that did nothing to quell the way Ben's cock throbbed in his shorts.

"Come in." He stepped out of the way and closed the door

after Thomas joined him inside. The man was older, like Ben had guessed, but that wasn't a problem. Ben appreciated a little seasoned experience now and then. And Thomas was handsome, classically and in every other way imaginable.

"Do you want a drink or something?" he asked. "We can talk or get comfortable first?"

Thomas scratched at his temple, looking around Ben's apartment with a nervous interest before his stare settled on the bulge between Ben's legs.

"How old are you?" Thomas asked him.

"Twenty-eight," he answered. "Is that a problem?"

"I'm older than you."

"With age comes experience," Ben said. His dick *hurt*, and he flattened it down with the heel of his palm. He barely stifled a groan and found himself hoping that Thomas didn't want to drink or talk after all.

Thomas's eyes tracked Ben's hand down between his legs, and his mouth twitched into the briefest hint of a smirk before falling away.

"No," Thomas answered him. "I don't want a drink."

CHAPTER 4
THOMAS

"DID you want me to show you the bedroom?" Ben asked.

Thomas swallowed down all of his apprehension and fear, wishing he could zap it from his bones, and answered Ben with a jerky nod. He had no idea what he was doing, no idea why he thought it had been a good idea to tell this ridiculously out-of-his-league younger man that he wanted to go to bed with him.

Thomas had spent nearly a week scrolling through One-Night, never quite ready to reach out to anyone, and no one had reached out to him either. But it was Valentine's Day and he was lonely, and apparently Ben was lonely too, and Thomas didn't really see the harm in taking care of his virginity once and for all. Not that he was really a virgin. He'd been with Jennifer for years, and girls before her too. He'd just never been with a man, and while he knew porn wasn't a fair indicator of what actual male-on-male intercourse was, he was fairly certain he'd be able to pick up the logistics of it.

"How do you feel about kissing?" Ben asked when they reached the bedroom. The room was small but cute, plain white walls decorated with ornately framed paintings and art. The bed was simple, and the nightstand and dresser looked like they were from a box store.

What a weird thing, Thomas thought to himself, that Ben only had one nightstand. Even after moving out of the house and buying new furniture to begin the next chapter in his life as a single man, Thomas had bought matching nightstands. He hadn't thought twice about it until seeing Ben's single nightstand on the side of the bed that he clearly chose to sleep on.

As for the question, he had a lot of feelings about kissing in that he'd never kissed a man, and that felt like it should be a special thing. Not that sex shouldn't be special, and he assumed it would be...the next time. Or worst case, the time after that.

"I'd rather not," he answered.

Ben reached behind him and balled his shirt in his hands, rucking it up and over his head before tossing it onto the floor between their feet.

"That's fine."

Thomas's shoulders sagged with relief that kissing wasn't a deal breaker, and he matched Ben's movements, taking off his own shirt and casting it aside. His gaze raked over the sharp angles and lines of Ben's body, and Thomas fought to not feel self-conscious about his own. He was older, he had more life on him, but it was hard to not compare. He knew picking out a guy like Ben might have ended poorly for him. It could still end poorly, but he tried to ignore that. Ben was considerably younger, extremely good looking, and clearly experienced. Most importantly though, he didn't want attachments, and neither did Thomas. Ben, for all of his benefits and leaps beyond Thomas's league, was safe.

"Are you nervous?" Ben asked him.

"A little," he confessed. "I don't make a habit of this."

Ben grinned and teased his fingers along the waistband of his shorts. "Should I feel special?"

Yes, Thomas thought emphatically, but he knew he couldn't tell Ben why, so he answered with a casual shrug.

"So, no kissing," Ben said, taking a step back toward the bed. "Any other limits?"

"I don't think so. You?"

"Just don't spit on me." Ben shoved his shorts down, revealing a thick cock that bounced toward his stomach after snapping past the elastic waistband. Thomas tried really hard not to stare, but it was the first time he'd looked at another man's cock in real life with a sexual intent.

He wanted to appreciate the moment, maybe savor it a little. And if he'd had any lingering doubt about his attraction to men, the way he got lightheaded when all of the blood in his body raced toward his dick eliminated it all. He popped open the button of his jeans and reached behind his underwear to palm his cock, unable to stop the groan that left his mouth.

"Do you like what you see, then?" Ben's voice was heavy with teasing.

"Very much."

"How do you feel about sucking cock?"

Thomas swallowed, another flare of nervous energy shooting up his spine. "Mine or yours?"

"Either?" Ben shrugged. "Both."

He didn't think he so much wanted to suck Ben's cock as he wanted to touch it and see it up close. He wanted to maybe lick it and taste it, explore the landscape of it. Ben shaved—or waxed—and the base of his cock disappeared right into a hairless swatch of skin as taut and tanned as the rest of him. Thomas wondered what he tasted like *there*, if Ben was salty or sweet, or if he'd taste like soap or sweat.

"We can try it," he said.

"Not big on foreplay, then?" Ben backed up to the bed until his legs hit the mattress. With his cock in one hand, he gestured for Thomas to come closer with the other.

Thomas's pants were still on and his cock ached for how hard it pressed against the zipper of his jeans. But he went to

Ben anyway and awkwardly lowered himself to his knees. Ben's cock bobbed in front of him, eye level and smelling like a surprisingly delicate floral soap. He didn't know what he'd expected, but somehow it wasn't that.

"Not rough, though," he said gently, taking Ben's cock into his hand.

The feel of an erection in his fist wasn't new. He'd spent a lifetime jerking himself off, but this cock wasn't his. The orgasm wouldn't be his. Thomas knew he had no idea what he was about to do, but he was eager and curious. He licked Ben's shaft from root to tip, then dragged his tongue around the underside of the flared tip. Ben grunted and steadied his hand on top of Thomas's head without grabbing or pulling.

Thomas made the decision to suck Ben's cock the way he liked his own cock sucked. Jennifer had been amazing at blow jobs until she decided she didn't like them anymore, so he did his best to wrap his lips around Ben's dick with the kind of gusto the event deserved.

"Shit." Ben shuddered when Thomas's lips wrapped around the head, and his fingers flexed against Thomas's hair.

He slid down Ben's length, using his tongue and as much spit as his mouth could manage. When Ben's cock thickened against the roof of his mouth and his hips began to pump in time with Thomas's movements, his own cock leaked against his underwear. He was good at it, or good enough. He was making Ben feel good, but more than that...

Thomas liked sucking dick.

He really liked it.

"Stop, stop," Ben rasped, tapping Thomas's head until he stilled.

Thomas's lips felt as swollen as his dick, and he looked up at Ben with one hand down his pants.

"I don't want to come yet." Ben's eyes rolled as he said it, like he hated the words more than anything in his life. "Let me suck you before we fuck. Can I?"

Thomas prayed his joints wouldn't crack as he stood up, but even if they had, the sound would have been lost beneath the positively ravenous sound that came out of Ben's mouth as he went to his knees. Ben made quick work of his pants, shoving them down to his ankles at the same time he swallowed the entirety of Thomas's erection into the back of his mouth.

"Shit." The curse left his lips like a prayer. His knees swayed, and Ben grabbed him around the hips, holding him upright while he used his mouth to lubricate Thomas's shaft. God, it had been so long since someone had sucked his cock. He didn't know if he'd forgotten how good it felt, or if it felt better because it was a man, but Ben didn't give him time to think about it.

A hot tongue swirled around the curve of his crown, snaking through his slit before Ben flattened it out and licked his way straight down to the salt and pepper curls around the base of Thomas's dick. It was good. Better than good, and he wished it was any other night, any other place, where he could do nothing besides take turns sucking and being sucked.

Before Thomas was able to stop him, Ben ended it on his own. He practically crawled up the length of Thomas's body and slid past him onto the bed.

"I don't want to come on my knees," Ben explained, arranging himself onto all fours and reaching for a bottle of lube on the nightstand. Thomas watched with rapt attention as Ben poured some lube onto his fingers, then reached back to tease at his own asshole. He moaned when he entered himself, back arched. "I love sucking cock, but I want you to fuck me."

Thomas could have happily spent the night watching Ben fuck his own hole open with his fingers, but again, that wasn't what he'd come over for. He'd come over to fuck. To lose his virginity.

He tried to play it cool and not fumble the condom application, but watching Ben writhe around the bed, impaled on his own fingers, was almost too much for him to survive. Thomas climbed onto the bed behind him and rubbed the latex-covered head of his dick against Ben's slick knuckles.

"Let me in, then," he whispered.

Ben withdrew his hand and dropped his head against the pillow with a groan. "There you are."

"What?" Thomas had barely heard him, his mind emptying when his eyes fell onto the shiny pink gape of Ben's hole. He pressed the head of his cock against the entrance, hesitating.

"I love a good talker," Ben said over his shoulder. "Dirty talk is so hot, but you don't say much at all, do you?"

Thomas tightened his hand around the base of his cock, doing his best to stifle the blood flow. Much like the other secrets he had to keep to himself, he couldn't tell Ben that he loved vocal sex, from both ways, but he had to keep his mouth shut because he was nervous, because he didn't want the adrenaline to make him fill the condom before his cock even made it inside.

"Sometimes," he admitted.

Ben shoved the bottle of lube toward him, and Thomas took it for the cue it was. He knew assholes didn't lubricate themselves. Thomas raised the bottle over his shaft and drizzled lube down, letting some of it slick over Ben's crack and run down around the head of Thomas's dick. He fisted himself, slicked the entire length of his cock and returned the tip to Ben's pucker.

"You ready?" he asked, unsure if he was asking Ben or himself.

"Do what you came here to do, Thomas, and fuck me."

Thomas pumped his hips, the head of his dick breaching Ben's achingly tight asshole. He stuttered as his cock popped through that searing hot ring of muscle, stilling so he could talk himself back from the embarrassment of a premature orgasm.

"You're thick," Ben whined.

Thomas eased his hips forward, in awe of the way Ben's body flexed and stretched around him. He kept going until he was fully seated, bracketing his hands around Ben's slender waist to get his bearings.

There.

He'd done it.

He'd had sex with a man.

Rather…he was about to.

"Please move." Ben fisted the sheets in his hand, pressing his cheek against the pillow with his eyes squeezed shut tight.

"Am I hurting you?"

"It's been a while since I've bottomed. It just takes some getting used to," Ben answered, lashes fluttering open. "Please just move. It helps. Just…"

Thomas pulled his body away, the length of his cock almost fully leaving Ben's body. He snapped forward, hips burying him back inside with more certainty than the first go. Ben's voice left him, and Thomas took over. He fucked into Ben with rough and short thrusts, the way *he* liked the best. Ben's hole gripped him tighter and tighter until Thomas worried he was going to lose circulation.

Sweat broke out on his temples and dripped down his face from the exertion, splattering against the top of Ben's ass. It was good. Better than good, but Thomas wanted more. He wanted to get deeper.

"Roll over," he grunted, tapping Ben's waist.

His cock slid out as Ben flopped onto his back, but he moved quickly and Thomas guided himself back inside. Like muscle memory, he took one of Ben's legs over his shoulder and surged forward, burying himself deeper than the last position allowed. Ben cried out, fingers digging into Thomas's back as he renewed his brutal pace. Now his sweat dripped against Ben's chest, and he could feel the way Ben's breath puffed out against his cheek every time Thomas bottomed out inside of him.

Ben reached between their bodies and took his cock into his fist, jacking himself off frantically as Thomas chased after his own orgasm.

"I'm close," Thomas warned, straightening his back and circling his hips as his breathing turned frenetic.

"Come, then."

A few more pumps of his hips and Thomas's orgasm crested, washing over him like a tidal wave. He stilled, buried deep inside of another man's body, and he spurted hot jets of cum into the tip of the condom. Thomas opened his mouth and tipped his head back, but no sound came out, only his ragged breath. Beneath him, Ben's fist still worked, and Thomas's eyes closed, focusing on the way Ben was moving their joined bodies with the force of his hand.

"Oh," Ben keened, back arching and hole tightening around Thomas's still pulsating dick. "Oh!"

Thomas watched as Ben came, unsure of where to look and wanting to see everything all at the same time. Ben's cheeks turned pink, shining under the dim ceiling light in the bedroom. His knuckles were white for how tightly he squeezed himself, his cock nearly purple from the pressure. Ben came with a shout, arching off the bed as streaks of cum painted the length of his obscenely sculpted torso and chest.

"Holy shit," Thomas muttered, dropping his weight onto his heels. Ben's hand kept moving until he shuddered so violently, his body ripped away from Thomas's barely softening cock.

Thomas pulled the condom down his length and tied it off, holding it in his fist as Ben caught his breath on the bed.

"I'll be right back," he said, scooting to the edge of the bed and then off. "Gonna throw this condom away."

Ben flung an arm over his face and nodded.

Thomas stood and looked down, wanting more than

anything to drag his finger through the mess on Ben's chest and taste his cum, but he also didn't want Ben to open his eyes. He'd done what he intended to do, and there was no need to make the rest of it weird. Ben kept his arm over his eyes, and Thomas quietly collected his clothes from the floor and snuck out of the bedroom.

He *did* throw the condom away.

But he also got dressed, and then he saw himself out.

CHAPTER 5
BEN

BEN RECOGNIZED the sound of his front door closing. He'd heard it enough over the past few months with all the slamming of it Cody had done. But Thomas didn't slam it. Not even close. He tried to close it so softly that Ben wouldn't even hear it. But he had. It was a shame that Thomas left so quickly—and without a word—because Ben would have gladly gone another round if Thomas had been up for it. Though, he suspected that wouldn't have been the case. They would have had to talk and look at each other during the recovery period, and Thomas seemed like he didn't even want to be in the same room as Ben half the time.

But Thomas definitely sucked cock like he wanted it.

With a tired grunt, Ben reached down and fisted his cock, still half-hard from the ferocity of his orgasm. His chest sat messy with drying cum and their mixed sweat, and he would have loved to wash the lube and salt away from both of their bodies, but he'd have to do it on his own.

When he stood, Ben winced, having forgotten how delicious the ache between his ass cheeks after a good fucking could feel. For no reason, he reached back and touched his hole. The skin was puffy beneath his fingers and still slippery from all the lube.

His finger would have pushed right inside if he'd tried, but coming alone had suddenly lost some of its appeal.

He took a quick enough shower, making sure he was as clean as he'd been before Thomas's arrival, then he climbed into bed. The night hadn't been anywhere near the loss he'd feared, and he swiped open to One-Night to fire off a quick message to Thomas.

BenO22: *Thanks for the orgasm.*
BenO22: *If you want me to return the favor sometime, you know where to find me.*

He was shocked to find Thomas replied.

TM45968: *You came while I was inside of you.*
BenO22: *Oh, I remember. I meant if you wanted to bottom. Do you ever flip?*
TM45968: *No.*
BenO22: *Well...if you want to fuck me again, I wouldn't tell you no.*
TM45968: *What about blow jobs??*
BenO22: *You're hot, Thomas. Nothing is off the table.*
TM45968: *Except spit*
BenO22: *Except spit.*
BenO22: *Goodnight, Thomas.*

Ben plugged his phone into the charger and set it on do not disturb. He'd never been a good sleeper and the annoying app notification vibrations were always loud enough to jostle him awake. He'd wait to see if Thomas had anything else to say in the morning, and Ben fell asleep hoping that he did.

Seven restful hours later, Ben woke up to the sun streaming through the slats of the horizontal blinds on the opposite wall of his bedroom. He needed curtains. He'd repeatedly said he wanted to get curtains, but always managed to forget them when he was at the store. He checked his phone to find Thomas had read his message, but hadn't replied. Ben tried to not feel bristled over the brush-off, but it was hard. They'd both agreed the hookup was only supposed to be casual, and it was very much unlike him to feel so attached to someone.

Especially on the tail end of everything that happened with Cody, Ben was looking for a rebound and nothing more.

While he brewed a cup of coffee, he texted his best friend, Lara.

Ben: *What are you doing today, slut?*
Lara: *Slutty things, ofc. You?*
Ben: *Need to buy curtains. Want to come?*
Lara: *Is this a sex thing?*
Ben: *No, just real curtains.*
Lara: *Let me check w/ the mister.*

Ben and Lara met in college and had been relatively inseparable ever since. In fact, it was Ben's meddling that had caused Lara and her husband, Spencer, to meet. It was a story she loved to tell, even if it made Ben look a little bit like a crazy person sometimes.

His coffee pot chirped at him at the same time his phone vibrated across the counter. He took a drink, then read Lara's text.

Lara: *Mister is doing car thing. Where do they sell curtains?*
Ben: *I hoped you would know.*
Lara: *I'm heterosexual, Benjamin.*
Ben: *Just come over then and I'll figure it out.*
Lara: *I need to wash my hair.*
Ben: *I'll see you when you're here.*

He left his phone on the counter and took his coffee into the living room. Collapsing gently onto his couch, he tucked his legs up beneath him and leaned against the arm while he waited for his streaming channel menu to populate on the screen. He put on something mindless because he didn't want to get sucked in knowing Lara was on her way…or that she would be eventually. It didn't matter, though. He could have put on the most riveting show on television and it wouldn't have been enough to distract him from the memory of Thomas's thick cock in his ass the night before.

Thankfully, Lara arrived before he could spiral too far back into the memory and he made her drive since she'd just bought a new Audi a few months before. She swore it had been a Christmas present, but he recognized the lie in her eye when she said it. Fact of the matter was, Lara had a lot more money than him, and her husband had more than both of them put together. She'd worked hard to have a comfortable life before meeting her husband, but she never wanted Ben to feel uncomfortable about the gap in their incomes.

After a quick stop at Starbucks, they pulled up to Target, which amused Ben to no end.

"Target?" he asked, pushing his sunglasses onto the top of his head. "That's surprising."

"Did you think I was going to take you to Ethan Allen?" Lara shoved her door open. "I told you to make a list of stores and you came up empty, so I'm just doing the best I can."

Ben laughed and followed Lara into the store, taking a cart because he knew full well he was going to probably leave with a thousand things he didn't need and not one single curtain panel.

"You look distracted," Lara mentioned as they rounded the corner into the makeup section.

"Do I?"

She nodded and reached for a dark red shade of lipstick, which she examined and then returned to the shelf.

"I'm fine," he said.

"Does this have to do with Cody?"

"Absolutely not," he swore, crossing his heart. "But also kind of."

Ben realized the official breaking point with Cody was so fresh he hadn't had time to tell Lara about it. He gave her a quick rundown of the fight the night before, hoping she would drop it when he finished his monologue with an extremely convincing, "I don't do cheaters."

"Cool, Ben, but what about all the narcissistic abuse? Can we not do that anymore either?"

Beneath the weight of her question, his cheeks heated with shame and embarrassment. He rolled the cart to the end of the aisle, walking away from her before she could see his face. She ran to catch up to the cart, her fingers curling around the handle and dragging him to a stop.

"I only say it because I love you." Her eyes dripped with sincerity and concern, and he sighed, shoulder-checking her into an end cap of Chapstick.

"I know. It's...I just don't want to talk about him. He was a bad decision and now he's just a blip on the radar."

"I believe you." She covered his hand with hers. "So tell me what has you floating in another galaxy then."

"Am I that obvious?"

"Did you meet someone else already?" she asked.

"Kind of. Not exactly."

"Well." Lara took the cart out of his control and headed toward the home goods section. "That sounds like it requires elaboration."

"I was feeling a little sorry for myself last night, so I went on One-Night and had a hookup."

"Go you." Lara came to a stop in front of some picture frames, picking them up one after another, only to examine them and return them back to the shelf.

"He was older. Really attractive." Ben leaned in close and whispered, "Great cock."

"We do love a good dick in these parts."

"He came by last night and we hooked up, but he snuck out while I was recovering from the ridiculous orgasm he'd just given me."

"So, a prince charming he's not," she teased.

"Even if he was, I don't need a prince."

"You're more in the market for a dragon, then?"

"I'm not in the market for anything." Ben took the cart out of Lara's hands and looped into the next aisle, surprised to see half of the space taken up by samples of hanging curtains. He knew they'd come to Target for *something*.

"Just dick," she said.

"I don't want a relationship," he clarified. "But I definitely wouldn't mind getting this guy into bed a few more times."

"Then make plans." Lara pulled one of the curtain panels out to look at the colors. It was coral and green with a splash of yellow and literally everything Ben hated about life. He smacked it out of her hand and pulled out a thickly woven navy blue panel with a gold-threaded diagonal pattern hidden between the folds.

"This one is nice," he said.

"It's dark."

"I hate pastels. You know that."

Lara reached for another panel, this one pale purple and cyan swirls like marble up the lower half of the material. It was less offensive than her first pick, but still not anywhere close to being his style. He let go of the navy one and dragged his fingers over half a dozen other fabric options.

"You didn't answer me," she observed when he finally found a fabric he liked.

"What about this one?" The curtain in question was a vibrant emerald green with an inlaid leaf pattern that, save for the thin silver thread work that lined some of the shapes, would barely have been visible for how dark it was.

"I'll give you my opinion if you tell me why you won't make plans with the hot hookup again," she said.

Ben ignored her and picked up four packs of the green curtains. He didn't need his best friend's approval to buy curtains for his own apartment anyway. He dumped them into the cart and turned his attention to the curtain rods.

"It's because you like him," she guessed.

He rolled his eyes at her. "I don't even know him."

"What's his name?"

"Thomas."

"That's a start. How old is he?"

"I don't know."

"What's he do for work?" she asked.

"I don't know."

Lara sighed and handed him an oil-rubbed bronze curtain rod that he did actually like a little bit.

"What *do* you know then?" she tried.

"I know he has a nice dick," he said. "I know he gives pretty great blow jobs too."

"I meant *about* him."

"Those are things about him."

"Ben."

"I don't know anything beyond his name and what he looks like. I could probably tell you what kind of soap he uses, but if I think about him too hard, I'll probably get an erection in the middle of the store and I think that would embarrass you." He paused to breathe and raised an eyebrow at her. "Did you want me to try anyway?"

"You're an asshole."

In his pocket, Ben's phone hammered with a staccato vibration and he pulled it out to check the alert. His screen remained black, which let him know it was a One-Night alert. A quick glance at Lara confirmed that *she* also knew what the alert was, and she grinned at him eagerly while waiting for him to read it.

He knew without looking it was from Thomas, and his finger shook a little as he tapped on the inbox icon. But in the deepest part of his chest, Ben didn't need to read the message. He already knew what it was going to say.

TM45968: *Can I see you again?*

CHAPTER 6
THOMAS

THOMAS REGRETTED LEAVING without saying goodbye as soon as Ben's door closed behind him. He regretted leaving Ben's messages unread, and he regretted reaching out and finally responding. He worried he looked desperate, answering Ben's texts with nothing more than a request for another hookup, but it should have been fine. Neither of them was looking for anything serious, and Ben was probably looking for something even more casual than him. Thomas wanted to experiment and Ben, with his tight and toned body, was a perfect test case.

In the hours that passed from when he'd woken up to when he'd finally grown the balls to reach out, he'd made a messy list of the things he liked the most, followed by some things he wanted to explore a little longer. He knew he couldn't go over to Ben's with the list in hand, so he'd come up with some ways to try and make things appear like they were happening naturally.

He still wasn't ready for kissing, though.

Hours turned into minutes and, before he knew it, he'd once again arrived at Ben's front door. They lived close, only a handful of blocks between their buildings, which Thomas hoped would prove useful in the near future. He knocked quietly and listened to Ben's footsteps thump louder and louder until the chain was detached and the door swung open.

Ben had a glass of white wine in one hand and the door in the other. He wore nothing more than a skimpy pair of purple shorts that left little to the imagination. Thomas took a breath to once again appreciate Ben's stature and form, doing his best to not gawk. Even in his own heyday, Thomas had never looked that put-together.

"Hey, you." Ben smiled and stepped to the side, making room for him to come in.

"Hey." He hadn't been nervous all day. Not even when he'd made his list and not even on the walk over. But back in Ben's apartment with the smell of his soap and their sex still fresh in his nostrils, Thomas's body turned tense. He straightened his back and tried to look away from Ben's penetrating stare.

"Did you want a drink?"

Yes.

"Not really."

Ben chuckled. "Just here for the business portion of the evening?"

"That's the agreement, isn't it?"

Ben scrunched his nose and studied Thomas over the rim of his wine glass before taking a decidedly large swallow. He nodded, like he'd made up his mind about something, and then jerked his head toward the bedroom.

"Come on, then," Ben said, starting down the hallway.

"It was the agreement," he repeated.

Thomas couldn't help but feel like he'd mis-stepped. Maybe there was a fine line between casual and disinterested and he'd just fallen firmly onto the wrong side of it. Ben didn't so much look bothered as much as he looked at Thomas like he was a puzzle with about seventeen missing pieces. Thomas got the feeling Ben wanted to find the pieces and he knew better than to allow that because he had no interest in being seen…being known.

"You're not wrong." Ben set his wine glass down on the corner of his dresser before sliding over to the nightstand and flipping on his bedside lamp. The room was dim, even in the light, and Thomas liked the feel of it. He didn't know Ben, but it felt like a Ben space. Whatever that meant.

"You got curtains," he observed, drawing an aborted chuckle from Ben.

"Today," Ben confirmed. "I was at the store when you texted me."

"I hope I didn't interrupt."

"You did." Ben pulled a condom and the lube out of his drawer. "But it's fine. Did you want to top again?"

Now it was Thomas's turn to scrunch his nose at the dismissive way Ben talked about the things they were going to do together. He almost opened his mouth to say something about it, but stopped himself before the words reached his throat. The last thing he wanted was to be called a hypocrite, and he had no intention of treating Ben any differently than he already had been.

"Yes," he answered gruffly.

Ben shoved his shorts down to his ankles, bending over so sharply his body folded completely in half. His ass cheeks spread apart just enough to reveal the hint of his smooth, pink pucker, and Thomas inhaled deeply, readying himself. He'd had an erection by this point the night before, and he fought back an unexpected surge of panic that his cock still hung relatively limp against his thigh.

It had to be nerves, he told himself as he reached behind him and pulled his shirt over his head. He dropped it onto the floor before discarding his pants. He left his underwear on, and Ben gave him another one of those thoughtful, decision-making looks.

"I didn't get a chance to tell you since you snuck out last night, but you have a really great cock." Ben reached for his own cock and tugged it straight toward the floor. He released it and it bounced back, slapping against his stomach and leaving a smear of precum against his navel.

"Do I?"

Ben chewed his lip between his teeth and answered with a small nod. "Can I suck it?"

"Y-yes."

Ben reached him before he had time to get his underwear off, and steady hands reached for Thomas's trembling fingers, stilling him before he could follow through.

"I can take it from here." Ben went to his knees with a measured grace, and he groaned, rubbing his cheek along the cotton-covered outline of Thomas's soft cock.

Thomas tried to steady his breathing, to close his eyes, to think about the things they'd done the night before, but nothing worked when it came to slowing his frantic heart. Ben mouthed around the tip of his dick, his underwear growing wet from Ben's tongue. Ben sucked him off like that, with the soaking cotton barrier between them, and finally...finally, Thomas's cock began to swell.

"Get on the bed," Ben whispered.

Thomas climbed onto the bed, settling against the soft pillows with an internal sigh. Ben was on him before his nerves had time to return, and this time he took Thomas's underwear down before taking his cock back into his mouth. The heat and the strength of Ben's tongue startled him and he cried out, hand flailing forward and grabbing Ben's hair.

"Is this okay?" Ben asked, mouth hovering over the shiny tip of Thomas's dick.

"Yes. Yes," he apologized. "Just caught me off-guard."

That earned him another one of those looks, but before it registered fully, Ben swallowed his whole cock down his throat.

It wasn't a difficult feat, Thomas mused, since he wasn't even that hard, but Ben sucked him the same as he had the night before. He sucked and lapped and hollowed his cheeks until Thomas's cock turned thick and long. Thomas closed his eyes when his vision went blurry and he felt the hard press of the sides of Ben's teeth and the roof of his mouth.

Like there'd been no issue before, Thomas's orgasm quickened, and with a burning heat in the base of his spine, it built until it was large enough to consume him.

"I'm really close," he warned. "I'm gonna…"

That was all he had time to get out because Ben groaned, a rough vibration that traveled from the base of Thomas's cock to every nerve ending in his body. He arched off the bed with a shout, holding Ben's mouth down around him as he spilled onto the back of his tongue.

"Shit," he cursed, falling back to the sheets.

Ben made a content little noise and let Thomas's half-hard cock fall out of his mouth.

"Shit?" Ben asked.

Thomas's breath caught in his throat because Ben looked… Ben looked sinful down there between his legs with his swollen lips and blown pupils. His cheeks were flushed and between his legs his cock sat hard and proud.

Ready.

"I came."

"That's the point of this."

"Now I can't fuck you."

Ben chuckled and straddled Thomas's waist, taking his cock into his hand. "Well, no. Not yet. But you could return the favor."

Thomas had wanted to suck Ben's cock again, so he didn't hate the idea, but he couldn't shake the worry about what kind of recovery period he was going to have.

"Alright," he agreed, catching how uninterested the word

sounded in response to the proposition. He forced a smile and reached forward, grazing his fingertips over Ben's fist. "I'm sorry. I didn't mean to sound like that."

"I feel like you're not sure you want to be here."

"I'm very sure I want to be here," he promised. "I just have a lot on my mind."

Ben cocked his head to the side, stroking himself slowly while he appraised Thomas again. He hadn't shoved Thomas's hand off, and his fingers moved in time with Ben's, up and down the length of his shaft.

"I can help you with that," Ben offered.

"I know." Nothing could have been closer to the truth.

"Can I come sit on your face?" Ben asked, scooching up his chest. "I want to feed this cock into your throat, Thomas. Is that okay?"

Thomas shuddered, managing a nod as his lashes fluttered closed.

"I like when you talk like that," he whispered.

"I won't stop then." Ben leaned over for the condom and the lube. "I want you to put this on first. Be ready because I want you inside of me as soon as I come."

"Not before?"

"After."

Ben moved higher up his body, and Thomas dragged his hands up Ben's thighs until he was hard to reach. Ben's balls dragged against his chin, then his asshole, and Ben raised up onto his knees enough that he could point his cock straight down onto Thomas's panting tongue. He fumbled between his own legs, only able to get the condom on blind because he'd done it so many times before. He dripped lube onto himself and cradled the heavy weight of his balls in his palm as his cock began to harden a second time.

"Ready?" Ben asked.

He nodded and flicked his tongue against the underside of

Ben's crown. Ben made a rough sound and angled downward, sliding his dick into Thomas's mouth.

"God, Thomas," Ben moaned, using his hand to cover the parts of his erection Thomas's mouth couldn't reach. "I love how you suck me."

"I can barely get my mouth around you like this," he mumbled. His latex-covered cock thickened in his hand.

"That's fine," Ben grunted, falling forward a little to get deeper. "Open me up while I fuck your mouth."

Thomas's body went rigid, a flash of fear tearing through him. He'd never done that before, not even to himself, and he didn't want to do it wrong. He didn't want to hurt Ben, but most of all, he didn't want Ben to know he was so new to this. It couldn't be that difficult to put a slippery finger inside of someone's ass, he debated himself, comparing it to a cunt just long enough for him to calm down and get his lube-slick fingers between Ben's ass cheeks.

He traced Ben's hot rim with the pad of his forefinger until Ben cursed his name. Thomas mentally crossed his fingers while actually putting one of them inside of another man's body for the first time. Ben's ass was hotter than he'd imagined, hotter than he'd even felt the night before around his cock. The latex had done an amazing job at dulling the sensation, and in response to feeling it for the first time, he sealed his mouth around the length of Ben's dick available to him, sucking ravenously.

Ben laughed softly, not in a mocking way, but sounding pleased and aroused, rocking back and forth to alternate between shoving his cock down Thomas's tongue and riding his finger.

"Another one," Ben rasped, and Thomas added his middle finger.

The second one was more of a stretch, and Ben made a high-pitched noise as he got it inside that had Thomas's cock pulsating with desperation.

"Just like that." Ben worked himself open with Thomas's fingers, precum leaking from his cock against Thomas's tongue and mouth to signal the approach of his orgasm.

"Thomas, I'm serious," Ben said, voice trembling. "Once I come, I want you inside of me. However it has to happen."

"Don't worry." Thomas speared his fingers deeper, teasing a third, but knowing it wouldn't fit. "You don't have to tell me twice."

Ben's hole flexed around his finger and his cock swelled, spurting hot jets of sticky white cum against Thomas's open mouth. He licked his lips, getting a taste of the salty release, and at the same time, he pulled his hand free. Thomas grabbed Ben around his slim waist and dragged him down, seating him on his now fully hard cock with one quick pump of his hips.

"Oh." Ben's lashes fluttered, but Thomas didn't give him a chance to recover. Ben was muscled, but still smaller, and Thomas bounced him up and down with such force, the last remnants of Ben's cum splattered out of his cock and painted both of their chests. It didn't take long for Thomas's second orgasm to sneak up, but he wasn't ready for the night to end.

He slammed Ben down, burying his cock deeper than he'd reached the night before, and he clenched his teeth, grunting from the pain and the force of staving off his own release.

"Don't stop." Ben smacked his hands like he was trying to coax a horse into a gallop. "Please don't stop. Please."

"I'm not," he growled, flipping Ben onto the bed and spreading his legs. All of his earlier nervousness was gone. The worry and the uncertainty vanished. It was like being with Ben —being inside of him—erased all of the noise and the nonsense in Thomas's head. He never wanted it to be over. He never wanted to leave. "I'm nowhere near ready to stop."

CHAPTER 7
BEN

BEN'S VISION whited out and the spit-soaked pillowcase plastered to his face made it impossibly hard for him to breathe. Behind him, Thomas rutted into him like a man possessed, the place their bodies joined together making the most unholy of sounds as Thomas's girthy cock plowed into his body over and over.

It was easily the best sex Ben had ever had.

Thomas fucked like he'd been wandering in a desert, lost for years without water or shade, and Ben's body was his long-sought oasis. It felt like hours since Ben had been able to form a coherent thought, but he'd managed to make a mental note that he should ask Thomas to jack off before they got together the next time because when he had one under the belt, getting to the finish line a second time was a marathon.

"I'm not used to these anymore. I hate condoms," Thomas muttered above him, hips snapping madly.

Ben raised his eyebrows in agreement, even though his face was mashed into the pillow. Thomas's fingers dug into his hips, sliding over the sweat-slick angles of his body before pressing deeper for purchase. It ached, but Ben found he welcomed it. There was something about the way Thomas fucked that felt messy and possessive all at the same time and Ben was drunk on it.

But through the haze, something in those three words attached itself to Ben's brain and wouldn't let go. He couldn't shake Thomas off, and the words had as much staying power as his dick.

Ben hated condoms too, but they were necessary when you were hooking up, which was exactly what they were doing. The only kinds of people who didn't use condoms were people in committed relationships, and if Thomas wasn't used to using them...

Before his brain could piece that thought process together, Thomas roared, his body going tense as he came. With his last thrust, he fucked into Ben so deep it lifted him off the bed, and he smacked his hand against the headboard to keep himself from going through it. Ben had already come again, and again, and when he'd finished, Thomas collapsed on top of him with a grunt.

Ben could feel the aftereffects of Thomas's orgasm as the cock inside his ass throbbed erratically until Thomas pulled out. They both winced at the movement, and Ben shouldered Thomas off of him, the reprieve giving his conscious mind enough time to make sense of the thoughts that had been tearing through it.

"Now you're the one running off?" Thomas asked, rolling onto his back as Ben stood up.

"It's my house," he answered back.

Ben pulled some clean underwear from his dresser and covered himself up before frowning down at Thomas sprawled like a starfish in the middle of his bed.

"We need to talk," Ben said.

"Already?"

"What's your deal?" He folded his arms over his chest defensively, like they could do anything to protect him from the conversation he was about to broach.

"What?"

Ben gestured at the man spread out naked and sweaty on his bed. He hated how good Thomas looked naked because it was hard to be stern when all Ben wanted to do was lick the sweat out of Thomas's armpits.

"I'm not an idiot," he said, adjusting his stance to look more confident. "My last boyfriend cheated me and I don't want to go through that again."

Thomas pursed his lips, a deep furrow appearing between his brows. He sat up and looked around, grabbing one of Ben's pillows and using it to cover his lap.

"You think that I'm cheating on you?" Thomas asked. "I thought this was…"

"No. I think you're cheating on someone *with* me."

Thomas barked out a laugh, his eyes narrowing as the sound tumbled out of him. "That's rich. I'm not in a relationship, though."

"How do I know?"

"How can I prove it to you?" Thomas shot back at him, holding up his left hand to reveal a pale white strip of skin where a wedding band would have sat. "I'm in the middle of a divorce. I'm not seeing anyone. I didn't even think I was seeing you."

"You're not," Ben said quickly.

He felt silly that he'd made an assumption, but there was still something about Thomas that *felt* off, even though Ben couldn't put his finger on it, and the look at Thomas's face confirmed it.

He had a secret.

"You can prove it by being honest," Ben said. "I can tell something is off, but I don't know what."

Thomas's face blanked, and he slid to the edge of the bed. He kept himself covered until he'd gotten his clothes off the floor and managed to get into his underwear and his pants. Ben watched silently, opting to put a shirt on when Thomas stood. Ben's first reflex was to touch Thomas, and he hated that. Thomas with his smooth skin and the hints of gray that salted his otherwise dark hair. He was handsome and he was a great lay, but he was messy and Ben didn't *do* messy anymore.

Not after Cody.

Ben sighed and jerked his head toward the doorway. "Let's go sit down at the table or something."

Thomas followed him down the hallway to the dining room, taking a seat at the table and folding his hands together in front of him like he was waiting for a lecture. Ben carried on into the kitchen, coming back with two glasses and a half-drank bottle of Chardonnay. He poured them both a glass and sat down opposite Thomas and waited for him to speak the truth.

"I'm not seeing anyone," Thomas said softly. He flattened one of his palms against the table and traced the tip of his pointer finger up and down each digit.

"So you said."

Thomas took a tentative swallow of his wine and mouthed something at his lap, but there was no sound to the words. He did it again and again, and then, "Can you excuse me? I have to use the restroom."

Ben pointed down the hallway and Thomas stood so fast, the chair almost clattered to the floor when he pushed it away. He watched Thomas go, sipping at his wine and trying to come up with what could possibly be so scary to admit that Thomas found himself unable to say the words.

The toilet didn't flush and the sink didn't run, but the bathroom door opened and Thomas returned with such purpose that Ben almost didn't recognize him.

"You're the first man I've ever been with," Thomas blurted as he sank back into the chair. And Ben had to admit that of all the things he'd expected to come out of Thomas's mouth, that wasn't one of them.

"I'm sorry, what?"

"You're the first man I've ever been with." Thomas frowned and looked down at his lap. "My wife and I are divorcing, and lately, recently, I was thinking that maybe I was interested in men. I think I've always known, but I was married and… so I just…"

"Thomas, calm down."

Thomas's shoulders heaved for how hard he was breathing, and at Ben's words, he caught himself and the motion slowed, growing less intense. Ben waited until Thomas's face turned back to its normal color before cautiously taking a drink of his wine. The admission caught him off-guard, but there was no shame in it and he didn't want Thomas to misinterpret any of his reactions as being negative, because they weren't. There wasn't anything wrong or shameful with what Thomas had confessed.

"I can go," Thomas offered.

"Did you want to go?"

"Not really."

"Then why would you say that?" he asked.

"This is a lot," Thomas said. "This has made things very not casual."

"We're not getting married. This doesn't really change anything," he lied.

It changed a lot of things.

"You were my first," Thomas said.

"Am I your last?"

"I hope not."

Ben leaned back and slumped in his seat, letting out a long and tired breath. This definitely wasn't what he'd signed up for when he'd let Thomas come over, but he wasn't sure he hated it. There was something powerful about being someone's first. Ben could teach Thomas to fuck the way that *he* liked, and it was childish, but there was a part of him that really liked the idea of Thomas making another man come one day doing things that Ben had taught him to do. Admittedly, he also didn't hate the idea of Thomas doing those things to make *him* come, but they'd agreed.

Besides, knowing what he knew about Thomas now, there wouldn't ever be anything between them other than this same kind of casual intimacy. Ben was still reeling from the breakup with Cody, and Thomas had a lifetime of repressed sexuality to unpack an explore.

"Do you want me to treat you differently?" Ben asked.

"Not really." Thomas reached for his wine, pulling the glass toward him without lifting it off the table. "Maybe some explanations of things sometimes, but you already kind of do that."

Ben's cheeks burned. "There's a difference between talking dirty and offering up a how-to guide."

"Do I need a step-by-step?" Thomas looked up at him with an arched brow. His expression was decidedly smug, like he knew he was good in bed without instruction. That if Ben did offer him a little guidance...he could be great.

"No," he conceded. "But it wouldn't hurt for you to finesse your technique a little."

"Finesse." Thomas looked at him in disbelief, taking a drink of his wine but not breaking away from Ben's gaze.

Ben, for his part, was enraptured. The Thomas sitting across from him was almost like a whole new version of himself. At least as far as Ben knew. To him, it seemed that giving Thomas the space to admit his sexuality had empowered him to speak freely about the things he wanted, the things he was good at. It wasn't arrogance or cockiness. It was confidence. It was competence.

It was fucking hot.

"There's things that you can learn," he said.

"Practice makes perfect."

Was Ben imagining things, or had Thomas's voice slipped down a register with that ask? Ben shifted his weight, thankful he'd put a shirt on, but regretful he hadn't opted for pants. The underwear did little to hide the interested bulge between his legs.

"Is that what you're looking for?" Ben asked. "Someone to practice on?"

"Practice with," Thomas corrected.

"Casually."

"Formally."

Now it was Ben's turn to arch a brow. That wasn't anywhere close to what they'd talked about the first time.

"Not committed," Thomas amended. "Well..."

"Exclusive," he supplied.

"But not serious."

"Right." Ben didn't have enough wine in his glass—or the bottle—to have this conversation.

"I'll go get tested," Thomas said.

Ben swallowed, dragging his tongue across the front of his teeth. "Why?"

"What I said earlier still stands. I don't like condoms."

"You're not the only person in this...this...formally exclusive casual arrangement."

"Did you want to keep using them?" Thomas asked.

"I feel like this conversation has gotten away from me." He topped off his wine and took a large swallow. "You were just coming out of the closet at me and now you're talking about fucking me bare."

"Well, when you say it like that..."

"Now I have to use the restroom. Let's talk about this another time," he muttered, pushing away from the table and walking down the hallway. He locked himself in the small room and studied his reflection like he would find the answer in his own face.

Thomas hadn't outright asked him for anything, but the conversation had made it clear Thomas wanted to keep sleeping with him. Ben didn't hate the idea, in fact he was quite a fan of it, but the continuation of their relationship did mean the bounds of it would change. He felt it was important for him to be as honest as Thomas was being so they would have a level playing field before making up their minds.

He returned to the dining room table, and Thomas gave him a knowing look about understanding the necessity for a bathroom pep talk to gather his wits.

"I just got out of a bad relationship," he shared. "I don't want another one. Good or bad. So this is just…it's whatever it is and that's all it's going to be."

"Are you proposing that you want to use me for sex?"

"That's what *you're* proposing," he corrected.

"I can be your rebound," Thomas said. "I'm kind of rebounding too, if it helps you to look at it that way."

It seemed they'd reached an agreement, though it might have been an impasse. They'd both laid their cards out on the table, and it was up to Ben to decide what happened next.

"No dates," he said, holding up a finger.

"That's fine."

"No one else." Another finger. If Thomas wanted to get tested, if he wanted to go bare…Ben had to know that he wasn't at risk. It was non-negotiable.

"Just you."

Something about the way Thomas said it, the way he looked at Ben as he said the words…

Ben swallowed and nodded.

"Fine," he agreed. "You have a deal."

CHAPTER 8
THOMAS

THOMAS LEANED back in the uncomfortable wrought iron patio chair and flipped his phone over onto its back. The screen stayed dark because he didn't have any messages. He flipped it back face down and sighed. He wasn't even expecting a message, but he'd hoped to hear from Ben before lunch time. He also knew that, as an adult, he himself was completely capable of reaching out and scheduling them some time together, but he didn't want to look too…

Eager?

Green?

Interested?

"You look distracted, old man."

Thomas tapped the back of his phone and looked up at the sound of his daughter's voice. He squinted into the sun until Kenzie stepped to the left and blocked it.

"I'm one of those things," he admitted, standing to give his oldest a hug. "Where's your brother?"

"Dakota said he couldn't get out of work."

Thomas wasn't surprised, but he was disappointed. He gestured to the empty seat across from him and waited for Kenzie to sit before he returned to his own chair.

"It's a Saturday," he said.

"I know." She shrugged helplessly and shoved her sunglasses onto the top of her head. "He's an asshole."

"So he got the best parts of your mom and the worst parts of me?"

Kenzie pursed her lips and reached for a menu. "Debatable. Either way, I'm here, so what did you want to talk about?"

"I just wanted to see how things were going."

"You could have called." Kenzie tossed the menu back down onto the table. "Or texted."

"You would have ignored me," he said.

She looked at him like that was the point. The waitress came by and Thomas ordered a refill on his beer while Kenzie ordered a white wine.

"You can go," he told her, counting back from ten in his head so he didn't say something regrettable. "I appreciate you being here. I want to have a relationship with you, but you don't have to stay. If it's that bad, Kenzie…If *I* am that bad…"

Kenzie let out an annoyed sound, but her expression softened—barely. "I just don't know how to do this with you."

"Do what? Have lunch?"

"Have a *relationship*."

"I love you, Kenzie, but that's a you thing. I've tried. For years. I'm either doing too much or too little—"

She cut him off. "Mom says…"

"Mom isn't here." Thomas held up his hands to stop that train of thought before Kenzie had a chance to get it out of the station. Even though he and Jennifer had agreed to not disclose the reasoning behind their divorce, he wouldn't put it past her to have done some underhanded things to cast him in a negative light with their kids. Kenzie and Dakota had never been his biggest fans and he knew a carefully dropped word or phrase would have done wonders to pull them both into her corner.

It wasn't his fault, or maybe it was, but it wasn't anything he could change. Jennifer had wanted to be a stay-at-home mom, so Thomas had done everything he could to make it possible. He'd worked the long hours and the double shifts to ensure he had enough money to provide for their family of four. Jennifer hadn't complained, at least not to him. He didn't want to know what she'd said to his friends, but he imagined it was far from kind. If the things he'd said to *his* friends were any indication, at least.

Thomas hadn't ever meant to be absent from his kids' lives, or his wife's life, but that was how it had turned out. The three of them had become a fully functioning family unit that he bankrolled until Dakota was in high school and Jennifer decided she wanted to go back to work.

He hadn't argued because he thought it would be nice to finally have some support when it came to the finances, but he hadn't anticipated Jennifer using work to find other men to sleep with. He hadn't anticipated a lot of things that had happened in his life.

Thomas sighed, rubbing the bridge of his nose. "How is your mom?"

"She's great." Kenzie sounded like she had more to say.

"Is she seeing someone?"

"Do you want me to answer that?"

The waitress brought their drinks and a bread basket. Thomas watched Kenzie tear the crust off a chunk of sourdough, just like she had her whole life. She tossed the crust back into the basket and rolled the center of the bread into a ball before shoving it into her mouth. He laughed under his breath as she chewed. Jennifer had always been grossly annoyed at Kenzie's relationship with bread, but Thomas found it endearing. Part of him flashed with an unspoken kind of pleasure about knowing it was something she still did. That even though he might not know his daughter the way he wanted to, he still knew parts of her.

"No," he said, taking a drink of his beer.

He didn't need Kenzie to confirm what he already knew.

Of course Jennifer had started dating now that they were divorced. She'd started dating years ago. He just hadn't known about it.

"He's horrible, though. If that counts for anything."

Thomas looked across the table at her, lips pursed. "I said you didn't need to answer."

"I'm just saying," she mumbled, taking a drink of her wine. "He's an idiot."

"You think I'm an idiot."

"Idioter," she said. "Bigger idiot."

"Impossible." Thomas pulled Kenzie's discarded bread out of the basket and began to pick at it. She smiled at him and rolled her eyes.

"Tell me about your apartment," she said.

He relaxed, the tension in his shoulders unwinding just enough for him to become fully aware of how painful the patio chairs at the restaurant were.

"It's walkable from here." He pointed toward the direction of his building. "Obviously smaller than the house, but it's just me."

"You should get a cat."

"I hate cats."

"You hated Mom." Kenzie smirked.

"Kenzie!" Thomas admonished his smug daughter, even though the sentiment was close enough to the truth to pass. "You mom and I...we just outgrew each other. It happens sometimes."

"I know." She sighed.

"I don't have bad feelings about what happened between us." That was a lie. "And I don't think she does either."

"Do you think it's weird she's dating already?"

"I honestly don't care."

Kenzie frowned, using her first two fingers to spin the stem of the wine glass, sloshing the liquid around the edges of the glass. "I kind of do."

"Have you told her?"

She nodded.

"What did she say?" he asked.

"She doesn't really care." Kenzie shrugged, and he could see the hurt in her face because it so closely resembled his own. The knit brows and the delicate lines around her eyes when she frowned, the tight lips and the way she tucked her chin to her chest like if she could just change the angle of her face, no one would know she was hurting.

"I'm sure she cares," he said. "She's your mother."

"She hasn't been the same since everything happened. She's just…very self-absorbed."

"I don't think it's unfair for your mom to want to put herself first." As he said the words, he hated himself—or them. Jennifer had been putting herself first for years, for longer than she'd ever admit. She'd been putting herself first since she'd asked Thomas to provide her with the life she wanted and then punished him for it in the next breath.

His phone buzzed and skittered across the table, and they both looked at it. Thomas grabbed it, finding a text with Ben's name on the screen. He bit the inside of his cheek to stop himself from smiling.

"What's that look?" Kenzie asked him, tone making it clear she knew.

"I don't think it's unfair for your mom to put herself first," he said again, setting his phone down on the top of his thigh. He'd deal with Ben after he finished his conversation with Kenzie.

"There's a difference between prioritizing yourself and disregarding everyone else."

"Maybe she's just trying to learn the difference between the two." His phone buzzed again.

"It's easy for you." She reached for another piece of bread and repeated her same crust-culling routine.

"Is it?" He didn't think anyone had ever noticed anything he did, let alone the things he'd sacrificed in the name of making sure the people he loved were provided for.

"Don't be modest." Kenzie stood up and dropped her bag onto her seat. "I have to go to the bathroom; I'll be right back."

Thomas waited until Kenzie disappeared into the restaurant before checking his phone to read the messages from Ben.

Ben: *It's a nice day today and I hate to spend it inside but do you want to come by later?*
Ben: *No pressure.*
Thomas: *What did you have in mind?*
Ben: *Honestly just wanted to get off with someone else's hand lol*

Thomas laughed and shook his head, appreciating how forward Ben was now that they'd laid their cards on the table.

Thomas: *I can give you a hand later today. I'm at lunch right now.*
Ben: *What time works for you?*
Thomas: *Dinner time?*

Kenzie weaved her way back through the maze of patio tables and sat back down, arranging the strap of her purse over the back of the chair and returning her attention to her bread ball and her glass of wine.

Ben: *Not a date.*

"Everything okay?" she asked. "You look crazy focused."
"Everything's fine. Just one sec."

Thomas: *Would you rather I wait until eleven so it feels less datey to you?*
Ben: *Datey???*
Ben: *Dinner time is fine.*
Thomas: *Six?*
Ben: *That's hardly dinner, but okay. See you then.*

Thomas set his phone down on the table and reached for Kenzie's next discarded bread crust.

"Everything's fine," she repeated.

"Yeah. So." He cleared his throat. "Tell me what's been going on with you. And your brother."

"I'm taking horrible classes this semester, but it's almost over and then I only have one year left."

"I know." Kenzie was in the third year of a bachelor's in Psych degree that she'd been chasing after since she was in elementary school.

Her focus on her life had always astounded Thomas. Once his daughter set her mind to something, there wasn't any coming back from it. Kenzie was headstrong and stubborn. She knew what she wanted and she didn't want to let anything get in her way. Dakota…his son…not so much.

"I've been trying to get in with a colleague of one of my professors who might have an in for an internship for me to do over the summer, which would be nice. Good experience for after I graduate."

"You've got this all planned out, don't you?"

Kenzie cocked her head to the side and smiled at him. "Don't I always?"

"And Dakota?"

Kenzie raised her shoulders toward her ears before letting them fall in a dramatic fashion. "He's a mess."

"Not everyone is as sure of what they want in their lives as you are," he reminded her.

"A house." She rolled her eyes. "Apartment, whatever. Steady paycheck. Job security. Emotional fulfillment."

"And which of those do you have?" he asked.

"Two and a half of the four."

"And Dakota?"

"One." She rolled her eyes, and Thomas was relieved for that because anything could be done with one of the four. "What about you?"

"Three and a half," he answered.

It was sad to say, but it had been years since Thomas has been emotionally fulfilled. There was a long period of time when he'd blamed Jennifer for that, but now with some space between them, he knew the truth. It wasn't anyone's fault but his own. If Thomas wanted to find any kind of fulfillment, emotional or otherwise, he would have to find it himself. And Ben was the first step in that evolution.

CHAPTER 9
BEN

BEN SLICED a red bell pepper into strips and dumped it all on a small white plate. This was fine. It was fine. It wasn't dinner. It was just…a snack. A snack for him, and maybe if he didn't finish it before Thomas showed up, he could have some too. But it wasn't dinner and it definitely wasn't a date. He knew they'd agreed to casual and experimental sex, but that didn't mean they couldn't conversate with their clothes on before and/or after the sexy things.

Thomas showed up ten minutes later, at six on the dot, and Ben did his best to ignore the complicated way his chest tightened when he opened the door. On the door mat, Thomas looked more confident than he had the other times he'd come over, and that change in his demeanor didn't do much to help the way Ben was feeling. But then again, neither did the way Thomas's snug khaki pants hugged his thighs.

"Hey," Ben greeted, wondering why his voice sounded so breathy. He wasn't a princess or a maiden in need of saving. He didn't *need* anything. He was using Thomas for sex and Thomas was using him as a study guide, and that was all they'd ever be. He stepped aside and gestured for Thomas to come in.

"You okay?" Thomas asked, closing the door behind him. "You look flushed."

Ben pressed his fingertips against his cheeks and shook his head. "I was just making myself a snack. Did you want anything?"

Thomas glanced toward the kitchen, his expression leery but open. "What do you have?"

"I was cutting up some peppers." He pointed at the plate on the table. "And hummus. Just something light and easy."

"I'm fine," Thomas said. "But you can eat. I'll take a drink if you have anything, though."

"Wine? Water? Juice?" Ben went into the kitchen and opened his fridge to make sure he hadn't missed any of the choices. Thomas sat down at the dining room table and tapped his fingers against the edge of the glass top.

"Whatever's easy."

Ben poured two glasses of wine and carried them to the table. He tried to not think about the last meal he'd shared with someone in his apartment, or the meal he'd been supposed to share at least. Cody's violent tone echoed through his memories and he winced, swiping a strip of bell pepper through the hummus.

"Are you sure you're okay?" Thomas asked.

"Just…a lot on my mind apparently."

"Did you want to reschedule?"

He huffed out a small laugh. "Not really. Sex seems to help me forget the shit in my head."

"I know what that's like."

"What about you?" he asked, swallowing the pepper and reaching for his wine. "You don't seem the same as normal either."

Thomas smirked, tilting his head to the side. "How do I look?"

"More…"

"More?"

Ben shrugged. "Just more."

Thomas answered that with a thoughtful noise, and he stretched his hand across the table toward the plate. "I had lunch with my daughter today."

"I didn't know you had a daughter."

"There's a lot you don't know about me," Thomas hedged. "That's the whole idea of this, right?"

"Well, yeah."

"I have two children. Rather, they're both adults now."

"How old *are* you?" Ben asked with a laugh. It didn't matter. Thomas's age wouldn't stop him from being interested and it surely wouldn't stop him from being aroused beyond measure at the idea of taking the older man to bed.

"How old are you again?"

"Twenty-eight."

"You're older than my kids, if that makes you feel any better."

"A little?" He chuckled and swiped another pepper through the hummus.

"I'm forty-five," Thomas said. "My kids are twenty-one and twenty-four. Does that change anything?"

"Not at all. I'm not in the market to be their step-dad."

Thomas barked out a laugh and leaned back in his chair, looking relaxed for the first time since he'd arrived. "I don't think they're looking for a step-dad, so that's fine. They don't even care for their actual dad if we're being honest."

"And are we?" he rasped.

Thomas studied him in silence from across the table before swallowing the rest of his wine down in one go. He gently set the glass down on the table and shoved it toward the half-eaten plate of peppers.

"Honest enough," Thomas said.

"Yeah." Ben cleared his throat and stood. "Ready?"

"Very."

Thomas followed him to the bedroom, not bothering to close the door. There wasn't a need for privacy. They were alone in Ben's small apartment. Just the two of them in the cramped bedroom with the new curtains and the lube on the bedside table. It felt like…something…had passed between them at the table, but it wasn't anything Ben could make sense of. So instead of bringing it up, he pulled his shirt off and tossed it onto the floor.

"Did you have any requests for tonight?" he asked.

Thomas held his hand up, waggling his fingers. "I want to use my hand."

"To what?" Ben shoved his pants to his ankles and stepped out of them, leaving him in a tight pair of briefs that didn't hide much.

"Make you hard. Make you come."

Ben bit the inside of his cheek and stretched his arm out, wiggling his fingers until Thomas got close enough for Ben to touch him.

"Do we get to kiss tonight?" he asked, working open the fly on Thomas's indecently tight khaki pants. Thomas stepped out of them and kicked them to the side, then added his shirt to the mix. He was in a pair of teal blue boxer briefs that looked soft as butter. The elastic band dug into his waist, and Ben traced his fingers over the soft bits of skin that swelled over the waistband. Thomas's skin was softer than Ben remembered and he closed his eyes so he could fully focus on the sensation of touching Thomas.

"Not yet," Thomas answered. "Is that okay?"

"It's fine. It's fine." Ben dragged his hands around to Thomas's front, reaching down and palming his growing erection.

Thomas sucked in a breath and grunted, pushing down his underwear and exposing himself to Ben's hand.

"Do you want me to tell you how I like it?" Ben asked. "Or do you want to try it how you like it and see how that feels to me?"

Thomas stepped closer, hooking his fingers behind the band of Ben's briefs and sliding them down. He studied Ben's cock like there would be a test afterward, and finally touched him, wrapping his long and gently calloused fingers around his thickness. Ben's breath left him in a rush and he tipped his head back, letting a moan tumble out of his mouth.

"I think I can sort you out."

"I have no doubt..." The words fell away as Thomas tightened his hand and used his body to walk them both back to the bed.

Ben's knees hit the mattress and he fell back, with Thomas coming down on top of him so close he could smell the wine on his breath. He closed his eyes because he wanted to kiss him and knew he couldn't. And even if he could, that he shouldn't. Between their bodies, Thomas worked his fist up the length of Ben's cock until he writhed against the bed, his orgasm so close, but also terribly far away.

"You're killing me," he whined, arching off the bed and pressing their bodies together.

For someone who'd never been with a man before, Thomas absolutely had a handle on the way to touch a cock. Not to mention he was one of the best fucks Ben had ever had, and that was saying something. He didn't dare think of what it would be like to bed Thomas once he got the hang of the male form.

"Can I kiss you here?" Thomas dragged his nose up the length of Ben's arched throat, hand still working quickly between their bodies.

"Yes."

Against his neck, Thomas's lips were warm, his tongue hot. Ben could feel the flat of Thomas's tongue as he gently sucked and licked his way up toward Ben's ear. A shiver tore up his spine, and he dug his fingers into Thomas's waist, holding on, pushing away, pulling him closer...

"You're gorgeous like this," Thomas whispered against his ear. "Messy and coming apart."

"You're gonna..." Ben's lashes fluttered, his eyes rolling back.

Thomas laughed softly against the tender spot behind his ear before nipping gently at the skin.

"I'm gonna," Thomas repeated back at him. "You're gonna what?"

"Come. You're gonna make me."

Thomas did something with his grip that caught the word in the back of Ben's throat before he could get it out. He flew off the bed, arms wrapping around Thomas's back like he'd be able to anchor their bodies together to stop himself from floating off into space for the force of his release. Thomas made a pleased sound and kissed his ear, a wet and sloppy thing with spit and tongue, and then with his hand still around Ben's cock, began to rut their bodies together.

"You're unbelievable," Thomas whispered, hand still working furtively up Ben's length.

"Can you come like this?" he panted, spreading his legs to make more room for Thomas between them.

Thomas dragged his nose along Ben's jaw, sliding his free hand to the top of Ben's head. He bracketed himself like that, hips pumping madly as he used the friction of their bodies and the slick heat of Ben's cum to chase after his own release. It was very nearly too much. So much contact and sensitivity and sweat. Thomas spread his fingers apart and added his cock to his fist, which only tightened his grip around Ben's already pulsing and tender length.

"Like this," Thomas said, fucking his cock into his hand.

Ben could see the look of concentration on his face, the way he was focused on using Ben's body to help get him off. And when Thomas's orgasm crested, the look on his face was utterly magical. Thomas arched away, his throat arcing into an elegant curve that had Ben flying off the bend to kiss him there. He licked and sucked at Thomas's Adam's apple until Thomas shouted, back bowing and his entire body buckling forward.

Hot jets of cum shot from Thomas's dick, splattering against Ben's sweaty chest, and Thomas released both their dicks, quickly catching himself on the bed so he didn't collapse and flatten Ben. Thomas's whole body trembled, his cock spasming madly between their bodies, cum still beading from the tip and leaking down his shaft.

"You're…" Ben closed his eyes and sucked in a breath.

Thomas flopped onto his back, pressing the outside of their forearms together while they both struggled to breathe.

"What am I?"

"You're unbelievable."

It wasn't the right word, but it was close enough. There were probably at least a hundred better words he could have used, but they all bordered on not enough or a little too much, and even in his post-orgasm haze, Ben knew better than to go there.

"You're going to give me a massive ego if you say things like that."

"Well, it's true. I'll feel sorry for everyone you fuck once you really learn how."

"Oh?" Thomas laughed and turned his head to face Ben.

"You'll ruin them for everyone who comes after." He rolled onto his side and tucked his hands together under his face. His nose was inches away from Thomas's and he took the silent moment to study the lines and coloring of Thomas's face. The way his features softened after he came and he looked happy, calm, peaceful.

Ben reached up and brushed some of Thomas's hair back from his sweaty forehead, and Thomas leaned into the touch with a breathy whimper. He pulled his hand back, digging his nails into his palm to bring himself back to the present. Ben sat up, practically leaping off the bed to grab his underwear from the floor. He stepped into them and shuffled to the dining room. He poured himself a fresh glass of wine and leaned against the edge of the table, taking a large swallow.

Like earlier, Thomas followed after him, hesitating in the hallway and giving him a long and slow onceover.

"You can't convince me you're okay," Thomas said.

Ben wasn't okay, but he wasn't ready to walk away either.

"Lust drunk." He waved his hand dismissively, hoping it would be enough to stop Thomas's line of questioning. "You make me a little crazy."

Thomas leaned against the corner of the wall and crossed his arms in front of his chest. He sighed heavily, his whole chest heaving as he let out an audible breath.

"Sorry?"

Ben rolled his eyes and took another drink of his wine. "Are you?"

"Not really," Thomas whispered. "I don't think I am."

Ben poured the rest of the wine down his throat and smacked his lips together. He needed to get out of his head and back into Thomas's pants. That had been the idea all along. The best way to get over Cody was to get under someone else, and that someone else was Thomas. It shouldn't matter how handsome he was, or how capable he turned out to be in bed. Thomas wanted him as a practice run and he wanted Thomas as a rebound, and that was what they'd both get. Thomas had delivered on his end of the deal; now it was up to Ben to do the rest.

"Anyway," he said, setting down his glass and heading back toward Thomas. He backed Thomas against the wall, crowding him in. Ben spit in his hand and reached behind the waistband of Thomas's underwear, curling his fingers and making a loose fist around his still plump cock. "Earlier was great, but let me show you another way to do it."

CHAPTER 10
THOMAS

THOMAS HADN'T MEANT to stay over at Ben's. But Ben had a gift for hand jobs that wrung every last ounce of energy from Thomas's bones and he'd fallen asleep in a puddle of sweat and cum. He'd woken up around midnight and tried to climb out of bed and make an escape, but Ben had flung an arm around his waist and pulled him back down. Thomas had settled without argument and quickly fallen back asleep.

He'd forgotten how nice it was to be held at night. It had been years since he and Jennifer touched each other that way, craved each other's touch and intimacy. He knew things with Ben weren't anything like that, but still, it was…nice.

But now the sun was out, creeping through the slit between Ben's new curtain panels, and Thomas didn't have the strength to face their relationship or, rather, their agreement in the daylight. Ben snored softly beside him, and Thomas carefully crept out of bed, gathering his clothes off the floor and balling them up against his chest. He carried them into the bathroom and quietly closed the door, the click of the lock deafening in the otherwise quiet of the apartment.

He dressed and thought he'd made a clean break, but

Thomas startled when he reached the main area of the apartment, finding Ben in the kitchen brewing some coffee.

"Morning," Ben mumbled, syllables slurred from sleep. He wore his dirty underwear from the night before and nothing else besides a streak of dried cum that tracked up the left side of his stomach. First thing in the morning, he looked even more muscular than normal, and Thomas tried not to stare. He was always *trying* around Ben, but he wasn't sure he hated it. There was part of him that liked the unyielding attraction he felt for the other man—as long as he could keep it under control.

"Hey." He stopped shy of his shoes near the door and ran a hand through his hair, meeting Ben's tired gaze.

"Did you want coffee?"

"No." He shook his head. "I was going to head out. I didn't mean to fall asleep."

Ben answered that with a thoughtful noise and a shrug. Thomas couldn't help but feel dismissed and his first instinct was to take offense, but he swallowed it back. He was the one trying to leave without a goodbye. He was the one feeling like he'd overstayed his invitation. Ben was merely going along with the signals Thomas had been sending.

"Do you want to make plans for next time or just..." Ben blinked slowly. "Play it by ear?"

"I'll probably be busy with work all week," he said.

"I don't think I know what you do." Ben's coffee filled his mug and he pulled it off the small single serve pot, turning to face Thomas head on.

"It's not important," he said, and he wasn't trying to be dodgy or deceitful. His job just...wasn't important. It was something he wasn't passionate about, but had made a career out of anyway because that's what his life had required of him.

"So you're replaceable?"

"Hardly. It's just..." Thomas shrugged. "Not relevant to who I am."

"That sounds miserable."

"It sounds like it pays the bills." He bent over to put his shoes on. Ben leaned against the wall, still barely dressed, still looking like he'd walked out of Thomas's most secret dreams. "What about you?"

"What about me?"

"What do you do for work?"

"I'm not an Olympic medalist, much to my parents' dismay," Ben answered, mouth twisting into a sad smirk.

"Swimming?"

"That obvious?"

"You have a phenomenal body."

Ben brushed a hand over his stomach, fingers making contact with the dried cum Thomas had spotted earlier. Ben picked at it, letting the evidence of their night flake away beneath his fingers.

"I work for a bookstore," Ben said. "Managing their marketing."

"That sounds…honestly a lot better than what I do."

"Well, it's not nothing."

"Is it what you wanted to do?"

"I wanted to swim," Ben admitted. "But I also wanted swimming to be fun. It was tearing my muscles up and getting unenjoyable, so I backed away from it my junior year."

"Second best, then?" he asked.

"Fourth or fifth maybe."

"As long as you enjoy it."

"I don't hate it." Ben sipped at his coffee, eyeing Thomas over the rim of his mug. "Are you sure you don't want coffee? I can make you some for the road if you want."

"I don't live far."

"Walkable?" Ben asked.

He nodded.

"That's convenient."

Thomas chuckled and looked down, suddenly feeling far too seen.

"Anyway." Ben cleared his throat. "Plans or play it by ear?"

"I'd like to see you again."

"I have plans on Saturday night with my friends," Ben said, head cocked to the side. "But they're not all night. I can come by when I'm done?"

Thomas hesitated, something about the idea of Ben being in his space feeling a lot more serious than what they'd been doing up to that point. But he didn't know why it mattered. Ben had opened up his home; Thomas could manage the same. After all, it wasn't like anyone was moving in. There were no closets or drawers being cleared, no room in the medicine cabinet being made.

"How late?" he asked.

"You turn in early?" Ben teased, no doubt a poke at Thomas's age.

He rolled his eyes and checked his pockets for his wallet, keys, and phone. "Just want to know when to be ready."

"Can I text you on Saturday and we'll figure it out? I won't leave you hanging, but I don't know for sure what we're doing yet."

"That's fair."

Ben took another drink of his coffee. "Are you sure you don't want one for the road?"

"I'm sure."

"Then I'll be seeing you on Saturday night." Ben mock saluted him before turning away and going back into the kitchen.

"See you then," he mumbled, seeing himself out of the apartment.

Thomas closed the door behind him a little harder maybe than was necessary, but there were feelings inside of him that seemed complicated and he didn't know what to make of them.

He needed the brisk morning air to shake him out of whatever had come over him in the entryway of Ben's apartment.

He walked slowly, but with purpose, cracking his knuckles one by one as he counted the steps between their apartments. He quit counting at one hundred because his building was in sight and he knew one hundred wasn't even close to being enough.

"You're being ridiculous," he told himself. "You're getting attached because he's the first man you've been with."

He didn't know if that was really true or not. It wasn't like he'd been a virgin when he met Ben and there was no reason for him to be so attached to him. But he couldn't deny he liked the other man's company. Even though they'd agreed they weren't looking for a relationship, and he knew Ben was only after a rebound anyway, maybe they could manage a friendship aside from the sex part.

Thomas made his way into his building and up to his apartment, his mood immediately calmed when he closed the front door behind him. The moody darkness of his space, paired with the luscious plants, was quick to put him at ease. He kicked off his shoes in front of the shoe rack before heading into the kitchen to make himself a cup of coffee. It brewed quick and he carried it to the living room where he settled on his overstuffed gray couch with a happy sigh.

He rested his head against the back of the couch and took stock of all the physical and mental feelings running through him while he waited for his coffee to cool. His shoulders were relaxed, his muscles loose. Between his legs, his balls ached and his cock was tender, and he shoved his hand into his pants to touch himself there. Even though last night all they'd done was exchange mutual hand jobs, his mind was quick to take him to penetration and he groaned, thinking about how good it felt to sink his cock into Ben's snug asshole.

In his hand, Thomas's cock pulsed, also remembering the

heat of Ben's body. The thoughts were welcome, and his brain started to play with things it hadn't ever entertained before. Thomas had never thought about what it would be like to be on the receiving end…to bottom, but he found himself wondering what it would feel like to take a cock inside of his body.

He'd never so much as had a finger up his ass before, and his immediate reaction was nervousness and trepidation, the earlier relaxation in his muscles gone as they tangled and tensed together with an unspoken fear of the unknown. Subconsciously, he knew it couldn't be *that* bad. Ben seemed to like having fingers and a cock inside of him. Thomas had watched how hard Ben got while stretching himself open to make room, and with that in mind, he let his own hand wander back behind his balls.

The angle was no good and his coffee had already gotten cold, so he cast it—and his pants—aside. He took his cock into one hand and reached further behind himself until his fingertips grazed over his pucker. Recognition unfurled up his spine as he pressed the pad of his first finger against his hole. Fear and desire and want all rolled into one. It was curiosity, he reasoned, and he tested the resistance with a gentle push. Even as his balls tightened, his muscles refused to give way. He needed a better angle, he needed lube, and he had neither in the living room.

He didn't even have lube in his bedroom, and part of him wondered if Ben wouldn't be a better partner for his little exploration. Ben seemed to know his way around a man's body and Thomas had no doubt he'd treat him with care and attention. His brain misfired at that, taking him quickly to a scene where he found himself in Ben's bed on all fours, his ass in the air and Ben's face buried between his cheeks, fingers squelching in and out of his hole.

Thomas shuddered, tightening his grip around his dick to stave off a surprisingly swiftly approaching orgasm. With one hand flat on the arm of the couch, he sucked in a desperate breath, focusing on the way his cock throbbed and burned against his palm and not the way his asshole clenched in anticipation.

He waited until his end drifted further out of his reach before he relaxed his fist with a pained grunt. He'd come so many times the night before, he was honestly surprised that there was any cum left in his balls and he worried another orgasm would have left him boneless.

This was…a lot.

It was more than he expected when he'd searched Ben out for the first time, and while part of him had known this was the road he'd end up on, it still felt unexpected and more than a little bit scary. He remembered what it had been like to lose his virginity as a teenager. He'd been headstrong and confident at the time, but hindsight and experience had proven him to be bumbling and awkward. He'd approached Ben with the same level of confidence as he had approached Jessica Gregory in high school after their sophomore homecoming, but inside, he'd felt much the same.

Why was it scarier now?

It was the same thing all over again, but this time he had a whole lifetime of the fundamentals under his belt. The parts were different, sure, but the ideas had to be the same. Make sure it's wet, go slow, get off. It was easy, wasn't it?

With a sigh, Thomas let go of his still hard cock, letting his hand fall against his thigh. He was glad there'd be a week until he saw Ben again because he needed to take the opportunity to get his head on straight. And if he couldn't manage that…then he'd have to call things off before they got out of hand.

And while he didn't know much about what was going on, he knew he absolutely hated the idea of that.

CHAPTER 11
BEN

BEN RESTED his head on Lara's shoulder, the noise in the restaurant getting to be a little more than he was interested in handling.

"You're tired?" she asked, raising her voice to be heard over the commotion of the room.

Ben wasn't so much tired as he just didn't want to be at dinner. The week had crawled by at a snail's pace and even though there'd definitely been nights when he'd wanted to get fucked, he didn't call Thomas. He didn't call anyone. Instead he spent so much time with his dick in his hand it was almost like he was a teenager again, discovering it for the first time.

"Ben looks bored," their friend Owen teased from across the table.

"I'm not bored." He pulled his head off Lara's shoulder and reached for his drink. They'd barely made it past appetizers before his attention started to waver and he felt like a horrible friend about it.

"Distracted?" Owen arched a finely plucked brow in his direction.

"Thinking."

"About?"

"A boy," Lara teased.

"A man," he corrected.

"Oh!" Owen leaned in, glass in hand. He nudged their other friend, Caleb, in the arm, drawing his attention straight to Ben.

"What?"

"Ben has a man."

"Oh, my God," he protested, rolling his eyes. "I don't have a man."

Owen squinted at Lara. "So, is he a boy?"

"Would you stop?"

"Only if you answer," Caleb said.

"Just a guy I met on One-Night. We've been hooking up for a week or so."

"How many times?" Owen asked.

"Three or four," he mumbled.

"Is he hot?" Caleb laughed.

"Very."

"And you're here with us instead of in bed with him? Is that right?"

Ben sighed. "Not exactly. I have plans with him later."

Lara plucked the last pork bun off the appetizer plate in the center of their table and shoved it into her mouth, looking at him with wide eyes instead of saying a word. He'd known her long enough to know what she *wanted* to say, though, because it wasn't anything he hadn't already thought to himself.

He liked having benefits with Thomas, but the more he had conversations with the man, the more he wanted to be actual friends with him. And while friends with benefits wasn't necessarily against what they'd agreed to, it was also a slippery slope to the one thing they'd both decided they did not want. And beyond that, Ben still had plenty of horrible feelings in his chest and they were all wrapped around Cody and the way he'd made Ben feel during their very brief relationship.

In the quiet hours he had alone, Ben had on more than one

occasion wondered if there was something he'd done wrong that provoked Cody's misplaced anger. Or, worse, he had *actually* done something wrong. He'd never doubted himself, what he deserved, or what he had to offer, but things with Cody had changed his opinion of himself in ways he hadn't been able to make sense of yet. Most likely because when he did have down time, he was thinking about Thomas.

That was the point of a rebound, wasn't it?

Get over someone by getting under someone else.

He was avoiding facing the negativity that things with Cody had brought into the forefront of his mind, and Ben knew he couldn't ignore it forever. But maybe for a little longer...

"When later?" Caleb asked.

"When I'm done here."

"Aw." Owen pretended to pout, looking at the appetizer plate in front of them. "And that's so far away."

"You're a jerk."

"I'm your friend," Owen corrected.

Ben rolled his eyes and finished what was left in his glass. He hoped the waiter showed up soon because he was going to need a lot more alcohol to make it through dinner.

It didn't take long for Owen to return his attention to Caleb, and Lara to return hers to him.

"Three or four times?" she whispered.

"A few," he confirmed.

"That's...not nothing."

"It's not something," he said. "We have an agreement."

"And what's that?"

"It's just a hookup."

"Is it?" There was the sarcasm-laced accusation he'd expected when she had her mouth full of pork bun, and he lamented there weren't more left to shove behind her teeth to shut her up again.

"I know what I'm doing," he lied.

"Physically, sure."

"I know that you are not about to give me dating advice."

"I'm sure he's better than the last one."

"We don't speak of him." Ben covered Lara's mouth with his hand and she pursed her lips against his palm, smacking him away.

"You deserve better than him."

"Do I?" He scrunched his nose, drink still empty, so he took hers and finished it off, sputtering at the disgusting sugary flavor that exploded in his mouth. "Jesus, Lara. What the hell is that?"

"It's called a Summer Slam." She laughed and took her glass out of his hand, setting it on the table beside his empty one. "And yes. You deserve much better than Cody. Do you really doubt that?"

"Sometimes," he muttered.

"Are you being serious with me right now?"

"It's new."

"It's wrong."

Ben sighed and shrugged. "In my heart, I believe that. In my head...I don't know. It's a little more complicated. Being with Thomas seems to help."

"But that's just a hookup." Lara tilted her head to the side and narrowed her eyes.

"A hookup," he confirmed. "A rebound."

"Does he know you're using him to get over someone else?"

"He knows that what we are is all we're ever going to be," he said. "It's fine. I promise you we've talked about it."

"Yeah, but the way you're acting makes me feel like you want it to be more than that."

The waiter appeared—finally—to refill their drinks, and Ben drank half of his in one swallow. How dare Lara be so intimately in tune with him that she was able to pick up on that without him even saying a word about it. And, sure, he'd thought on a few occasions what it would be like to be more than friends with Thomas, but he'd done his best to nip those thoughts in the bud before they bloomed into something untamable.

"He's not the one," Ben said.

Lara inclined her head to the other side, expression still tight with disbelief.

"He's not," he said again.

Their meals arrived, and Ben wondered the whole time if maybe moving things along with Thomas wasn't as bad of an idea as he'd originally worried. Not like he wanted to be boyfriends with him, but if Thomas was new to being with men, he'd need a friend. He'd surely want someone he could confide in or talk to about his experiences. Ben could be that person. Maybe seeing Thomas outside of the bedroom without any intent behind it was what he needed to draw his mind back from racing toward imaginary fairy tale finish lines that could never exist for them.

And that was what he told himself when he drove home and parked in his assigned parking spot. When he sat in his driver's seat with the engine off to text Thomas and ask for his address. When he locked his car and started in the direction of Thomas's building, which was closer than he'd ever thought. Even when Thomas had said it was walkable, this wasn't what he'd imagined.

He stopped in front of the building and looked up, already knowing Thomas lived on the fifth floor, that he had a balcony, that he was so close. Ben pulled out his phone and fired of a text.

Ben: *Do you want to come downstairs?*
Thomas: *Are you here? I can buzz you in.*
Ben: *I am, but like... do you want to go for a walk? There's a gelato place a little further down the road.*

Thomas didn't answer, but less than two minutes later he appeared in the lobby, legs covered in dark and tight denim, paired with a simple and plain black t-shirt with a v-neck that exposed the tease of the top of his coarse chest hair. He wore Converse on his feet and held his phone in his hand. Thomas joined him on the sidewalk, expression slightly confused.

"I didn't think we did things like this," Thomas offered in lieu of a hello.

Ben wasn't drunk, but he was a little buzzed. He probably shouldn't have driven home, but the alcohol had ebbed and flowed over the course of dinner, finally hitting him in full force when he caught a whiff of Thomas's cologne. Had he worn cologne the other times they'd gotten together? Ben couldn't remember. He knew Thomas smelled good, but he didn't remember him smelling like this, like clouds and pine trees and petrichor.

"Like what?" Ben slipped his phone into his pocket.

Thomas gestured at the night sky like it meant something.

It did, Ben knew.

"I'm a little..." He paused and swirled his finger near his temple, hoping it got the message across. "I drank a bit and I just want to clear my head before we..."

Thomas licked his lips and it looked utterly sinful. Ben had to have seen him lick his lips before. It had to be the alcohol talking, clouding his vision, telling him it was sexier than it had been before, that it...

No.

Nope.

Absolutely not.

"Gelato?" Thomas asked.

"Anything to settle my stomach."

Thomas swallowed visibly, audibly, then he nodded and tipped his chin toward the corner. "Lead the way."

"Have you been there before?"

"I haven't lived here long," Thomas answered, and Ben remembered his circumstances. Why Thomas was living in a city apartment and not a sprawling house in the suburbs somewhere with his loving wife and two children.

"Right." Ben started toward the gelato shop with Thomas beside him. "So, how was your night?"

"Uneventful. Yours?"

"Dinner with some friends," he said. "We had Japanese."

"Sushi?"

"Ramen."

"I don't think I've ever had ramen," Thomas admitted.

Ben scoffed and stopped, grabbing Thomas's bicep and dragging him to a halt. It wasn't the first time he'd had his hand on Thomas's body, but he'd never realized how muscular he was. Or maybe he had and it just hadn't mattered.

"How have you never had ramen?"

"I mean, I've had the dollar stuff from the grocery store," Thomas said. "I had a lot of that when I was younger and Dakota was a baby."

"Dakota? Is that your son?"

"Yeah. My oldest."

Ben flexed his fingers, tightening them around Thomas's arm until he registered the heat radiating against his skin. He dropped his hand to his side and started to walk again, not waiting for Thomas to follow. He could or not. Ben wanted him to, but also hoped he wouldn't.

"Real ramen isn't anything like that shit," he said.

Thomas chuckled and caught up to him. "I didn't think it was."

"You should try it sometime."

"You'll have to take me," Thomas said quickly. He made a painful noise and followed up with, "Since you know where to go. Or you can just tell me."

Ben bit the tip of his tongue between his sharpest teeth,

desperate for some clarity. He knew he was riding the line of what was acceptable between them, of the things they'd agreed on. But he would be a liar if he said he didn't want to see Thomas more than he had been. That he wanted to see Thomas differently than he had been.

"I can take you," he said, rounding the corner with Thomas at his shoulder.

The lights of the gelato shop glowed a bright yellow and pink neon, and Thomas glanced at him, barely more than a flick of his head that Ben was aware of in his peripheral. Ben stopped in front of the store and returned Thomas's stare. There was something there, something he was sure Thomas wanted to say, but the door to the gelato shop opened and a group of girls poured out, laughing and chattering, completely unaware of anyone else around them. Their exit jostled Ben as the girls weaved between them and around them, but Thomas held his stare and Ben returned it in kind.

He couldn't breathe.

He couldn't think.

The noise of the group quieted to a background hum, and Thomas reached for the door to the gelato shop and pulled it open.

"After you," Thomas said, his voice low.

Ben blinked and forced a smile, tearing his gaze away and severing whatever had passed between them. But his skin prickled, senses heightened, and when Thomas settled his hand at the small of Ben's back to walk with him to the counter, Ben didn't shy away from it.

CHAPTER 12
THOMAS

THOMAS TRIED to ignore the slope of Ben's throat as he spent entirely too long perusing the dozen gelato flavors available to choose from. He took his time, looking from the bins of gelato in the freezer case and up to their names scrawled in chalk marker on a blackboard on the far wall of the shop and back again.

It had been a long week. Jennifer was combative when the topic of her new boyfriend came up and Thomas had dared to ask if he was someone she'd slept with while they were still together. While their divorce had been amicable enough, her answers to him turned malicious and cruel, and that was as much of a yes as he needed. On top of that, Kenzie had stopped answering his messages, and that was probably what hurt him the most. He was sure they'd made real progress over brunch on Sunday, so her silence was perplexing. He hadn't heard a peep from Dakota, but he hadn't heard from him since Christmas, so that wasn't as surprising as the rest of it.

Work had been work, and he hadn't been able to get Ben's line of questioning out of his head. He sat behind his computer, day after day, answering phone calls and dealing with supply chain issues, wondering if he was destined to spend the rest of his life in a job that made him miserable. He didn't have a family to provide for anymore. Only himself, and his rent, and his plants.

But was it too late to change?

"I can't decide," Ben said softly, his nose scrunched. "What are you going to get?"

Thomas huffed, hoping his cheeks didn't darken from his embarrassment. "I haven't even looked yet."

"There's almost too many choices," Ben said.

"Have you narrowed it down?"

"Mint chocolate, I think. But the caramel cake one sounds good too."

Thomas finally looked at the gelato descriptions on the wall. "The caramel one sounds really sweet."

Ben made a disgusted face and nodded, decision made. "You're right. Mint chocolate it is."

Thomas gave a cursory glance to the menu, opting for cookies and cream, which was a pretty consistent flavor as far as he'd ever been able to tell. They each got a single scoop, then took them onto the sidewalk and settled at one of the small cafe tables in front of the window.

"There's something to be said about green mint ice cream," Ben muttered, spoon hanging off of his tongue.

"Better or worse?"

"It's far superior."

"I'm inclined to agree," Thomas said.

Ben leaned his head back, again displaying the unnervingly sexy arch of his throat while he stared up at the night sky. It wasn't terribly cold out, but it was cloudy, and the neon gelato shop sign reflected off Ben's face like a rainbow kaleidoscope. Thomas gnawed on the inside of his cheek, forcing his attention down to his gelato so he didn't stare.

"So, how was dinner?" he asked.

Ben sucked another flat spoon of gelato against his tongue, making an indecent popping sound as he let go.

"It was..." Ben pursed his lips and shoveled another bite of gelato into his mouth. "It was fine."

"That doesn't sound fine."

"My friends were just..."

Thomas sensed the discomfort radiating out of every part of Ben's body, almost thick enough to cut with a knife. "You don't have to talk about it."

"They brought up my ex. Or not my ex...whatever he was. The guy from before you."

"The bad one," he supplied.

Ben nodded. "He came up, and I have mixed feelings about the whole thing, and I was drinking and it's distracting. That's all."

"Do you still want to be with him?" Thomas asked, even though he feared the answer. He shouldn't have cared if Ben still had interest in his ex because Ben had already said he didn't have interest in Thomas beyond what they were doing together, so what difference should it make?

"Definitely not." Ben rolled his eyes like the concept was absurd and something in Thomas's chest relaxed. "He's not a good person."

"I'm glad you're not with him anymore, then," he said softly.

"Me too." Ben set back to work on his gelato and Thomas looked away.

"What's your ex like?" Ben asked after a few more bites.

"She's not who I thought she was," he said.

"In what way?" Ben glanced at him quickly. "If you don't mind me asking."

"I don't mind." He leaned back against the uncomfortable square back of the chair, allowing the sharp corners to ground him in the present and remind him who he was and what they were to each other. "She...she wanted everything and offered little in return. I thought that was what I wanted. To provide for a family, but…it felt so one-sided."

"That sounds as unfulfilling as your job."

Thomas snorted, rolling his eyes and letting out a long breath. "It was a good life until it wasn't."

"Have you always been interested in men?"

"I don't know," he said, turning his attention after Ben's toward the sky. He couldn't tell if it was coming on a storm or not, but there wasn't a single star in sight. "I never really thought about it because I had her. She started cheating on me, or I found out she had been, and after that I allowed my mind to wander more than I had before."

"And it wandered to men?" Ben licked off the last of his gelato and dropped the spoon into the empty bowl. Thomas had barely touched his and it had started to melt around the edges, creating a milky white pool at the bottom of the cup.

"It wandered a lot of places. Men was the only one worth exploring."

"And you set up a profile on One-Night?"

He nodded and picked a chunk of chocolate cookie out of the melting mess of gelato.

"And I was your first," Ben said.

"You know you were."

"I just like hearing it."

"Is that so?"

Ben smirked, suddenly looking shy. "A bit."

"What about it do you like the most?" he asked.

"Oh, God." Ben covered his face with his hands. "Are we doing this?"

He laughed. "Doing what? It's just a question."

"It's exposure."

"You don't have to answer," he said. "I know none of this is part of the deal."

"The deal." Ben sighed and stretched his legs out, letting his hands fall together in his lap. "The fucking deal."

"Is that something else to talk about?"

Thomas hated the worry that sparked up his spine at the way Ben referenced their arrangement and it wasn't a conversation he wanted to have, but he couldn't *not* ask. A lifetime of not asking Jennifer was what had gotten him an apartment the size of his former basement and a costly divorce.

"It could be," Ben squinted, a half wink expression that Thomas couldn't make sense of. "But later. I can answer what I like about it if you want."

"I am curious," he said, glad to not have *the talk* yet.

Ben leaned closer, raising one hand to shield his mouth, even though he didn't lower the volume of his voice. "I like it because I know my body is the first you've ever had. My mouth is the first male mouth around that gorgeous cock. My hand, the first male hand..."

Thomas thought of all the things they hadn't done that Ben could maybe one day add to his list. The first man he'd kiss, the first man he'd let inside of *him*. He shivered, remembering how hard he'd come with his fingers dancing against his asshole and wondering how Ben would have touched him.

"I get the idea," he rasped.

"You're my first virgin."

"I'm hardly a virgin." He scoffed.

"You know what I mean."

"I'd never..." He trailed off, unsure of how much he wanted to say, but also well aware he'd already said too much to come back from. "Not just with a man, but I'd never..."

"Use your words," Ben coaxed, eyes glittering in the light.

"Fucked someone's ass before," he said, throwing up his hands. "I've never fucked someone's ass."

"We'll get you better at it."

He feigned hurt. "Are you saying I'm bad?"

"I'm saying we'll get you better." Ben chewed his lower lip between his teeth. "That gives me an idea."

"Should I be scared?" By this point, Thomas's gelato was a melted pool of stale cookies and quickly warning milk.

"I wouldn't be."

"What's your idea?"

"How familiar are you with your prostate?" Ben asked.

The tips of Thomas's ears warmed under the cool night air. "Excuse me?"

"Your prostate."

"I know it exists," he sputtered.

"Have you ever found it?" Ben leaned in again. "Touched it?"

"No."

"And I know you haven't touched anyone else's either."

"Obviously not," he said.

"Well, there's a first time for everything." Ben stood up and tossed his empty cup into a nearby trash can. "Was yours not good?"

"I wasn't that hungry," he lied, adding his into the trash.

"Should we head back to your place and do a little exploring?" Ben wiggled his fingers and laughed, threading his arm into the crook of Thomas's elbow and pulling him away from the gelato shop.

"You wanted to talk about our arrangement," he said, committing the feel of Ben's hand against his arm to memory.

He knew it didn't mean anything, or that it wasn't supposed to, but it felt so easy and so right, and he was so thankful for it. For the cool February night, and the cloudy sky, and the melted gelato, and all of it.

"I don't really want to," Ben corrected, giving him a squeeze.

"But do we have to?"

"Probably. At some point."

Thomas sighed, and together they turned the corner.

Without warning, lightning flashed above them at the same

time thunder clapped, shattering the quiet of the night. The clouds parted and it started to pour. Rain splattered around them, on them, and Thomas looked up as drops landed in his eyes and on his cheeks. Beside him, Ben laughed, water streaking down his throat, his shirt immediately soaked and plastered to his lithe, swimmer's chest.

"Come on." He raised his shoulder and cocked his elbow forward, trying to urge Ben along down the street. His building was in sight and he wanted to get out of the rain. "Hurry up."

"Why?" Ben asked with a laugh, shaking his hand free from Thomas's arm. Thomas tried to not mourn the loss of the affectionate touch, but found it near impossible.

"Why?" he repeated Ben's question. "Because it's pouring rain! We're getting soaked."

"We're already soaked." Ben laughed again and hooked his arms around Thomas's neck, spinning them in a circle on the sidewalk. He looked up and inhaled deeply, his dark lashes fluttering as he breathed.

"We're already soaked," Ben said again, "But now the whole night smells like you."

"Excuse me?"

Their rotation slowed to a stop and Ben's nose dragged up the side of Thomas's neck. It wasn't a kiss, it wasn't anywhere near to being a kiss, but it felt as intimate as he'd always worried a kiss could be. He and Ben were nearly the same height, with Thomas only having an inch or two on the younger man and he stayed still as he could, letting Ben breathe him in.

"You smell like the rain," Ben said. "Even before now. When you came outside earlier, you smelled like the rain."

Thomas's breath hitched in his throat and as Ben slowly pulled his face away from his neck, he looked down. They were terribly close, painfully close, and he could smell the mint from Ben's gelato against his lips. Thomas swallowed hard, closing his eyes, unsure of if he wanted Ben to lean up to meet him or put space between them.

"Now you smell like the rain too," he whispered.

Ben made a quiet sound that puffed against Thomas's mouth.

His heart slammed against his ribs, and he could feel Ben's match his, beat for rapid beat, from the other side. Ben's arms slid down his shoulders, his biceps, his forearms, until their fingers tangled together in the barest of holds. Thomas swore if Ben asked to kiss him, he would have said yes. He would have begged for the other man's tongue in his mouth, their bodies hot and aligned in the unexpected storm.

But for as immediately as the rain had started, it stopped, and the stillness of the experience shattered between them like glass. Ben cleared his throat and chose to step back, putting space between them. Thomas realized in that moment how much he'd been hoping for a kiss, and he understood the urgency of the conversation about the bounds of their agreement.

"We should get inside before it starts up again," Ben said, starting down the street. Thomas wasn't sure if he was walking to his place or if he'd keep going on to his own. He followed a step or two behind, relief flooding him when Ben came to a stop in front of his building instead of carrying on.

"Are you sure?" he asked, not willing to speak about what had passed between them, but not able to ignore it.

Ben smiled, even though it didn't meet his eyes.

"I'm positive," he said. "Take me upstairs, Thomas. Show me your bed."

CHAPTER 13
BEN

THOMAS'S APARTMENT was somehow nothing and everything like him all at the same time. Ben didn't get much of a chance to survey the living area because Thomas walked him right into the bedroom and closed the door without so much as a word. Ben leaned back against the door and watched Thomas as he discarded his clothes with no preamble. Long gone was the nervous man who'd shown up at Ben's place no more than two weeks before with his eager confidence and hidden insecurities.

"I didn't picture you being a black room, white sheets kind of guy," he mused.

"Are you surprised?" Thomas stood before him in a pair of white boxers, tented from his growing erection.

Ben tilted his head to the side, appraising Thomas with careful and quiet thought. His initial response would have been affirmative, and he knew he didn't know much about Thomas, but something about the space felt entirely fitting to the other man.

"Honestly, no," he said. "The plants in the other room are a bit unexpected, though."

"Jennifer hated plants. Said they attracted flies."

"Do they?"

"Did you really come over to talk about plants?" Thomas asked, palming himself over the nearly see-through fabric of his underwear.

"No." Ben pulled his shirt over his head and dropped it onto the floor. "I came over to teach you all about anatomy."

"Did you want a pointer stick for the lesson?"

He chuckled and popped open the button on his fly before shoving his pants down to his ankles. Ben held up his first two fingers and took a step toward Thomas. "I have that covered."

"Who's up first?" Thomas asked.

Ben hadn't thought that far, and now in the close confines of Thomas's bedroom, he found it hard to think about anything beyond how messy he wanted to make that ridiculously luxurious-looking white bedding.

"How about I show you mine and then you show me yours?"

"There's lube in the nightstand."

"Alright." He had to get his head on straight and get his act together. There were a thousand ideas running through his head of the ways he wanted to make Thomas come and none of them were casual and few were friendly. He brushed past Thomas on his way to the bed, allowing himself a breath to grimace before throwing himself onto the comforter and spreading his legs. "Get the lube and come here."

Thomas eagerly obliged, shoving out of his boxers and settling between Ben's thighs. Ben bent his legs at the knee and reached between his legs, cupping his balls and raising them up to expose himself. There was something oddly hot about the clinical nature of their engagement and, for the first time in a long time, Ben wondered about role playing games. He chuckled to himself and shook his head, scooting back so he was half sitting and half reclined.

"What's funny?" Thomas asked.

"I was just thinking about role playing in the bedroom," he

answered. "First I'm the teacher and now it feels like you're the doctor."

A deviant look flashed across Thomas's face and he flipped open the cap on the lube. "If only I had rubber gloves."

"You're going to kill me with that mouth."

"I could."

"Thomas."

Thomas squirted lube on his fingers and smeared it around until his skin shined under the dim light of the bedroom.

"You're just going to go in easy, palm side up." Ben had to drop his head back and close his eyes or he was going to come just from the way Thomas looked at him. "Probably to the middle knuckle. You'll feel it when you press up."

Thomas braced himself with one hand on Ben's hip, then he swirled his slippery fingers over Ben's bare hole. He shivered, squeezing his eyes closed as Thomas eased one finger inside of him. It wasn't anything he hadn't taken before, from other people or even himself, but the penetration paired with the heady weight of Thomas's stare on him felt like something different entirely. When the pad of Thomas's finger pressed against his prostate, gooseflesh tore across his body so violently he shuddered, fisting the sheets to keep himself on the bed.

"I found it," Thomas whispered.

Ben nodded. "You did."

"Can I..." Thomas licked his lips and dragged his stare away from Ben's cock toward his face. "Can I suck your cock?"

A nervous laugh fell out of Ben's mouth and he collapsed back against the pillows and the headboard. "You don't ever have to ask to suck my cock."

"Am I good at it?"

"What you lack in talent, you make up for with enthusiasm."

"Should I be offended?" Thomas arched a brow and curled his other fist around the base of Ben's dick.

"You should put my dick in your mouth," Ben rasped,

threading his fingers through Thomas's hair and encouraging him downward.

Thomas continued his gentle exploration, pressing and prodding around Ben's channel and prostate, adding a second finger at the same time he sealed his lips around the flared head of Ben's cock.

"Shit," he muttered, every muscle in his stomach convulsing.

Thomas hummed a pleased sound and slipped lower, hollowing his cheeks and sucking as he moved.

Ben groaned, licking his lips and trying not to count the strands of gray in Thomas's hair. The interest didn't have anything to do with Thomas's age, merely his proximity. While they, of course, had been that close in the past, Ben hadn't ever allowed himself to watch so intently, to study, to focus. It was clear Thomas was doing the same, his brow furrowed as he bobbed up and down the length of Ben's cock, his fingers swirling a devastatingly enjoyable circle around the soft bundle of nerves inside of Ben's body.

"Do you want to fuck tonight?" he managed to ask, fingers tightening in Thomas's hair.

With an agonizing slowness, Thomas licked his way toward the tip of Ben's cock before letting it slide out of his mouth. His lips were shiny from spit and swollen, and Ben wanted more than anything to kiss him. Instead he bit his lips together between his teeth and waited for Thomas's answer.

"The way we have been," Thomas said.

"I wasn't asking if you wanted to bottom."

"Maybe another time."

"I'm talking about tonight," he said.

"Yes." Thomas shifted, revealing his own erection—long, and thick, and swollen between his legs.

"Then you have to stop. I don't want to come yet."

"Was it that good?"

He huffed out a quiet laugh. "Yes, but also the prostate."

Slowly, Thomas withdrew his fingers, nostrils flaring when Ben's hole gaped after his exit.

"I don't want to come before we fuck," Thomas said with a small frown.

"Do you think it feels that good?"

"You look like you ran a mile and I've only been between your legs for five minutes."

"Did you want me to show you what it feels like?" he asked.

"I have a toy," Thomas suggested.

Ben was suddenly aware of the sweat on his forehead and his temples. He really had been doing the work to fend off his orgasm apparently. He hadn't even realized because he'd been so transfixed watching the way Thomas's burgeoning confidence turned him into a sexier version of his already sexy self, but those four simple words caught him entirely off-guard.

"A toy?" Ben reached between his legs and tugged his balls away from his body with a grunt.

"A prostate massager," Thomas said. "It's small. The man at the store said you just put it in and it vibrates against you there."

"I know what a prostate massager is," he said. He just didn't understand why almost-virgin Thomas would have one.

"I haven't gotten up the courage to try it yet."

"Did you want to now?" he asked. "You could wear it while we…"

"Fuck," Thomas filled in the blank.

"Yes."

"Will you put it in for me?" Thomas's cock spasmed against his stomach, precum beading at his slit. "I've never done that before."

Ben scrubbed a hand down his face and sat up. "Yeah. Stand up and bend over the bed. That might be the easiest way to get it in. Where is it?"

"Top drawer, in the back."

He scrambled off the bed and went to Thomas's dresser,

digging around through Thomas's underwear drawer until he found the small black massager. Ben had one like it at home, and it was one of his favorite toys. He loved to wear it on nights when he wanted to spend hours with his cock in his hand. It was a little bit torturous, but he loved the way the constant vibration put him on edge while he teased his cock and balls. He checked the batteries, leaving it on the lowest setting while he poured some lube over the tip.

Thomas had bent over the bed, and Ben smoothed a hand down the subtle curve of the small of his back and over his ass. "I hope one day you want to see what it feels like to have a cock in your ass."

"When I'm ready, you'll be the first to know." Thomas's thighs trembled and so did his voice. Ben let out a slow breath and gently pressed the tip of the massager against Thomas's hole.

"I'll go slow. The vibration will help, but if you want me to stop, just tell me and I will."

Thomas spread his legs wider. "Don't stop."

Ben pressed harder, the puckered rim of Thomas's ass flaring out to make way for the small, bulbous end of the toy. Thomas sucked in a breath and Ben steadied him with a gentle hand against his back.

"Bear down a little. That'll make it easier."

Thomas did, and the toy sucked into him after that with surprising ease. Thomas gasped, but the breathy sound turned into a shocked moan as Ben settled the flared plug base between the cheeks of his ass.

"Are you okay?" Ben asked.

"I could come like this."

"It's even better if you don't," he promised. "If you fight against for a little bit."

"I want to fuck you."

"Then put on a condom and fuck me."

"Get on the bed." Thomas straightened, grunting as the toy adjusted inside of him. He went to the nightstand and opened the drawer, producing a condom that he opened without so much as another word.

Ben climbed onto the bed, on his back again with his legs spread. His cock burned against his hand like a branding iron and he kept his balls in the cradle of his palm so they didn't get any ideas about premature orgasms. He watched with rapt attention as Thomas covered his cock with the condom and once again settled between his legs. Thomas used his shoulders to lift Ben's legs into the air like it was a position they'd done hundreds of times before and not just once.

Thomas lined the slick head of his cock up against Ben's hole and eased forward with a slow pump of his hips. He breached Ben gently, more gently than he would have wanted considering his brain was headed right for a dangerous and undoubtedly emotional place.

"Go on," he coaxed, egging Thomas on. "Don't be scared. I won't break."

"I'm so close to coming," Thomas answered him through gritted teeth.

"That's the point."

"I want you to come."

Ben let go of his balls and gave a slow tug up the length of his erection. "You don't have to worry about that."

"Do you think..." Thomas's words came out scratchy as he set a devastatingly slow rhythm. "I know we talked about it before, but do you think that one day I could come inside of you?"

Ben's balls churned, hot and tingly between his legs. He tightened his fingers around his cock and stroked himself quicker. The simple thought of Thomas's cum flooding his hole after that tender and cautious prostate massage from earlier was enough to bring him to the very brink of his release.

"If we get tested," he said. "We'd need to have rules."

"More rules." Thomas's body shuddered, his ab muscles contracting.

Ben knew the strength of the vibrator and he also knew that Thomas was most likely as close to coming as he was.

"We can talk about that later," he promised.

"I'm embarrassingly close to coming," Thomas mumbled, falling forward and bracing himself with a hand on the pillow beside Ben's head. They were close, so close. Their noses brushing and their lips no more than a handful of inches apart. Thomas pumped his hips, a slow gyration that dragged the head of his cock against Ben's prostate like their bodies were designed to do nothing more than exactly what they were already doing.

"Me too," he chuckled. "So, please get on with it."

Thomas's breath puffed hot against his mouth, but he didn't change his pace. He kept at Ben with the same agonizing slowness he'd started with, drawing Ben's orgasm out of him like a string unraveling from a ball of yarn.

"I'm coming." Ben arched off the bed, their chests connecting and mouths coming even closer together. Thomas held his stare, eyes hooded as they scanned the depths of Ben's eyes. It was the most serious look Thomas had ever given him, the most intimate thing they'd ever done, and Ben whimpered, a gentle cry against Thomas's mouth as his balls emptied onto his stomach.

"You're so gorgeous." Thomas brushed his hair back from his face, hips finally faltering as his cock thickened and swelled at the onset of his orgasm. "Your body. Your…"

Thomas didn't finish his thought, the words falling off into a long and low groan as he came. In that moment, Ben also wanted to know what it would feel like for Thomas to come inside of him with no barriers between them. But how absurd, to take Thomas's seed into his body and not his spit.

"Thomas," he whispered, tilting his head back. He slid his hands around Thomas's ass and pulled him deeper, wrapping his legs around the small of his back and holding him in. In the quiet of the room, he could hear their breathing, nearly in sync, and the gentle hum of the massager still buzzing against Thomas's prostate.

"Thomas," he said again, ready to ask permission, but Thomas beat him to the punch.

"It was a stupid rule."

"What?"

Ben barely had time to get the word out before Thomas closed the space between them, slanting their mouths together. He didn't use any tongue; instead the kiss was a gentle press of parted lips and shared breath. It was enough to wring the last of Ben's orgasm out of his body, and he trembled, tightening his arms and legs around Thomas. He wanted more. More of the kiss, more of his body, more than just friends, but…

But.

He took what he was given, their breaths falling completely in time with each other the longer their mouths were connected. Ben shifted, puckering and ending the kiss only to press his lips against the corner of Thomas's mouth. It wasn't even close to how much he wanted, but how did you ask a stranger for everything? It was enough for now and as far as first kisses went, it would always be his best.

"Are you okay?" Thomas asked, cock still pulsing inside of Ben's body.

"I should ask you." He couldn't stop himself from peppering a flurry of kisses against Thomas's mouth. He didn't know if he would get another chance.

"That felt…that wasn't anything like I expected."

"The kiss?" he asked.

"The kiss. All of it."

Ben reluctantly let his legs slide away and Thomas pulled out of him with a frown. On his knees, Thomas pulled off the condom and knotted it in the middle, throwing it into a small trash can beneath the nightstand. He reached behind him and pressed the power button on the plug before drawing it out with a comparable wince. Thomas dropped the toy onto the floor and shouldered Ben out of the center of the bed, then lay down beside him.

"Are you okay?" Thomas asked again.

Ben turned his head to the side, giving himself the space to study the sweaty dips and lines of Thomas's body. He reached out and traced his finger in a delicate circle over one of Thomas's nipples. Thomas shuddered and reached down, snatching Ben's hand away from his chest and kissing his fingers before dropping both of their hands back down to the bed.

No, Ben thought to himself, he wasn't okay at all.

CHAPTER 14

THOMAS

IT HAD BEEN TWO WEEKS, and Thomas was having no luck getting Ben to nail down a time to get together again. They'd exchanged some text messages, but Ben had been just shy of dismissive and Thomas worried he'd done something wrong the last time they were together.

On a warm Friday night, Thomas surveyed his apartment, wondering if maybe the fault lay in his decorations. Had his decor inadvertently revealed something about him that he wasn't ready to share or had Ben read into something that wasn't there? Had their talk about getting tested and foregoing condoms been too much?

He worried that was the case.

Even in the few weeks they'd been…doing whatever they were doing together…the nature of their relationship had changed a lot. What started as a one night stand had turned into an ongoing—and exclusive—hookup and then into something more like friends with benefits? Thomas knew his feelings toward Ben went far beyond friendly, but he also knew that Ben was freshly out of a bad relationship and he wasn't looking for anything more committed than what they already had. And, honestly, Thomas was still legally married, even if for all intents and purposes it was over, so he had no right trying to get into a relationship with anyone.

Ben had wanted a rebound and Thomas was fine for that to be him. In a sense, Ben was kind of like a rebound for him as well, if you counted him rebounding from an entire life that didn't mean anything close to what it used to.

None of that changed the fact it was a Friday night and Ben was blowing him off, and he was utterly bored. Thomas hadn't been great about keeping up with his friends as the divorce with Jennifer progressed, and he debated how horrible it would be to reach out to one of them now. The divorce had made things weird, considering most of his friends were part of his and Jennifer's couple friends. He'd expected that people would want to pick sides, but he hadn't expected it to be so jarring to lose as many as he had.

He decided Friday night wasn't the best time to try and reconnect with old friends and instead decided to go treat himself to a cup of gelato at the shop Ben had taken him to down the street. He definitely wasn't hoping to run into Ben, and genuinely didn't even know what he would say if he did. Thomas just wanted out of the house and the gelato shop was the first place he thought to go. He checked his phone one last time for any messages from Ben, watered his plants, and locked his apartment.

Thomas was half a block away from the gelato shop when he heard a laugh he immediately recognized. He debated turning back before Ben saw him, but it was already too late. Ben turned, head thrown back in a laugh as he reached across the table and smacked the arm of the woman he was with. Was Ben on a date? Was that why he'd been avoiding Thomas?

When Ben saw him, his face fell and he turned to his friend and whispered something. The woman looked over his shoulder toward Thomas, a curious expression on her face. That was enough for him. He turned to go, but Ben called after him, and against his better judgement, he stopped. Ben's footfalls grew louder against the sidewalk until he was so close Thomas could smell him.

"Hey," Ben said softly.

"I didn't mean to interrupt your date."

"I'm not on a date." Ben laughed gently. "Lara is my best friend."

"Friend date, then."

"Still not a date."

Thomas scrubbed a hand down his face and turned sideways to look at Ben. "Either way, whatever it was, I didn't mean to interrupt."

He started to head back home, his desire for gelato forgotten, but Ben reached for him. It wasn't much more than a soft press of fingers against his forearm, but it was enough to bring his stubborn feet to a standstill.

"Thomas."

"Yeah?"

Ben's fingers slid up his arm and curled around the tense muscle. "Don't make this weird?"

"Are you asking me not to?"

"I haven't been ignoring you," Ben said.

"Ben?" A woman's voice came between them softly, and Thomas let his stare drift toward Ben's friend. "I'm gonna head out."

"I didn't mean to interrupt," Thomas said again.

She smiled at him, her eyes a vibrant and mischievous green even in the dim light of the streetlamps. "You're not interrupting anything."

"Lara," Ben sighed warily.

"In fact, we were just talking about you," she said.

Thomas looked from Ben's friend—Lara— back to him, question in his eyes. "You were talking about me?"

Ben's lashes fluttered and he gave Lara an exhausted look.

"I'll talk to you later."

"Hopefully much later," she said, kissing Ben on the temple. "Nice to meet you, Thomas."

"We didn't meet," he said.

Lara's mouth twitched into a smile before falling away. "Well, until we meet *again*, then."

Thomas listened to the wedges of her heels clunk down the sidewalk until she disappeared out of sight and around the corner, leaving him and Ben alone.

"What were you saying about me?"

Immediately, he feared the worst. He imagined Ben and his friend laughing over cups of gelato while they talked about how closeted he was, how new, how embarrassed.

"I don't want to say," Ben muttered.

"You won't hurt my feelings."

"It's nothing like that."

Thomas jerked his arm, but Ben didn't let his hand fall away. He tightened his hold, both of their stares moving to the place where they touched.

"You don't have to lie," he said.

"Thomas." Ben let go of him and shoved his hands into his pockets, looking away. "It's not like that."

"What then?"

"I was telling her how much I like you." Ben raised his voice a little and frowned, letting out a long breath and walking in the direction of their apartment buildings.

Thomas found himself momentarily stunned, but managed to recover and caught up with Ben before he'd reached the corner. He fell in step beside him, listening to their footsteps and the harsh cadence of Ben's jagged breaths.

"You like me?" he asked.

"Apparently."

"So you've been ignoring me?"

"I wasn't supposed to like you." Ben turned the corner, Thomas at his side. "That wasn't part of the plan."

"The agreement," he said.

"The whatever."

"You like me?"

Ben came to a stop and looked up. They were in front of Thomas's apartment building. He hadn't realized they'd walked so fast.

"I'm sorry for it," Ben said. "I know it wasn't supposed to happen."

"It's not…it's not bad that you like me."

"I've never been one for unrequited romance, Thomas." Ben rolled his eyes and sidestepped him, leaning against the side of the building and folding his arms in front of his chest. Ben slumped down, his entire body telegraphing his defeat. Thomas would have been lying if he'd said Ben's reaction to his own confession didn't feel like a wound. No one had ever been upset about liking him before. Actually, no one had ever liked him before at all, besides Jennifer, and she hardly counted anymore.

"Who said it was unrequited?"

"You're married."

"Divorcing," he corrected.

"And I'm on the rebound," Ben reminded him.

"You don't have to be," he said. "You know, what we've done so far could have been a rebound thing. What happens from here out doesn't have to be."

"I don't even think you know what you're saying." Ben gave him a tired smile.

"I'm pretty sure I know my own mind."

"But you don't." Ben shoved off the wall and walked a tight circle in front of the door. "You're…you're not even out. You're not even sure you like men."

"Oh, I'm sure I like men."

"You're sure you like *me*."

Thomas sighed, unable to dispute it and relatively sure his interest in gay porn wouldn't be enough to convince Ben otherwise.

"I don't feel right asking you to be in a relationship with me when you don't even know what that would mean," Ben said.

"I was married for years. I know how to be in a relationship."

"But not with a man."

"Is it that much different?"

"Socially?" Ben tilted his head to the side like it was an ignorant question, and Thomas supposed that it might have been.

"I'm not scared of it," Thomas said. "We already agreed that even if things were casual between us, they would be exclusive. I went and got tested this week, and…"

"You did?" Ben interrupted.

"Of course. It was what we talked about before you disappeared."

"I didn't disappear."

Thomas rolled his eyes and folded his arms over his chest.

"Fine," Ben conceded. "I did disappear."

"I'm negative." Thomas waved his hand flippantly. "But apparently that doesn't matter anymore."

"It matters," Ben whispered. "It matters that you went even though…"

"Did you?"

Ben nodded.

"All for nothing, then?"

"I don't know what you want me to say," Ben replied softly.

"I want you to make sense." Thomas tapped his temple with the tip of his pointer finger. "You like me, you like being with me, you went and got tested so I could come inside of you—but now that I know about all of this, you don't want it anymore?"

"It's not that simple."

"You know what?" Thomas stepped away, growing more frustrated with every word out of Ben's mouth. "I like you, I like being with you, I got tested so *I* could come inside of you because those were things we'd talked about and agreed on, but this isn't it for me. I am too old for games like this."

"I'm not trying to play games!" Ben surged toward him, wrapping his fingers around Thomas's arms and backing him against the wall. He was close again, so close. As close as he'd been the last night the two of them had spent together when Thomas had wanted more than anything to kiss him.

"I'm too old to not be honest with myself and the people around me," he said.

"So does your ex-wife know you've been sleeping with a man? Your kids?"

"It's not their business. If I was seeing a woman, I wouldn't tell them that either."

Ben exhaled and pressed his forehead against Thomas's. Thomas allowed himself to reach forward, gently sliding his hands around Ben's slim waist. He felt the firm lines and muscles beneath the soft fabric of his t-shirt, and he wanted more. He rucked it up just enough to get contact with Ben's warm and smooth skin. At the first touch, Ben sucked in a breath and groaned like he was in pain.

It wasn't anyone's business who he took to bed or who he jacked off to. Thomas knew that if things progressed with Ben, there would come a day when Jennifer, Dakota, and Kenzie would eventually find out, but it was so far down on the list of concerns he hadn't paid it any mind. Their reactions surely wouldn't be enough for him to change his mind or alter course.

"Am I sending you mixed signals?" Ben asked, sounding confused and defeated.

Thomas tightened his grip on Ben's waist. "A bit."

"I don't want to settle," Ben said. "I wasn't looking for a relationship after my last one and you deserve better than me just sliding into the comfort of being with you."

"Isn't that the point?"

Ben continued, uninterrupted, "And you deserve the certainty of knowing who and what you want."

"You think I don't know my own mind?" he asked again.

Ben dragged his hands up Thomas's arms, his shoulders, his neck, until he reached Thomas's face and traced his fingertips across his cheekbones. The touch sent a shiver through his entire body and he closed his eyes, relishing the emotions Ben brought out in him. Thomas felt powerful and handsome. He felt capable and desired. They were all heady feelings and he wanted more of them.

"I know you do," Ben said softly.

"Then what is the problem?"

Ben brushed their noses together, letting out another small breath. "I'm not sure I trust mine."

"How so?"

"I want to believe you, Thomas. I really do. But I don't understand how I can be your first choice when I'm also your only choice."

CHAPTER 15

BEN

THOMAS BLINKED HIS EYES OPEN, the confusion clear on his face. "What does that mean?"

"I'm the first man you've been with, but I'm also the only man you've been with."

"Right."

"There wasn't a choice." He bit his lower lip, knowing he needed to put space between them, but not able to make his feet work. What was it about Thomas that had him so full of wanting?

"I would choose you if there was," Thomas said.

"And I want to believe you." Against his will, Ben's mind went back to Cody and the disaster of that relationship. He remembered all too well the false sense of comfort and security he'd been lulled into before things went to shit. It wasn't that he expected Thomas to treat him that bad, but things with Cody had made him more aware than ever of what he wanted and what he deserved.

Ben had wanted a casual hookup because he'd wanted to clear his mind. But Thomas had gotten under his skin and made him think different ways and want different things. And the whole while, he'd been there wanting Thomas and the promise of what a relationship between them could be, even though he couldn't shake the nagging doubt that he wasn't more than a passing mid-life crisis for the other man.

Cody had robbed him of his ability to trust.

It wasn't fair to ask Thomas to do work to repair the damage caused by his ex, but he didn't know what else to do.

"But it's not that easy?" Thomas asked.

"I just want to be sure. I want *you* to be sure."

Thomas pulled him closer, their fronts colliding so Ben became achingly aware of the hardness growing between Thomas's legs. "How can I make you sure?"

The idea sat on the tip of Ben's tongue, but even as he thought to verbalize it, he hated the taste.

"Dating," he choked out.

"I'll date you."

He shook his head. "Not me. Or at least, not just me."

"Excuse me?" Thomas's fingers gouged into his waist and he pushed Ben back into the middle of the sidewalk. He didn't let go, though. He came off the wall, straightening his back and stepping after him.

"I just want you to be sure," he said again.

"You want me to date other people? We just talked about being exclusive. I don't understand."

Ben wanted to kiss the frown off Thomas's face. Why had the other man said no kissing? Why did he care? Why was he insisting on such a horrible idea? The only person who would get hurt in this was himself. If Thomas went out with another man, met someone else and realized that Ben wasn't so great or wasn't worth it, he'd be gone. But even if Thomas did come back to him, Ben would only be the first and last, but maybe not the only.

"It was a bad idea," he said, already wishing he could take it back.

"I know." Thomas scoffed. "But did I understand you right? Is that what you were saying?"

"I'm confused, and I'm sorry." He closed the space between them and wrapped his arms around Thomas's waist, holding their bodies together so tight there was no atoms or air between them. Thomas didn't hesitate. He returned the hug, holding Ben just as tight, if not tighter.

"Is that what you want?" Thomas sounded like Ben had sucker punched him, and the breath left Ben's own lungs in kind.

"No," he answered quickly. "It's not."

"Then don't say it." Thomas grabbed his face and jerked his chin so they were forced to make eye contact. The hurt on Thomas's face was apparent, and Ben would have given pretty much anything to go back and erase the last ten minutes from their lives so he would have never mentioned the idea to Thomas in the first place.

"I'm sorry."

"Don't be sorry," Thomas said to him. "Just be honest."

"I want you," he rasped, leaning into Thomas's touch.

"You can have me." Thomas bumped their noses together, the hurt in his features softening just enough to make Ben stop wishing the sidewalk would open up and swallow him whole.

"Thomas." Ben reached up and hooked his fingers around Thomas's hands. He didn't know if he was holding on or pulling closer. "Please, can I kiss you again? Like a proper kiss?"

"Yeah." Thomas answered with a quick nod, a thousand emotions flashing through his eyes too fast for Ben to make sense of any of them. "Yeah, you c…"

Ben didn't wait for him to say anything else. He surged forward, taking Thomas's half open mouth in his. He kissed him like that. Different from the last time because he could feel the heat of Thomas's tongue against his teeth, but not what he wanted because it wasn't enough. It was nowhere near enough.

Thomas's fingers pressed harder into his cheeks, and Ben moaned, his lips parting. He drew a shocked breath when Thomas's tongue was the first to move, sliding into his mouth with the same tentative but confident curiosity he applied to everything else he did.

When Ben returned the kiss, swirling his tongue around Thomas's, he swallowed down the resulting moan and walked him back into the wall to get a better angle. He kissed Thomas, deeper and harder, until his cock stuck to his underwear for how slick the tip was with precum, and only then did he pull back for air. He didn't go far, keeping their mouths pressed together with only enough space to breathe.

"Do you want to come in?" Thomas asked, a little breathless.

"Yeah. But I won't."

"What?"

"If you mean what you said and I mean what I said, then I want this to be more than it has been, and if I go upstairs with you, I'll want to take you to bed."

Thomas grinned and pressed a kiss against the corner of his mouth. "Can't it be both?"

"Yeah, but…"

Thomas kissed him again. "It's okay. I know what you mean."

"I *really* want to." He slid his hand down between their bodies, giving Thomas's erection a squeeze to prove his point.

Thomas's lashes fluttered and he followed Ben's hand down, grabbing him by the wrist. He didn't move him away, but he didn't let him go either.

"Let me take you out for a drink or something, then," Thomas offered.

"You were on your way for gelato, I think, when…"

"But you've already had some."

"I didn't eat it."

"Let me take your for a drink," Thomas said again. "Someplace dark and quiet."

"Mahogany wood and whiskey?" He arched a brow and watched Thomas answer with a nod.

"If you like."

"Do you even like whiskey?" he asked.

"Sometimes. I was going for the ambiance."

He chuckled under his breath. "Are you trying to get me someplace dark so you can feel me up under the table?"

Thomas squeezed his wrist. "I'm trying to get you somewhere quiet so I can listen to every word that comes out of your mouth."

Ben kissed him again, crashing their mouths together and shoving Thomas once again into the wall. He held Thomas by his cock, the grip meant to be a promise and a question all in the same breath. He kissed Thomas with long and slow strokes of his tongue until Thomas's hips bucked forward, pushing his cock into Ben's hand.

"Drinks," he murmured, regretfully ending the kiss. He would have gladly gone upstairs with Thomas if he'd allowed it, but he wanted to respect him and not push.

Ben knew he'd been a little frantic and scattered when they'd run into each other at the gelato shop and he'd done much more than send mixed signals. He wanted to believe they'd gotten to someplace level and good, even if it wasn't where they'd intended to go.

"I've wanted that for so long," Thomas whispered, pressing his fingertips against his lips.

"You have?"

"I didn't at first because everything was so new, but...yeah."

Ben cleared his throat, feeling relatively choked up with emotions for a reason he couldn't put his finger on. For as much as it had taken for him to back down and admit his heart, he knew it had been just as much—if not more—of a leap for Thomas. They were both taking a risk on each other and things were getting serious.

"I know a bar," he offered, clearing his throat. "I don't think it's mahogany inside, but they have an extensive liquor menu."

"Walkable?" Thomas asked.

"Sadly, no."

"I can drive."

"We can get a car," he suggested. "So we can both drink."

"If you like." Thomas pulled his phone out of his pocket. "What's the name of the bar?"

"The Brentwood."

Ben watched Thomas's fingers swipe and tap across his phone while he ordered the car, then nervously reach for Ben after he returned his phone to his pocket. Ben offered up his hand freely, in awe of how *right* it felt in that moment to be standing on the sidewalk holding Thomas's hand.

The car came and they sat in the back together, so close the outsides of their thighs brushed. Thomas didn't let go of his hand and he didn't say a word. The silence was gentle and enjoyable and it was new to Ben. He couldn't remember a time he'd had that kind of comfort with another person. Certainly not with Cody and not with anyone before him either.

The bar came into view and Thomas squeezed his hand. Ben returned it, and once the car stopped alongside the curb, he pulled Thomas out after him and into the building. He found a small table in the back corner of the space, almost removed from the low hum of conversation that filled the room. In the middle of the table sat a thick, leather-bound drink menu, and he handed it off to Thomas to browse. Ben already knew what he wanted to get so, like earlier, he took advantage of the time to watch Thomas.

No more than thirty seconds passed before Thomas closed the menu and dropped it back down on the table in front of them.

"Did you find something you liked?" he asked.

"You."

Ben couldn't help but laugh at the ridiculousness of the pick-up. "Does that line work on women?"

"It wasn't a line." Thomas leaned back in his chair with a smirk that told Ben it might have been a line.

"Did you find a drink you wanted?" he asked instead.

"I did."

"Are you going to keep me in suspense?" Ben smiled. "You can tell a lot about a person by the drink they order."

Thomas laughed and leaned in. "I'm getting a scotch."

"I believe it."

"Are you going to enlighten me as to what this reveals?"

"Scotch drinkers are proud and confident," he said, and Thomas looked at him as he spoke, proud and confident. "They have a dedicated attention to detail."

Thomas arched a brow, the tip of his tongue darting out to lick the corner of his mouth. "Is that so?"

"They like to take their time with things. Savor them."

"Is that true? Do I take my time?"

Ben cleared his throat. "You've been thorough when allowed."

"When allowed?"

"I think that things between us have been developing under false pretenses," he said. "Both of us trying to pretend that there wasn't anything between us when there was. Now that things are more out in the open..."

"Now I can stop and savor," Thomas said.

"Hopefully," he rasped, voice cracking.

"What about you?"

"Gin and tonic," he answered.

Thomas reeled back, eyes still heavy with tease, but now colored with a flash of surprise. "You didn't strike me as the type."

"No?"

"What do they say about a gin drinker?" Thomas asked, reaching under the table and settling his hand on Ben's thigh.

"That I'm stubborn as a mule."

"And are you?"

"Clearly not, because we're here."

"You say that like it's a bad thing."

"It's not bad," he corrected. "It's just...obviously not what I had planned."

"Speaking of plans, we're both tested, so does this mean..."

Ben's throat flushed warm at the implication in Thomas's half question. "We can forego condoms. Yes."

"And does this also mean we're dating?"

Ben leaned back in his seat with a sigh. That was the question of the hour. He'd admitted his interest in Thomas, and Thomas had shared his view of whatever was happening between them, but dating felt like such a big and scary thing for him. Even though he knew in his gut that Thomas wasn't ready to be in a relationship with a man, he couldn't say no. He didn't want to continue to deprive himself of the things he wanted or enjoyed out of fear of losing them.

"Did you want to date me?" he asked. "Like, are you sure you're ready to be in a relationship with a man?"

"I'm ready for *you*," Thomas said, his face looking as confident and sure as it had when he'd told Ben he drank scotch.

"Then, yes," he said. "We're dating."

CHAPTER 16
THOMAS

THOMAS STUDIED his reflection in the mirror, wondering if going on a date with Ben was a mistake. Not that he wasn't interested, because he was. It wasn't that he was nervous about being out with a man, because he wasn't. The problem was his age. He wasn't an old man, but he was much older than Ben, who was closer to Dakota's age than Thomas's own. In his gut, he knew if his age was an issue for Ben, Ben wouldn't have been interested in dating him, but it was still a hard feeling to shake.

The date was also a departure from what they'd gotten used to. There would be no walk to the other's apartment and no trip to the gelato shop. Ben had planned the date and it involved nice clothes and a car ride, and all of the nerves Thomas could contain in his chest without imploding.

His phone buzzed on the counter with a text from Ben letting him know he was five minutes away, and then immediately buzzed again with a phone call from the absolute last person he wanted to talk to.

Thomas frowned and accepted the call, leaving it on speaker. "Hi," he said.

"Hey." For so many years, Jennifer's voice had brought him

comfort, but now it only put him on edge. "Do you have a minute?"

"Not much more than that." He turned off the lights in the bathroom, tired of his reflection. He grabbed his phone and carried it into the living room.

"I just wanted to do you the courtesy of telling you that I'm seeing someone."

"Your daughter beat you to it."

Jennifer sighed, and he could picture the expression on her face down to the three fine lines that fanned out below her right eye when she was frustrated. "I asked her not to tell you."

"And I asked her *to* tell me," he said, which was close enough to the truth.

"I didn't think you cared."

"I don't. It was an oversight in my thought process." Thomas put on his shoes and checked his pockets for his wallet and keys.

"I wanted to see if you were interested in meeting him."

"I don't," he said quickly. There was no world where he felt it was important for him to meet his ex-wife's new boyfriend. Especially since there was a chance she'd fucked him while they were still married.

"Kenzie likes him."

"Does she?" He knew better.

"I don't want there to be animosity."

"This isn't a blended family, Jen." The screen on his phone lit up with a message from Ben, indicating his arrival. "You made your choices and we are where we are, but you and I? We don't need to do this."

"Tom—"

"Your minute is up," he said. "I have to go."

She let out a long breath "Alright."

He ended the call instead of offering her any other platitudes. Jennifer had taken up enough space in his brain for the majority of his life. He didn't want to think about her anymore, so he tried to wipe her out of his head as he rode the elevator down to the front lobby of his building.

Ben stood on the sidewalk, his long and slim legs wrapped in a pair of tight, charcoal gray slacks. He leaned against the passenger door of his car, arms folded across his chest while he waited. When he saw Thomas, he dropped his arms, mouth spreading into a wide smile that served to erase Jennifer in a way he hadn't been able to do on his own. Thomas strode out of the building and across the sidewalk, seizing Ben with both hands and slanting their mouths together. Ben let out a surprised moan, and Thomas slid his tongue into his mouth, pressing him back against the car and kissing Ben until he couldn't breathe.

"That's quite a hello," Ben murmured when Thomas pulled away to catch his breath.

"I'm happy to see you," he said.

Ben's stare flickered down, kiss-swollen mouth twisting into a sly smirk. "Are you now?"

"Yes, but figuratively too."

"Everything okay?" Ben slid to the side and opened the passenger door, gesturing for him to climb inside.

"I just talked with my ex."

"Hold on." Ben closed the passenger door and jogged around to the driver's side. He climbed in and buckled up, turning the car on before giving Thomas a sideways glance. "So, your ex?"

"She called."

"About?"

"To tell me she was seeing someone."

"Why?" Ben asked.

"Because she assumes I care?"

Ben licked his lips, swallowing and gripping the steering wheel so hard his knuckles turned white. "Do you?"

"I don't." He reached over the center console and settled his hand on Ben's thigh, giving the solid muscle a squeeze. "Not in the slightest."

"Then why would she call and tell you?"

"Because she would care if I was seeing someone else."

"Why?"

"Because the only reason we divorced was because of her cheating on me. She still wanted to be with me." He leaned his head against the headrest and watched the lights of the city whir past while Ben drove. "She just wanted to be with everyone else too."

"Her loss."

He smiled softly. "I'm glad you think so."

Ben rested his hand on top of Thomas's and they finished the drive to the restaurant in silence. It wasn't awkward, and Thomas found he enjoyed the ease of it. The restaurant was cute and cozy, located up the hill from the city in a small and quiet tourist town. Thomas didn't often make it up there, but Ben seemed to know the streets well enough.

"Ready?"

Thomas nodded and followed Ben out of the car and into the restaurant. Ben had made reservations, which sent a pang of feeling straight through Thomas's chest. He hated to compare Ben to Jennifer, but he couldn't think of a time in their years-long marriage that she had ever taken the initiative to schedule a date for him. At the time, it hadn't even bothered him, but being on the receiving end was exciting, he realized.

They navigated through a maze of café-size tables to a small booth in front of a window. They sat opposite each other and Thomas settled in with a quiet sigh.

"This is nice," he said.

Ben flipped open the menu and looked up at him. "Is it?"

"I've never been *taken* on a date."

"Ever?"

"Ever."

Ben leaned back, shoulders wide and head tilted back. "I like that I get all of your best firsts."

"Best?" he teased. "That's yet to be seen."

"Ouch." Ben dropped the menu and clutched his chest, pretending to be injured. "You wound me. And here I was, about to ask you to choose a wine."

"Not a sommelier, then?"

"Not so much."

"I should have known with your gin and tonic order on our last outing." He turned his attention to the wine list at the back of the menu, searching for a bottle that would be good enough to go with whatever they decided to order.

"What's wrong with gin?"

"Are you serious? What's wrong with gin?" He rolled his eyes. "It tastes like paint thinner."

Ben shoved his menu forward. "I can't believe you're over there saying I have no taste."

"To each his own."

"Gentlemen," the waiter interrupted their back and forth. "Can I get you started with some drinks this evening?"

"A bottle of Burgundy, please," he said, glancing at Ben. "Did you know what you wanted to eat?"

"I'll have the vegetable lasagna," Ben ordered, handing over his menu.

"I'll have the herb roasted chicken," Thomas added.

The waiter tipped his head in thanks and left them to their conversation.

The words between them flowed freely and easily, with Thomas talking about what it was like having two kids under five in his early twenties, and Ben sharing what it had been like to walk away from a swimming scholarship a year from gradua-tion. Even though they had little in common to be found in their backgrounds, it was impossible to ignore the ease with which they got along. It was nice to be understood the way Ben understood him. And at no point in the evening did he even allow himself a second to think about the fact Ben was a man. Ben was a person whom he was attracted to, physically and intellectually, and Ben was a man who returned that interest. It may not have been what they'd intended, but it seemed to be working.

After the plates were cleared and the waiter had dropped off a dessert menu, Ben excused himself to use the restroom. Thomas scanned the 5x7 cardstock to see if anything sounded good, but he realized all he wanted was a cup of gelato on an uncomfortable chair with Ben in front of him.

The waiter returned, but Ben hadn't, so Thomas waved him off, starting to worry about Ben's absence. When five more minutes went by, Thomas decided to go check on Ben. He made it to the bathroom that led to the hallway in time to catch Ben, who appeared a little flustered and plenty unhappy.

"Hey." He caught Ben by the arms and straightened him up. "Are you all right?"

Ben smacked his lips and shoved his hair out of his face, looking over his shoulder before staring down at their shoes. "I'm fine, but I'm ready to go."

"You're not fine," he said, "but we can go."

Ben nodded and trailed behind him back to the table. They hadn't discussed who would pay, but Ben looked ready to jump out of his skin and Thomas knew he had to get him outside. He dropped a stack of bills on the table and ushered Ben out of the restaurant and onto the street.

"What happened?" he asked. "You don't have to go into details if you don't want to, but I can tell something is bothering you. I didn't do anything wrong at dinner, di—"

"What?" Ben fluttered his hands between them and shook his head. "No, nothing like that. I just...I ran into my ex and..."

"The one who cheated on you?"

"Yeah."

Thomas wanted to go back inside and give whoever it was a piece of his mind. He'd never seen Ben as upset as he was, so unsettled and frantic.

"What did he say to you?" he asked.

Ben wagged his finger and frowned. "No. He just...he said some messed-up things, trying to get me back. It's his usual MO."

"Messed-up things?"

"God, this is embarrassing." Ben shoved his hands into his pockets, once proud shoulders now slumped and curled. "Can we walk at least?"

"If you like."

They made it around the corner before Ben spoke again. "He cheated on me, but he also...he wasn't *nice*."

The emphasis on the last word was enough for Thomas to understand the story Ben was trying to tell. Immediately, heat flared up his spine, surging through him in a barely controllable way. He reached over and grabbed Ben's hand, twining their fingers together and kissing his knuckles. The contact between them and the subtle taste of sweat on Ben's skin were the only things stopping Thomas from turning around and going back to the restaurant.

"He wasn't nice," he repeated.

"No."

"Did he..." Thomas didn't want to ask, but he needed to understand—he wanted to understand.

"Did he hit me?" Ben glanced at him, cheeks flushed.

Thomas nodded.

"No. But things broke. Or he broke things. Whatever."

"It's not whatever."

Ben came to a stop, forcing Thomas to look at him. "It's whatever. I need it to be whatever, please?"

Every bone in his body urged him to fight Ben on this. It was impossible to picture Ben in a situation like that, and then not to wonder what if Kenzie or Dakota ever found themselves in an abusive relationship. He thought about what he would do if anyone ever dared to raise a hand to either of his kids...

"If that's what you want," he finally said, jaw clenched.

"We weren't together long." Ben smoothed his hands down the front of Thomas's shirt, trying to settle him like a skittish horse. "It was just a blip."

It had been more than a blip, he realized. Ben had been so accusatory about the cheating, and now that he looked back, Thomas could see the little ways Ben had reacted to *him* that had clearly been triggered as a result of whatever had happened with the ex. But he didn't want to stick his finger in the wound and make things worse. If Ben wanted to move on from it, Thomas wasn't going to stop him. Thomas was trying to do his own kind of moving on, and while Jennifer hadn't been abusive toward him, their engagements in the marriage had been far from perfect. He appreciated the importance of being able to put space between bad relationships and good ones in order to save the latter.

"It was just a blip," he repeated, pulling Ben close and kissing the top of his head.

Ben leaned against him, heart beating frantically, and Thomas held him until his pulse slowed and then steadied.

"Thank you," Ben murmured. "For understanding. For just... letting me be."

"Why wouldn't I?" He tipped Ben's chin up and dropped a gentle kiss against the corner of his mouth. "You've given me space to be; you deserve the same."

Ben closed his eyes, long brown lashes fanning out against his cheeks. He looked peaceful, but Thomas could feel the tension that still lingered just beneath his skin.

"Are you ready to get home?" he asked, dreams of gelato long forgotten.

"Yeah. Thank you." Ben reached into his pocket and pulled

out his keys, pressing them against Thomas's chest. "But can you drive?"

He nodded, taking Ben's hand and walking the long way around the block back to where Ben had parked. He drove them back to Ben's apartment in silence, walked him upstairs and offered to leave, but Ben pulled him inside and kissed that idea right out of his mind.

CHAPTER 17
BEN

SEVEN DAYS after running into Cody, Ben still wasn't sure his heart rate had returned to normal. Thomas had been lovely in the way he handled things—perfect, even—but the fact that the encounter had left him feeling so unsettled was enough to make him realize he needed to do some work on dealing with the fallout of that relationship.

He went to the pool, thinking that a few laps would be enough to help him clear his head, but the time underwater only forced him to think longer and harder about it. Ben went to the sauna to work out the tightness in his muscles from swimming because he'd been out of the water for so long, and even though he loved the way he sweat and burned in the wet heat of the sauna, it also wasn't enough.

So, he called Lara.

She showed up at his apartment an hour after they hung up, bearing gifts in the form of a tray of iced coffee and a bag of cupcakes slathered with so much frosting they made his teeth hurt just looking at them. His hair was still wet from the pool, and he shoved it away from his face while Lara wiggled the cups of coffee out of the cardboard carrier.

"Why did you get four coffees?" he asked, watching her reach into his cabinets and pull out all of his clean glasses.

"We're having a tasting." She proceeded to pop off the lids and split the four coffees between eight glasses. He didn't even realize he had eight drinking glasses.

"I would have preferred wine or champagne if that was the case."

"You sounded upset."

"Exactly."

She rolled her eyes at him and gathered as many of the glasses in her hands as she could. "Come help me. Be useful."

Ben followed her to the dining room, returning for the cupcakes so Lara could arrange the coffee flights in whatever manner she felt best suited them. He sat down at the table and let her fuss over everything until she took the empty seat beside him.

"Our first coffee is a dark cold brew with maple cream." She slid one of the glasses toward him and he took a small sip. It was good enough, and the maple wasn't cloying. "Now tell me what's wrong."

He chuckled and set the coffee down on the table. "You're not even going to let me get warmed up?"

"It's not alcoholic so it doesn't matter, but nice try."

"You planned this," he groaned.

"Once you start talking, we can finish the tasting."

Ben took another drink of the maple cream cold brew, unsure of the best place to start. "Uhm, well…"

"Does this have to do with the guy from the gelato shop?"

"You don't need to play coy. You know who he is."

"Thomas," she said.

He nodded.

"Did he do something wrong?"

"Not at all," he muttered, drumming his fingers on the table. "He's honestly done everything right."

"Impressive, considering he's so new to all of this."

"It's not *so* different than being with a woman, you know."

Lara eyed him while she sipped the first coffee. "That's not what you told me last time we talked, and it's not what you told him either."

He hated when she was right.

"We're dating now. It's more serious," he said.

The ice in his coffee melted a little, shifting and crashing against the glass. He took another swallow, hoping all of the sugar she was about to dump into him wasn't going to ruin his stomach.

"That's good?"

"Yeah? Yeah." He cleared his throat. "We were on a date last weekend and I ran into Cody."

"What now?"

"I went to the bathroom before dessert and Cody was there."

"Was he with someone?" she asked.

"I honestly don't know. I didn't ask." He pushed the now empty first coffee glass toward the center of the table. "He approached me."

"Did he hurt you?"

"No. Nothing like that. He just...you know. He was extremely apologetic. Told me how much he missed me. How he knew he'd messed up—"

"But you know he's a liar, right?"

Ben sighed. "What's the second coffee?"

Lara arched a brow. "Number two this afternoon is an iced lavender and honey latte."

He scrunched his nose, but gave it a try. The lavender was soft and the honey was barely sweet. It was infinitely better than the maple cream.

"I know he's a liar," he answered her earlier question. "But the way he was talking to me, the things he said. It just...mixed up some feelings."

"This one is good." Lara smacked her lips.

"It is. And seeing Cody just spooked me a little and I made Thomas leave the restaurant." He took another drink, wishing for more.

"Did he see Cody?"

"No. He wanted to go in after him, though."

Her eyes widened. "Does he know about everything?"

"He didn't at the time," he said. "But I told him about it after. Because I was so upset."

"So, what I'm hearing is the problem isn't that you saw Cody. It's that you're still upset from seeing Cody. Is that it?"

He pointed toward the row of coffees and she groaned, pushing the third glass in the row toward him.

"This one is…shit." Lara chuckled. "I don't remember. Try it and tell me what you think it is."

"Cupcake me." He pointed at the cupcakes on the kitchen counter before taking a sip of the coffee. It was lighter in color than the rest, but definitely had a noticeable flavor profile. Ben smacked his lips and took another swallow.

"I think…I think it's almond maybe? Almond and…"

"Marzipan!" Lara shouted, setting the cupcakes down on the table amidst the scattered coffee glasses. "It's marzipan and pistachio."

"That is quite a mix."

"Is it good?"

"It's different." He unwrapped one of the cupcakes and picked some crumbs off the bottom of the treat. "I'm upset that I'm upset. Or I'm upset that I *was* upset."

Lara adjusted herself in the chair, folding her left leg beneath her and bending her right leg at the knee. She propped her chin up and gave him one of her basically trademarked stares. He loved Lara, but hated that look and he knew she was waiting for him to talk through whatever he'd meant by the last statement.

"I shouldn't have stayed with him as long as I did," he muttered. The marzipan coffee was too sweet on his tongue, and he slid the half-drank glass toward Lara.

"It's…nothing that you can change now, Ben. No matter how hard you regret it, you can't undo it."

"I didn't want anything serious with Thomas at first because I was reeling from how Cody treated me." He scrubbed a hand down his face and sighed. "How fucked up is that? I almost missed out on him because of something completely out of his control."

"But you didn't."

"I could have."

"We don't live in a world where that happened." Lara gestured toward the fourth coffee. "That one has Baileys in it."

He feigned shock. "So you *did* bring me alcohol?"

"Baileys is hardly alcohol."

He grabbed the last glass anyway, taking a grateful swallow. The liqueur didn't do anything to soothe his nerves, but he appreciated the attempt nonetheless.

"Do you want the hard talk now?" Lara swiped her finger through the inch of frosting on one of the cupcakes and popped it into her mouth.

"I suppose." He didn't, but he knew he needed it.

"Cody was abusive to you, and that has no reflection on you at all. The only thing that tells anyone is Cody is a prick and you're better off without him."

"It says I tolerated his behavior," he interrupted.

"It says you did what you had to do until you found a way to get out of the situation," she corrected.

Ben dipped his chin toward his chest in defeat. His entire body ached, from the swim and the stress, and a little bit from the overwhelming nervousness that wrapped itself around him like a weighted blanket.

"I'm mad that seeing him still affected me," he said.

"I know things with him are in your past, but they're not *that* far in your past. Be a little nicer to my best friend, please." She took another swipe through the cupcake frosting, and he snatched it away from her.

"Stop defacing the dessert."

"You don't even like frosting. I'm doing you a favor." She grabbed it back from him, finished her assault on the frosting, then returned the naked cupcake to his hand.

He broke off a piece and chewed on it thoughtfully, trying to work his way back through the barrage of emotions the conversation with Lara had brought him. She wasn't wrong so much as he found it nearly impossible to believe her. He heard her say things weren't his fault, but he didn't see how that could be true. He'd facilitated his own abuse by tolerating and welcoming Cody into his life over and over.

Ben swallowed the cupcake and rubbed his temples, dropping his head back so it hung off the edge of the chair.

"I know you don't believe me right now." Lara reached over and rubbed his thigh. "But you'll see it one day."

"I hope so."

"Will you tell me more about Thomas now?" She stood up and stacked all the empty coffee glasses together and carried them into the kitchen. He glanced up at her and then ate some more of the cupcake.

"What do you want to know?" His mouth softened around the corners while he chewed, the tension unwinding as his brain moved from Cody to Thomas.

"I want to know why he makes you smile like that."

"How am I smiling?" His cheeks burned and he turned away from her, dragging the edge of his hand across the table to scoop up the cupcake crumbs.

"Like you're in love."

He jumped up so fast, his chair almost toppled. "I'm not in love with him."

"Sure." She turned on the water and started to wash all of his glasses. "Tell me your favorite thing about him then."

Ben crumpled the cupcake wrappers in his hand and joined Lara in the kitchen, dumping the trash into the can before grabbing a dish towel off the oven handle so he could dry as she washed.

"I love how earnest he is."

"In what way?" She passed him a glass.

"He's just really confident? I don't know. He knows what he wants and he isn't scared to go for it."

"And you feel like you're scared to go after the things you want?"

"I am." He finished drying the first glass and set it down on the counter. "Or I was."

He'd made progress at least, going from wanting a rebound to wanting a partner. He'd never intended for Thomas to fill that role, but he wasn't mad about it. Thomas made him feel like he was doing the right things, making the right choices.

"I feel less scared with him now," he whispered. Lara passed him another glass and he took it, drying it quietly while he thought about what he'd just said.

"What else do you like about him?" she asked.

"He's funny. He's hot." Ben chuckled under his breath. "He's really great at sucking cock."

"I thought he was straight."

"Well, bisexual now, but for a beginner?" Ben set the dry glass down and kissed the tips of his fingers and thumb. "Chef's kiss."

"Practice makes perfect, they say."

"If he practices too much, he'll likely suck my soul right out of my body."

Lara laughed and cleaned another glass. "I can think of worse things."

"Yeah," he agreed, finally starting to feel better about where his head was at over Cody and where his heart was at with Thomas. "Me too."

CHAPTER 18

THOMAS

THOMAS SCANNED THE MENU, looking for something with enough alcohol to take the edge off, but not enough to leave him too drunk to hold a conversation with Kenzie. He'd almost cancelled their brunch, but their relationship was on thin ice already and he'd been surprised enough when she texted to get together. She'd always reached out to Jennifer, and he'd gotten used to it, but Kenzie seemed to be trying and he didn't want to push her away by making her feel unimportant.

Unfortunately, keeping their Sunday brunch date meant he'd left Ben alone, naked, and asleep in bed. The relationship with Ben was such a new thing, and while the sex between them was great, Thomas looked forward to enjoying the quieter moments together. The lazy Sunday mornings with game shows on low volume and hot mugs of coffee between them. Bitter-tasting kisses, sharp from sleep, and lust on the couch during commercial breaks. He wanted lunch ordered in so they didn't have to get dressed and afternoons that led into quiet evenings alone at home.

But brunch with his daughter was a reminder that he had a life outside his new relationship and he needed to pay them both the attention they needed. He didn't know when he would see Ben again, but he knew he would. Things with Kenzie felt more uncertain.

"Sorry I'm late." His daughter flung herself into the empty seat opposite him, her massive purse landing at her feet. She looked a little flustered and tired, much like her mother.

"It's okay." He tried to not think about the extra fifteen minutes he could have spent in Ben's arms.

Kenzie looked around, tucking her hair behind her ears. She flagged down a waitress and asked for a third chair.

"Bringing a date?" he asked.

"Yeah." She rolled her eyes. "My brother."

"Dakota?" Thomas sat up straighter, looking around to see if he could find his son.

"Are you more excited to see him than me?"

"You know I love you both the same," he said.

Kenzie snorted and dropped her phone onto the table beside her condensating water glass. "I know I'm your favorite."

"My oldest daughter."

"Only," she corrected him with an arched brow.

He smiled and nodded, relaxing into the ease with which she teased him. It had been so long since things felt safe enough between them for that kind of banter. He was eager to see Dakota too, even though things between them were much more tense than between him and Kenzie. He knew both of his kids thought he'd been an absent dad, and maybe he had, but...he didn't want to be anymore.

"While we wait for him, how's school going?"

"Good, but like—"

"Hey." Dakota's voice cut Kenzie off, and she let out an exasperated breath.

"But, like, Special Topics in Cognition is really tedious and it's hard for me to focus on the content of the lecture because the professor has the drollest tone of voice," she finished her statement and flicked a quick glance up at her brother.

"Dakota." Thomas stood up and gestured to the open seat the waitress had brought over.

Dakota sat, and Kenzie eyed him while he got settled. Thomas sat back down and smoothed his napkin back over his lap because he wasn't sure what to do with his hands. What a weird experience, to feel so nervous around and judged by the humans that he raised.

The waitress returned, obviously flagged by Dakota's arrival, and took their drink orders, leaving them alone in a relatively awkward silence.

"How have things been?" he asked his son.

Dakota gave him a tired look. "Things are...fine."

"You're a liar," Kenzie said.

"Trent has just been a little argumentative lately," Dakota said.

"Trouble at home?" he asked.

Dakota hadn't ever come out, so much as just come home one day with a man and said they were getting married. Thomas had been caught off-guard by it, only in so much as before Trent, Dakota had only dated women. At least, as far as Thomas and Jennifer had known. They'd been together for quite a few years, to varying degrees of success, but for as much as Dakota was flighty and non-committal, he seemed dedicated to Trent.

"We're just fighting," Dakota said, glaring at Kenzie.

"You're sleeping on my couch," she shot back.

A different server brought their drinks and a basket of bread. Thomas held out his palm while Kenzie promptly divested the first piece of its crust. She discarded it in his hand and shoved the insides into her mouth, eyes narrowed on her brother. Thomas picked at the crust, dropping it on the small plate in front of him. For as estranged as he was from his kids, he didn't want them to use their relationship with him just when they needed something and he had the sneaking suspicion that was exactly what was about to happen.

"That bad?" he asked, not ready to jump to conclusions, even though he knew better.

"No." Dakota scratched at a spot behind his ear. "Besides, it's not like you've never slept on the couch before."

He sighed, taking a long breath to stop himself from saying something regrettable.

"That was rude," Kenzie said softly.

Thomas looked at her, surprised by her defense.

"It's true," Dakota protested, gesturing flippantly at him. "He was horrible to Mom and I caught him on the couch more than once. You don't remember because you're younger."

"I wish you wouldn't presume to know the inner workings of your mother's and my marriage," he said.

There had been many occasions he'd slept on the couch, but mostly because they were nights he had to get up early for work and didn't want to wake her earlier than her alarm. Or times when he'd come home late, and sometimes the occasional event when he'd drank too much and fallen asleep to the *Late Show* because anything was better than crawling into a bed covered with another man's sweat. But the latter scenario was toward the end of things, long after Dakota had gotten married and moved out.

"Oh, come on." Dakota rolled his eyes. "You're not over here winning any husband of the year awards."

"Are you?" Kenzie accused.

"Kenzie, I appreciate it, but it's done," he told his daughter.

"It's not." She reached for another slice of bread, furiously ripping the crust away. "It's not. You know what I'm in school for and the more I learn, the more I notice the stuff the two of you think you're hiding."

Thomas rubbed at the bridge of his nose and stared down as she tossed another crust onto his plate. He hadn't even touched the first one yet and he didn't know if he would. His appetite had vanished as soon as Dakota sat down and opened his mouth. Thomas felt horrible for thinking it, but the sinking tension in his stomach was hard to ignore. What was wrong... what had he done wrong to feel so uncomfortable around one of his own children?

What about unconditional love?

"Kenzie," he warned. "There's plenty that you don't know."

"You want to try me?"

Dakota countered with a derisive snort of a laugh. "Yeah, let's hear it."

His phone vibrated in his pocket, and he knew it was Ben, but he also knew he couldn't look. Not in the middle of the most awkward meal of his entire life. His mind raced with worry over whatever observations Kenzie thought she'd made over the years, and the impending realization that he needed to talk to Jennifer. Sooner rather than later. They'd mis-stepped by not being honest with the kids, and even though he'd agreed to protect their relationship with her, it was grossly unfair for him to have to bear the brunt of their misdirected anger.

"Well, to start with, since you brought it up." Kenzie leveled a glare at her brother. "You're an asshole. You treat Trent like shit."

"Excuse me?"

"I've heard you on the phone with him the past two nights and you are so fucking manipulative."

"Fuck you, Kenzie," Dakota snapped.

"Hey." He held up his hand. "Don't talk to your sister like that."

"Are you going to tell her not to talk to *me* like that?" Dakota asked, the vitriol in his voice a near carbon copy of Jennifer's.

"I think it's unfair you want me to unload on Dad, but you can't take it yourself," she lobbed back at him.

"Are we going to talk about your holier-than-thou attitude and all the pretentiousness?"

"If you even knew what that word meant, you would know it's the wrong one."

"Kids," he interrupted, but they were too far gone, bickering as bad as they had when they were teenagers. This wasn't the brunch he'd expected and it was almost as awful as the one he'd feared.

Dakota said something to Kenzie that set her off, and she stood up, grabbing the corners of the table to support herself, and leaned over her older brother to whisper-yell at him, "I was doing you a favor about letting you stay with me, but you can put your shit back into your backpack and get out of my apartment. See if Trent hasn't changed the locks yet."

"Kenzie," Dakota immediately tried to backpedal.

"I'm not *like* Dad," she said, sitting back down, but not letting go of the table. "I'm not going to let someone talk to me like that."

Thomas's heart sank.

In that moment, he knew Kenzie had picked up on all of the things he and Jennifer thought they'd been so skilled at hiding. He'd been so focused on trying to present both of the kids with the model of a cohesive family unit, he hadn't even stopped to think about the way he was presenting *himself* and what kind of example that set for both of them. He glanced at Dakota, whose face was red with anger directed explicitly at Kenzie.

"It's okay," he said, meaning to direct it at both of them.

Kenzie relaxed her fingers from the table and dropped her hands into her lap. "Please go get your stuff out of my apartment and leave the key on the counter."

"You're a—"

"Don't," he interrupted his son. "Don't even think about it."

"I did you a favor and you took advantage, and besides that, you're just mean." Kenzie smoothed her hands down her thighs anxiously, and Thomas recognized it as the same gesture he often used to calm his nerves. "You're older than me, and you can go take care of your marriage now."

"I knew this was a bad idea," Dakota mumbled under his breath, standing up and glaring at them both. He pointed at Thomas, anger now directed at him instead of Kenzie. "I don't care what she thinks she knows. I know what kind of man you are."

"And what's that?" he asked.

"You're weak."

Thomas bit the side of his tongue to stop himself from reacting to Dakota like he was anyone besides his son. He recognized how he could have appeared that way by taking Jennifer's accusations and bad behavior on the chin for so long. He should have stood up for himself. That would have set a better example to his kids. But instead he'd offered fake apologies to hide Jennifer's indiscretions from them. He'd settled for far less than he deserved and, in doing so, taught them that happiness wasn't something worth fighting for. Kenzie could barely stand him, though he wondered if she was on the verge of changing her opinion of him, and Dakota thought him the worst person in the world.

"You're right," he agreed. "I let a lot of things happen that I shouldn't have."

He should have left Jennifer as soon as she cheated. He should have worked less. He should have been more present. He should have fought harder for balance.

Dakota looked flustered, his cheeks still red and his eyes wide, like he didn't expect Thomas to agree and he didn't know how to fight back when he did.

"I think it's time your mother and I were honest with you," he said. "So you can understand what happened between us."

"You don't have to, Dad," Kenzie said, and he knew she knew.

He knew she knew everything.

"We do." He gave her a reassuring nod. "And it's okay."

"Go pack, Dakota," she said, angling her face toward her brother.

Dakota stomped off without a word, and Thomas reached for his drink, swallowing half of it in one go. The ice had melted and the liquor was watered down. It was nowhere near enough to calm him down as the adrenaline spiked through him.

"I know Mom cheated on you," Kenzie said.

Thomas rubbed the bridge of his nose and let out a long breath, turning to face his daughter once Dakota was out of sight.

"I never meant for either of you to know what happened between us."

"Why not?" she asked.

"I didn't want…*we* didn't want your opinions of either of us to change."

"But they should have changed. I grew up thinking you were just completely removed from everything going on and, in reality, Mom was the one who was being horrible and Mom was the one saying mean things and she was the one out there sleeping around.

"She's still your mother." He sighed.

"That doesn't make it less true."

"How did you find out?" It didn't matter, but there was a nagging voice in the back of his mind that was curious how Kenzie had put the pieces together.

"I had dinner with Mom and Jarrod and he made a comment about something they'd done last year, but you and Mom were married last year. I asked her about it and she denied it, but I could tell by their faces, and it was like a lightning bolt. So much other stuff just clicked into place when I realized."

He tried to not be angry that Jennifer hadn't taken Kenzie's question as proof their plan had been a bad one. But he felt proud that he'd raised a daughter so smart and intuitive she'd known what to ask and she'd seen the writing on the wall.

"And Dakota is cheating on Trent," she said, sending Thomas's heart back into the ground. "I've heard them on the phone and I can tell by how he's acting. I let him stay because he said Trent threw him out, but it sounds to me like he deserved it."

"He doesn't deserve it," Thomas protested, out of instinct.

"You haven't heard him on the phone," she said, lips pursed. "He's…Dakota can be really mean."

"That's my fault." He picked up one of the bread crusts and tore it off into smaller pieces, needing to eat even if he didn't want to. "I should have set a better example for him."

"You set a fine example," she interrupted him before he could finish the thought. "I mean, I turned out all right, didn't I?"

Kenzie gave him a sweet smile and he couldn't help but laugh. "Yeah. You're pretty all right."

"I know." Kenzie took a sip from her drink and wiggled in her seat. "And I'm sorry, by the way. I thought it would be good for Dakota to come and be around family. I thought that maybe he would hear me out about what Mom had done to you and see how it affected you and realize what he'd done to Trent was wrong."

"You meant well. You don't have to apologize."

"It wasn't fair for me to spring that on you," she said.

"Kenzie." He reached across the table and patted her hand. "It's really okay. I promise."

"Okay." She swallowed and shrugged like she was trying to change the subject.

"Did you want to talk about something else?"

"Please. Anything." She looked relieved at the out.

He picked up his glass and took another swallow, ready to finish the watered-down disaster and get a fresh one. "Have at it."

"So." Kenzie cleared her throat. "I told you what's going on with school. What's going on with you? Anything exciting?"

Thomas licked his lips, phone vibrating once again in his pocket. "Actually, yeah."

"Anything you want to tell me about?" Kenzie started in on a third piece of bread.

"Actually..." He leaned back and listened to his heart slam against his sternum, eager and scared—and ready. "Yeah."

CHAPTER 19
BEN

IT TOOK Thomas an hour to answer Ben's texts and another hour before he showed up, looking tired and hopeful at the same time. Ben greeted him with a kiss, then let him inside.

"Sorry it took me so long," Thomas apologized.

"You're fine. Kids are important."

"Well, they're adults."

He rolled his eyes. "You know what I mean. How was brunch?"

"It was…" Thomas toed off his sneakers and went into the living room. He collapsed onto the couch with a sense of ease that had something in Ben's chest constricting. He…liked it? He liked that Thomas felt comfortable enough in his space to make himself at home that way. It was a big thing, though. He knew that much. A big feeling.

Ben sat down beside him and rested his head against Thomas's shoulder. "It was?"

"Interesting."

"Do you want to talk about it?" he asked, not wanting to push.

"I think Kenzie is finally warming up to me," Thomas said. "But I worry Dakota is a lost cause."

"Why?"

"He's cheating on his husband. He was sleeping on Kenzie's couch until she threw him out." Thomas closed his eyes and leaned his head back, and Ben turned, dropping a kiss below his ear. "I need to talk to Jennifer and we have to talk to the kids. They have a really skewed perception about what's happening between us."

"How long until your divorce is final?"

Ben honestly didn't care. He knew the legality of Thomas's marriage was a technicality and had no bearing on anything between them. But he had the suspicion the date meant something to Thomas. That it would bring him closure and maybe allow things between them to move forward in a more serious way.

"A few weeks is all. My birthday actually. The tenth of May."

He did some math on his fingers and made a mental note to not forget Thomas's birthday was coming up.

"A double celebration, then," he said.

Thomas nodded and scooted into the corner of the couch, taking Ben with him and arranging him so Ben was half on top of him.

"That can't be comfortable."

"It's exactly what I need right now." Thomas closed his eyes and let out a long breath, the rise and fall of his chest moving in time with Ben's own breaths. "What about you? How is your morning? How was your week?"

Ben hadn't wanted to have the conversation, but he didn't want to avoid it either.

"It's a little heavy," he admitted.

"I'm strong enough for it," Thomas whispered, stroking fingers through his hair.

Ben closed his eyes and settled against Thomas's chest, listening to his breaths and his heart. "I have a lot of messy feelings about my ex-boyfriend."

"I have a lot of messy feelings about my ex-wife."

"I feel like sometimes...I think that what happened with us was my fault." Ben paused, and Thomas didn't answer, instead giving him space to think and speak. "Lara assures me that's not the case, though."

"It's not."

"But I let it go on."

"You tried to have a relationship with someone who didn't care about you and didn't respect you," Thomas countered. "Trust that I know what that looks like because I was in it a lot longer than you were. You can't change people like that."

"I didn't want to change him. I just wanted him to want me. To like me."

"Something he's clearly not capable of, so it would have been a change."

That stopped him, and he took time to think about the truth of Thomas's words. He hated to admit it, but something about the simple words Thomas had just said caused everything else to click into place—the things Lara had tried to force him to make sense of, the tangled mess of his own feelings that surrounded Cody, and the way their relationship evolved and ended.

"Oh," he said softly.

Thomas huffed out a gentle laugh and tightened his arms around Ben's back. "Did something in there resonate with you?"

"All of it," he admitted, pushing himself out of Thomas's hold so he was sitting upright. "Like, the whole thing turned a spotlight on how I felt about it."

Thomas matched his sitting position, one eyebrow raised in question. "And?"

"You're right." He shrugged. "Lara was right. It's...it wasn't me."

"You can't make people love you. You can't change people who don't deserve the honor."

He scoffed and rolled his eyes, shoving Thomas's arm and pushing him into the side of the couch. "It's hardly an honor."

Thomas grabbed his hand. "It would be."

Ben swallowed, the rest of his body turning to marble as the implication in Thomas's words sank in. He didn't move, save to lick his lips and wiggle his fingers to check and make sure Thomas's hand was still beneath his. No words passed between them, but Ben knew there weren't enough to say what he wanted anyway.

"It would be," Thomas said again, more insistent. "I hope you know that."

He cleared his throat and Thomas yanked his hand away, giving Ben the idea the moment that had just passed between them wasn't one-sided. He mourned the absence of Thomas's skin beneath his, so he turned and reached for him, grabbing his face and crashing their mouths together. Thomas moved quickly, hauling Ben onto his lap while breaking the kiss only long enough to get both of their shirts off.

Thomas moaned into his mouth, opening wider and giving Ben room to explore. His tongue dove deep and his hands roamed wildly, tracing their way over every inch of Thomas's exposed skin that he could reach. Thomas reached down lower, hands fumbling nervously at the buttons and zippers on their pants and then, blessedly, he got Ben's dick out and into the hot grip of his fist.

Ben grunted, circling his hips and fucking himself into Thomas's hand, and Thomas kissed down his chin and jaw, sucking against his neck and his throat while he pumped his fist up the length of Ben's quickly thickening erection. He arched his back, a groan falling out of his mouth as Thomas twisted his wrist with a rough jerk around the tip of his cock.

"I want you," he panted, grabbing Thomas's hand and stilling his movement. "Please."

With a sense of reluctance so heavy Ben could feel it,

Thomas released his cock. He wound Ben's legs around his waist and shoved up from the couch. When he straightened, Ben laughed, clinging with arms around his shoulders and face buried in the crook of his neck.

"I'm too heavy," he protested.

"Not at all," Thomas assured him, laying sloppy kisses on whatever parts of Ben's neck he could reach. He carried Ben into the bedroom and set him down on the bed, stepping back to kick free of his pants and his underwear while Ben scrambled out of his own at the same time. He rolled over to the nightstand and snatched the lube, tossing it into Thomas's waiting hands.

Thomas's cock was hard as ever, thick and sturdy, and this time…bare.

It had been days, weeks maybe, since they'd talked about foregoing condoms, but this would be the first time they actually did it. He'd found it refreshing that they'd managed to cool the severity of their sex life while still exploring intimacy with each other in different ways. They'd obviously had sex with each other since their first real date, but this would be the first time Thomas took him without a condom.

Thomas's cock shone under the bright lights of Ben's bedroom and he'd never cared so much about whether the lights were on or off during sex, but this time he wanted to see absolutely everything.

"Can I get you ready?" Thomas climbed onto the bed and Ben spread his legs apart and cupped his balls. He raised them up, putting himself on display for Thomas's eager eyes.

"You don't have to." He dropped his head back against the pillow. "I like it without sometimes."

"I want to," Thomas rasped.

"Then yes."

Thomas's hand was already slick with lube and he wasted no time burying his two longest fingers inside of Ben's hole. He rotated his wrist and pressed against his prostate, drawing a sharp gasp from Ben's throat.

"Did I find it?" Thomas asked, hair falling on his face and cheeks already flushed red.

"Yeah." He nodded and untangled the sheets from his hands. "You found it."

"I'm glad I had a good teacher." Thomas started to move, sliding his fingers in and out, scissoring them apart and twisting, doing his best to drive Ben into an absolute frenzy. Thomas prepped him with his entire body, using the momentum of his hips to drive his hand forward, pushing Ben further up the bed with every thrust of his fingers. It was indecent and it was decadent, and when Ben felt sweat trickle down his temple, he begged Thomas to stop.

"I'm ready," he promised, reaching down to force Thomas's fingers away from his hole. "I want *you*."

"I'm yours." Thomas lined up and pushed his hips forward. The head of his cock popped through with ease. Ben didn't even feel the burn until Thomas was already halfway inside of him.

"Oh, shit," he gasped, grabbing Thomas's waist in his clammy hands and steadying himself. Steadying them both.

"Oh shit is right." Thomas stared down at the place their bodies came together, eyes wide with wonder, but heavy with lust.

"How does it feel? How do I feel?"

Thomas swallowed, dragging Ben down the bed so his asshole enveloped Thomas's cock like a glove. When he was fully seated, Thomas blinked a few times, then caught Ben's stare.

"How do I feel?" he asked again, fingers tightening around Thomas's waist.

Thomas nodded, like he didn't have the words.

"You too," he said.

Thomas withdrew until the head of his cock popped out of

Ben's hole. He quickly shoved back in, burying himself balls deep in one thrust. Ben whimpered, scratching his nails up Thomas's back and pulling him down for a kiss. Thomas tilted his head to the side to align their lips, and as he licked his way into Ben's mouth, he started once again to move.

In and out and in and out.

His tongue mirrored his hips with a steady pace that was clearly meant to make Ben lose his mind. This felt different, and not just because there wasn't a condom keeping them apart. This felt bigger, monumental, like for all the words that had passed between them, the unspoken ones being said in that very bed were the most important of all. His mind recalled him back to the couch when Thomas vowed so solemnly it would be an honor to love him, and Ben wondered how he knew.

He spit in his palm and made a loose fist around his cock, letting the rough pumps of Thomas's hips drive his cock in and out of his hand at the same pace Thomas moved in and out of his body. His orgasm was already dangerously close, and the slide of his palm quickly brought him to the edge. At least, he told himself it was his hand—not his heart.

"You're close," Thomas grunted before Ben could even open his mouth. "You get so tight when you're about t—"

Ben cried out as he came, the force of his orgasm bordering on catastrophic as cum shot out of his dick. His release painted his knuckles, his chest, all the way up to his chin. He thrashed beneath Thomas until a hand on the front of his shoulder steadied him enough to ground him back in the present. Thomas clenched his jaw, his cock thickening and pushing at Ben's already stretched and well-fucked channel, and then with a low growl, Thomas came inside of him.

Heat flooded the deepest parts of him, pushing the rest of his own cum out of the tender tip of his dick. Thomas grimaced, teeth grinding together, abdominal muscles clenching and contracting as he spilled into Ben's asshole.

For an eternity, neither of them moved, neither of them said anything. Their breathing returned to normal, and Ben's cock began to soften in his hand. He released himself and grabbed Thomas, hauling him down and kissing him once again. This time he moved his mouth with a languid and satisfied kind of pleasure that sent shivers up the length of his spine. Thomas held onto him, returning the kiss with all of the same emotion Ben was pouring into him.

"That was..." he whispered against Thomas's mouth, the words that came to mind not feeling like enough.

Nice.

Great.

Everything.

Perfect.

Best.

None of them even came close to saying what he wanted to say, so instead of using words, he kissed Thomas again. He touched him, he moved with him and beneath him, until Thomas's cock turned hard again, and then Ben let his body say the rest.

CHAPTER 20
THOMAS

THOMAS HAD PUT off calling Jennifer as long as he could manage, but by the time Thursday rolled around and he hadn't heard from her, he gave in. He texted her on his way to work asking if they could grab lunch and she agreed—which surprised him—but it was what he wanted. That didn't stop his nerves from taking root at the base of his spine through two hours of morning meetings and half a dozen text exchanges with Ben about all the ways he wanted Thomas to fuck him the next time they saw each other. Thinking about Ben's bare ass wasn't even enough to distract him from the conversation he was ramping up to have with his very soon-to-be ex-wife.

When he'd told Ben about his lunch plans, Ben sent him a series of skull and coffin emojis, quickly followed by a message with four simple words—*Will you be okay?*

Of course, he'd answered, even though he didn't believe it. He was forty-five years old, and a conversation with the woman he'd spent his entire life with shouldn't have felt as daunting as it did. But he was a different man than he was when he met her, when he married her, when he divorced her. Ben had made him a different person, or maybe he'd always been this man and understanding what it meant to be with Ben was like a permission slip to let himself learn more too.

Either way.

He'd picked a place close to his office so he walked there, rolling up his sleeves so he didn't sweat too profusely on the way over. Jennifer had gotten there before him, already seated at a table with a half-empty glass of water in front of her. She glanced up, her expression taut with wrinkles around her eyes and pursed lips.

"You're late," she said.

"I'm not." He slid into the empty side of the booth opposite her.

"What did you want to talk about?"

"Why you're so combative, for one." He sighed and let a breath out the corner of his mouth.

"Thomas."

"We need to talk to the kids," he said.

"About?"

"You." He gestured between them. "Us. This."

"What about it? We agreed. You can't just go back on that." Jennifer leaned forward, her voice an angry whisper.

"Dakota thinks that I cheated on you and that's why we split up."

Jennifer's mouth twitched.

"Kenzie knows I didn't," he went on. "But she knows you did."

"We *agreed*," she said again.

"I didn't tell her." Thomas leaned back, trying to put whatever space between them he could. Had Jennifer always been this selfish and demanding, and he'd never noticed? It couldn't be. There was no way he could have been this blind for that long. "Your little boyfriend slipped up and said something that sent up the red flags and she figured it out."

"His name is Jarrod."

"I don't care." He didn't. "It's important to me that the kids know the truth. I thought that not talking to them about it was the right thing to do and I was wrong. They're both adults and they deserve the truth."

"If you think outing me as an adulterer is going to make Dakota love you, you're mistaken."

He'd never thought that at all, but hearing the insult lobbed at him with such an intense ferocity hit him like a knife in the chest.

"I don't think it'll change his opinion of me in the least," he said. "But it might change his opinion of you and that's not my problem anymore."

Thomas knew it wouldn't, though. If Kenzie told him the truth, that Dakota was having an affair behind Trent's back, he wouldn't be fazed by his mother's own infidelity.

"Actually." He cleared his throat. "I don't think it will, but it's important to me that they know the truth. So I can tell them on my own, or you can come along."

"So I can defend myself?" she balked.

"There is no defense for what you did to me." Thomas was already tired, and he stood, no longer interested in trying to remain a unified front with his ex. "I know I wasn't a perfect husband or father, but I don't deserve this hate. Not from them and not from you."

"Thomas." Jennifer slumped in the booth a little, a fraction of the fight going out of her. "I don't want them to think less of me."

He wanted to feel sorry for her, he really did, but...

"I know I worked too much when the kids were younger, but I did that for you and I did that for them. You cheating on me was for you. You didn't think about me and definitely not about them." He reached into his pocket and pulled out his keys, testing the weight of them in his hand. "That's just something you'll have to deal with now."

"When are you going to tell them?"

"Like I said, Kenzie already knows. If you want to talk with her about it, you can. I don't think it will make a difference to Dakota. My only intent is to stop lying to them about it if and when it comes up, but honestly, Jennifer, I try to not think about you, let alone talk about you."

With that, he turned on his heel and walked out, leaving Jennifer alone in the booth and for the rest of her life. He was grateful that when his birthday rolled around, it would be like a magic page flip on a calendar. Married one day, divorced the next. He didn't have to see her ever again if he didn't want to and, in that moment, he didn't. She had treated him horribly and he deserved more than her. He understood that now. He didn't know if someone like Ben was what he deserved, but he was enjoying their time together, and that was enough.

Though... something in the back of his head told him it wasn't, and on his walk back to the office, Thomas found himself faced with the worry that his relationship with Ben was unfairly imbalanced. Sure they'd talked and agreed what things would be between them, but Ben was on the heels of a nasty break-up and Thomas knew how much it took for him to admit his interest in something serious. Was he as "all in" on things as Ben was?

He stopped at the sandwich cart in front of his building and bought a fruit bowl, but his worries plagued him the whole ride up to his floor. Back in his office, he closed the door behind him and dropped his phone and the fruit on his black leather desk pad. He rubbed at the bridge of his nose and swiped the screen open to text Ben.

Thomas: *Talked w/ Jennifer.*
Ben: *And?*
Thomas: *She's honestly horrible.*
Ben: *But how are you?*

Thomas: *I'm here.*
Ben: *Here? What does that mean?*
Thomas: *It means I'm here. At work. Moving on with things.*
Ben: *You're really bad at this.*
Thomas: *At what?*
Ben: *Give me an emoji or three that describe how you're feeling.*

Thomas furrowed his brow at the demand, but sent back the yawning smiley face, a peach, and beer mug.

Immediately, the phone rang and he picked it up on the first ring.

"Hey," he greeted.

"Those are horrible answers," Ben chided. "You are horrible with texting."

"I text just fine," he protested, stabbing the thin plastic fork into a quarter of peach.

"You don't emote well."

"What's wrong with my emoting?" Thomas bit the peach and chewed while he waited for Ben's answer.

"Tired, sure. I get that one. Exes are exhausting. But the peach is slang for ass, so are you out cruising or something?"

"*What?*" Thomas choked as he swallowed, smacking himself on the sternum until his throat cleared. "No, I'm eating a peach!"

"A peach is an ass!"

"An actual peach. I'm eating an actual peach right now."

"You're *the worst*," Ben said with a laugh.

He went after a cube of watermelon next. "You'll have to teach me. Next, you'll tell me that eggplants are sexual too."

"They aaaaaare. Oh, my *God*. Sometimes I forget you're so much older than me."

"Not that much," he grumbled.

"Clearly enough."

That little comment landed in the pile alongside his earlier worries about things in their relationship being uneven, and the scales tipped a little more in the wrong direction.

"Uhm, speaking of that." He dropped his fork and wished he had some water. "I was thinking on the way back to the office."

"About?"

"You. Us. I don't know."

Ben sighed. "Out with it."

"I just want to make sure that you and I have made the right decision about being together."

"Are you having second thoughts?" Ben's voice went quiet.

"Not at all," he said quickly. "Nothing like that. I just…I know it was a lot for you to admit you wanted more than something casual with me, and I want to make sure that, like…things are fair between us."

"Fair how?"

"I worry we're at different places in our lives—" he started.

"Are you breaking up with me?"

"Absolutely not."

"Then shut up," Ben snapped.

"Excuse me?"

"You're being ridiculous, everything with us is fine. It's how I want it. Isn't it how you want it?"

Thomas huffed out a tired breath. "You sound desperate to believe it."

"I do believe it," Ben said. "And I'm not desperate. I just want to stop you before you slide deeper into whatever rabbit hole of doubt your ex-wife kicked you into."

"She hardly…" He stopped himself, closing his eyes. Ben was right. At least, right enough. For the moment.

"You done?" Ben asked.

"For now."

"What are you doing tomorrow night?"

"Hopefully you," he said.

Ben rewarded the change of topic with a throaty laugh that went straight to Thomas's cock.

"If you're good, we can arrange that. But I wanted to see if you felt up to meeting Lara tomorrow night."

"From the gelato shop?"

"One and the same."

This was...a big deal and it played right into everything Thomas was worried about within the limits of their relationship. Meeting friends was something serious and were they serious? He knew he didn't want to be casual with Ben, but was he ready for a meet the friends kind of thing? Because after meet the friends came meet the kids, and then...

"Stop it," Ben said.

"Stop what?"

"Looking in that rabbit hole."

"I'm sorry." He exhaled long and slow. "I'm just in my head a little more than normal about things."

"You don't have to apologize."

"Do you think it's too soon for me to meet her?" he asked.

"I've already told her about you. She knows how I feel about you and how things are between us."

He grimaced, stabbing his fork over and over into a piece of pineapple until he turned it into a macerated puddle of stringy pulp.

"How are things between us?" he asked.

"Not casual," Ben answered. "But I'm not thinking about marriage yet, if that's what you're worried about."

"I'm not worried."

"Are you a liar too?" Ben teased him, and he closed his eyes, dropping his fork.

"You're my first after her," he said.

"I remember. I'm your first lots of things."

"Don't remind me." Thomas groaned.

"I like to remind you." Ben dropped his voice to a whisper. "And I like to remember too."

"I'm at work," he warned.

"I'm not."

"Are you…" He couldn't even ask, but Ben answered him anyway with a low moan. Thomas adjusted himself, shifting his weight beneath the cover of his desk within the secrecy of his office. "What exactly are you remembering?"

"How thick your cock is." Ben answered, and then moaned again, no longer trying to hide what he was doing on the other end of the call. "How it stretches me out when you fuck me."

"What else?"

"Thomas."

"What else?" he asked again.

"I'm fantasizing now," Ben panted. "About eating your ass and then burying myself inside of your hole."

"I'm at work," he said again, palming his quickly growing erection and trying to will it away.

"Now I'm thinking about eating your ass and burying myself inside of you in your office. On your desk. Like in the movies, when they…" Ben trailed off, and if Thomas strained, he could hear Ben's hand working up and down his cock. "Is your desk big?"

"Yes." He undid his fly and pulled his cock out of the hole in his boxers. It wasn't much, but he got a hold on himself and followed suit.

"Do you ever wonder what it would feel like to have me inside of you?"

He arched off his seat, balls already hot and tight in their sac. "More often than not."

"We can try it."

"Okay," he rasped.

"Really?"

He nodded, even though Ben couldn't hear his agreement,

and he moaned when he came as quiet as he could keep himself. He knew Ben heard that because under his breath he muttered a curse, and Thomas knew he'd also found his release. Thomas gave himself a handful of breaths to steady himself, then wiped his hand on a brown paper napkin from the sandwich stand and tucked himself back into his slacks. His cock was far from soft and his mood far from sated, but it would have to hold him over.

"Really, really?" Ben asked again.

"Yes."

"Tomorrow, then? You can meet Lara and as a reward for surviving her, I'll show you how good it feels to have a tongue and a cock inside your asshole," Ben promised.

Thomas balled up the soiled napkin and tossed it in the wire trash can under his desk before offering Ben his approval...and his consent.

"It's a date."

CHAPTER 21
BEN

BEN WAS NERVOUS, and Lara wouldn't stop laughing at him.

"Isn't Thomas the one who is supposed to be nervous?" She picked at her cuticle and rolled her eyes. "It is Thomas, right? Do you call him Tom? Tommy?"

"I'd never."

Ben looked around the expansive park, eager and terrified about Thomas's arrival. He'd suggested they go get dinner or drinks, but Lara, in her infinite need for adventure, suggested they head to the park for a picnic. She even offered to make the charcuterie board, which left Ben with little grounds to protest. He arrived early because he wanted to warn her to play nice, and it looked like she'd already been there for hours. The largest blanket he'd ever seen sprawled across the low sloping hill on the west end of the park and she'd laid out boards of meats and cheeses, and three plastic glasses for wine.

"Don't say it like that. I'm sure he calls you Ben, not Benjamin." Lara worked at loosening the screw top on the bottle of red wine she'd no doubt carefully curated for the event.

"Nobody calls me Benjamin," he reminded her. "Except you when you're being a jerk."

"Would you let him if he wanted to?" she asked.

"Let him what?" Thomas asked from behind him. Ben straightened and turned his head to the side, only to be met with Thomas's profile as he leaned down and pressed a quick kiss against his cheek.

"Call him Benjamin," Lara offered, finally getting the cap loose.

Thomas rubbed his hands down the front of his thighs and sat down on the blanket so close to him their thighs touched. He tipped his chin down toward his shoulder and leaned close, his voice barely louder than a whisper, "Do you want me to call you Benjamin?"

Up until that moment, he hadn't.

But…

"It's up to you," he rasped.

Thomas kissed his shoulder and shifted his attention to Lara. "Is this the part now where you ask me about my intentions with your friend?"

Lara smirked, pouring wine into the three glasses. "I'm not concerned. Ben is a big boy and can take care of himself."

"Thank you," he grumbled.

"It just seemed appropriate that we officially meet since we're clearly the two people Ben spends the most time with."

Thomas leaned forward and held out his hand. "I'm Thomas. Nice to meet you."

"Lara." She shook his hand and then passed him one of the glasses of wine. "So, what's your favorite color?"

"Are you serious right now?" Ben grabbed the last glass of wine and hoped the alcohol would be enough to make him stop wanting to murder his best friend.

"It's a fair question."

"Dark blue," Thomas answered, not missing a beat.

"Movie."

"*Vertigo.*"

"Season."

"Winter."

Lara raised her lip in disgust. "Why?"

"I like the cold," Thomas answered.

"Also why?"

"Because I like fireplaces and warm blankets," Thomas said.

Ben leaned against him, resting his hand on Thomas's thigh.

"It doesn't get that cold here," Lara said.

Thomas shrugged. "I have a car and the mountains aren't far."

Ben fought back the wave of jealousy that rolled over him when he pictured how many vacations Thomas had taken in his life with his family. How many winter nights he'd spent under blankets in front of fireplaces with Jennifer on his lap or by his side. He didn't want to erase her from his past, but he also did? It was something he couldn't make sense of, but he vowed to find a way to make new and better memories to overwrite the ones he knew caused Thomas the kind of pain some of his past with Jennifer had to have.

If he made it to the winter, his subconscious reminded him. It was April and they were having a picnic at sunset and hadn't even bothered to bring coats. Winter was a long way away and he had no idea what the next months would bring.

"Fair," Lara conceded.

"What about you?" Thomas asked.

Lara's mouth crawled into a slow smile, and he immediately knew Thomas had passed her test. He'd watched her give the runaround to Cody once and he'd failed miserably. That should have been a sign to call things off, even before they'd gotten bad. But Lara swore her methodology was simple. She asked to learn, but where she gained the most insight into someone's personality was if they turned the questions back on her.

Give and take, she'd told him.

"Yellow and fall," she answered.

"Yellow?" Thomas laughed. "That's rare."

"Not sunshine yellow. Like mustard yellow or golden yellow."

"Fair enough, a color that runs rampant in the fall," he said.

"Jewel tones, you know." Lara plucked a circle of salami off one of the cutting boards, rolled it up, and dropped it into her mouth.

"What about you?" Thomas asked, the question directed at him.

"Blue," he answered.

"Dark?"

He nodded.

"And the season?"

"Spring," he said.

"Why?"

"I like the idea of being able to start over. No matter how things were in the winter, spring brings a new chance for things to grow. And they don't always look the same, but they're there. They've survived."

Thomas regarded him thoughtfully, a small crease between his eyebrows, and Ben worried he'd said too much and given away much more than he'd meant to with the answer. But Thomas didn't push him on it, instead changing the subject.

"So, Lara." He took a small drink of wine. "Tell me about our charcuterie."

"Salami, prosciutto, peperoni, brie, gouda, cheddar, pickles." She swirled her finger in a circle above the board. "Olives, figs, honey."

"Surprisingly basic," Ben quipped.

"It's impressive," Thomas countered, tucking a cube of gouda alongside a slice of prosciutto. "Do you work with food as a job?"

"I don't work at all," she answered with a laugh. "I married for money."

"That's a lie." Ben threw a blueberry at her.

"I married someone much smarter and more focused than me for love, and after a few years, that turned into money. Which works for me. I can do what I love until I don't love it anymore."

Thomas dragged his tongue across the front of his teeth, his entire expression tight like he had something he wanted to say, but he didn't want to offend.

"Spencer hates it when I work," Lara went on. "He says I get too stressed out, so I just do things on the side to bring in extra money when I feel like I'm not contributing."

"Charcuterie," Thomas said, and Lara nodded.

"Sometimes that. I make wreaths, which sounds so silly, but I sell them online for a lot of money and I enjoy making them. It's like stress relief."

Thomas's expression softened, but not in a real noticeable way.

"Lara has a degree in Accounting," Ben offered.

"And I hate to waste it, but Spencer is Spencer." She shrugged and finished off what wine was left in her glass.

Ben knew something she'd said must have hit a nerve about Thomas's ex-wife, but he recognized the stoic way Thomas reined his commentary in.

"It's nice that your husband supports you like that," Thomas said.

"Honestly, he doesn't even have to work. His family is old money from a town up north called Mallardsville. He wanted to do more with his life, though. And when we were in college, Ben was kind enough to think the more could be me."

"A little matchmaker?" Thomas asked, shoulders relaxing.

"Spencer seemed like the kind of man who could handle her."

"I'm a big personality." Lara nodded sagely, if not a little mockingly. Ben had told her as much for years, half in jest, but Lara could be a lot when she set her mind to it. It was one of the things he'd always loved the most about her. She'd never shied away from being honest with him about when he was doing something wrong.

"And how did *you* meet this Spencer?" Thomas asked. "How did you meet Lara?"

"Spencer and I used to swim together in college," he said, recalling the story. "And Lara used to copy my notes in one of our first year finance classes."

"Please don't tell this story," she interrupted.

"One time I got strep throat and I was out sick for a week. When I came back, I had to ask Lara to copy her notes and they were an absolute disaster."

"Ironic, since I'm the accountant and you're not," she said.

Ben held out his glass for her to refill. "She shoved a stack of papers at me when I asked, not realizing that she'd given me more than just her finance notes."

"Please stop," she begged, cheeks flushed in the pink light of the sunset. "I'd been stalking him a bit, not in an unhinged way, but I thought he was hot. I found out he was on the swim team, so I had the swim schedule written on the back of some of my notes and he found it."

Thomas chuckled, obviously aware of where the story was going.

"Lara isn't my type," Ben picked up the story again, "But I knew Spencer would like her, so I circled the time for the next practice and told her to come. I introduced them and the rest is history."

Lara held up her hand with the massive pear-cut diamond sparkler on her ring finger as proof.

"Sounds like everything worked out then," Thomas said.

"Could have been worse," Ben agreed.

"And we've been friends ever since." Lara topped off

Thomas's wine, unasked. "What about you? How did you meet your best friend?"

Thomas's face fell, but he pulled it back together so quickly Ben almost didn't even notice the change in him.

"I don't think I have one anymore," he said with a frown. "Most of my friends were couple friends with Jennifer and when we split up, the wives all went with her, and…"

"Good husbands do as they're told," Lara supplied with a matching frown.

"Really?" Ben turned to Thomas, his eyes worried. "You don't have any friends?"

"I mean, I'm sure I do. I'm sure there are people I could call."

"But not like this?" he asked.

"It's fine." Thomas tried to shrug it off. "I'm old anyway. I don't even know how to go about making friends anymore. And honestly, after the talk I had with Jennifer yesterday, I think it might be safe to reach out to some of the guys again."

"You don't look like you want to," Lara hedged.

Thomas chuckled, leaning back on the blanket and dropping his head back to stare up at the sky. "I don't."

"Why?" he asked.

"They've shown their true colors. They didn't care to ask what happened between us. They went with whatever their wives told them, which I can't be mad about. I spent years taking Jennifer's word about things." Thomas closed his eyes and inhaled, his shirt stretching across his chest as his lungs filled. "I'm sure she told her friends horrible things about me, and her friends told their husbands, and here we are."

"Gossip is insidious," Lara agreed.

"I don't see it as a loss." Thomas reached over and patted Ben's hand, reassuring him when Ben felt like he was the one who should have been consoling Thomas. He couldn't imagine the loss Thomas had faced, was still facing. To lose your home, your friends, your family, your whole life. He hadn't been able to comprehend the leap Thomas had taken to walk away from so much in order to embrace the truth of himself, and he admired that in ways he didn't have words for. He looked at the chance Thomas was taking on him and the massive commitments Thomas had made, and he felt undeserving beyond measure.

"And now you have Ben," she said.

Thomas looked down, eyes lighter than Ben had expected considering the weight of what they'd been discussing. "And now I have Ben."

CHAPTER 22

THOMAS

GETTING home after Lara's picnic was a welcome blessing. He liked her enough, but all he'd been able to think about, even through the dark thoughts of the life he'd left behind, was Ben.

"Are you okay?" Ben asked, closing the door behind him.

"Of course. Your friend is nice."

"She can pry."

"She didn't." He reached out and slid his hands around Ben's waist, pulling him closer. Their chests bumped, and Ben studied him quietly.

"She didn't," he said again, kissing the corner of Ben's mouth. "I didn't tell her anything that made me uncomfortable."

"How did it feel to be out around her?"

"Out?" He slid his hands down Ben's back to his ass, cupping the small mounds of flesh and digging in his fingers.

"Like, with me. With a man."

"Is it the wrong answer to say I didn't even think about it?" Thomas tilted his head to the side. "I was just enjoying a picnic with my bo...with you and your best friend."

Ben's mouth twitched. "Were you going to call me your boyfriend?"

"Is that what we are?" They'd never talked about titles, but the assumption had always been there for him.

"You tell me." Ben licked his lips, the tip of his tongue peeking out just below his Cupid's bow.

"I like the sound of it."

"Then yes," Ben agreed.

"And, no, it didn't bother me. It was normal. Wasn't it?"

"I'm trying to be mindful that this is all new to you," Ben said, looping his arms around Thomas's neck. He brought their foreheads together so close that Thomas could still smell the wine and cheese on Ben's breath.

"If something makes me uncomfortable, I'll tell you," he promised. "But being with you, privately and publicly, does not."

"Okay."

"Did she like me?" he asked, taking a step backward and pulling Ben with him. He started the walk down the hallway to the bedroom, his mind unable to focus on anything else.

"Very much."

"How do you know?"

Ben kissed the side of his neck. "Because I know Lara."

They finally reached the threshold of his bedroom, and Thomas came to a stop. Their arms were still tangled around each other, and Ben continued to watch him with a careful focus that made Thomas feel like a caged animal in need of tenderness and affirmations.

"We don't have to do this if you're not ready," Ben said.

"I'm more than ready," he said, taking another step backward, their first step into the bedroom. "I'm nervous. But I want this, and I want it with you."

"I'll take the lead, then?" Ben asked.

Thomas nodded. His palms were clammy and his heart raced. He didn't remember ever feeling as anxious as he did, and he was confident the only thing keeping him grounded was the overwhelming way he *wanted*.

Ben stripped out of his clothes, then reached for Thomas, divesting him of his in the same slow fashion. Every move Ben made was calculated and Thomas found himself feeling desperate for things to move along faster. It was hard for him to relax, to let go, but he trusted Ben to know the right speed.

"I'm going to talk you through this."

"I'm fine," he protested, and Ben reached up to cover his mouth.

"I know you're fine. I'm going to talk you through it so you stay fine, and I'm going to talk you through it because I think it's fucking hot."

"Right." The word came out on an exhale.

"Get on the bed. All fours, but like…" Ben trailed off as Thomas climbed onto the bed, pressing his hand against the small of Thomas's back to flatten his chest against the sheets. "There you go."

Thomas buried his face in the pillows, noticing the way they smelled like an even mixture of his and Ben's shampoos. It settled him and he closed his eyes, relaxing as much as he could manage. Ben crawled up behind him, never breaking contact. His fingers trailed along his back and town, tracing a gentle circle around the exposed whorl of hair around his asshole. Thomas found himself feeling self-conscious, fighting an urge to reach back and cover himself.

"Your ass is as sexy as your cock," Ben whispered, his breath burning hot against Thomas's backside. His face burned from embarrassment, but then Ben kissed his hole and a shudder of unanticipated pleasure ripped through his entire body.

Thomas's mind raced, and then Ben licked his hole, sealing his lips around it and kissing him there. Ben *kissed* his asshole, and his mind went utterly blank. He grunted, fisting the sheets and lifting his ass higher into the air as Ben speared him with his tongue. Ben's hands on his cheeks spread him open and held him down, kissing and licking his rim and the skin around it until Thomas's cock was so hard it ached.

From behind him, Ben made the sounds of a starved man at a feast, and that only served to ratchet Thomas's own arousal further out of the stratosphere. By the time Ben eased a finger into him, he was ready to cry for the relief of it all. He'd had a finger in him before. He'd had two, both of them belonging to Ben, and so he knew Ben would waste no time feeling out his prostate and...

But this was different.

This was Ben's fingers inside of him, his tongue swirling around the place their bodies joined, and his mouth sucking loudly as he rimmed his hole. Thomas wasn't able to stop himself from humping the air, desperate for any kind of friction beyond what Ben was offering him. He shifted weight onto his shoulder and reached down to take his cock into his fist, only for Ben to release his ass and smack his hand away.

"You'll come," Ben muttered, mouth full.

"I want to."

"Not yet." Ben licked a long stripe from his balls to his hole. "I want you to come when I'm inside of you."

"You should hurry then."

"I'm enjoying myself."

Before Thomas could answer to that, he felt Ben smile against the hot pouch of his sac. "Aren't you?"

Before Thomas could answer, Ben sucked his balls into that same deviously hot mouth, drawing a surprised shout out of his mouth. Thomas buried his face into the pillows, gripping and twisting the sheets to stop himself from once again reaching for his cock. The pleasure Ben granted him was great, and not nearly close to enough. Ben didn't relent, though. He sucked Thomas's hole, his balls, and the base of his cock until he fit a third finger inside, burying it knuckle deep.

"I wish you could see yourself, spread open for me," Ben murmured, tracing his finger along the tender edge of Thomas's rim. "My cock is going to look so good inside of you."

"Please," he all but begged. "Please."

"Please what?"

"Please. I need you inside of me."

Slowly—almost hesitantly—Ben withdrew. One finger, then another, then the last. Thomas's hole gaped, sucking after the intrusions that his body immediately yearned for.

The lube bottle opened, and Ben grunted, slicking his dick with so much that Thomas could hear the way his shaft squelched in his fist. The tip of Ben's cock against his hole was cold and slippery, and his body immediately tensed.

"Relax," Ben whispered, smoothing a hand down his back and over the curve of his ass.

"Can..." Thomas swallowed, the sheets soaking wet in his fists.

"What do you need?"

He looked over his shoulder, mouth going dry at what he saw. Ben behind him, cock in hand, with that lithe swimmer's body Thomas loved so much. His lips were swollen, and Thomas wondered what he would taste if they kissed. His cock lurched at the thought and he squeezed his eyes closed to fight back the overwhelming waves of emotion and want that threatened to drown him.

"I just want to see you," he managed.

Ben gave his hip a little push and Thomas rolled onto his back, bending one leg on either side of Ben's kneeling form.

"This is better," Ben said, stare drifting down Thomas's body to his cock. "Now I can see all of you."

"I'm ready," he whispered.

Ben lined himself up again, cock a little warmer than before, but just as threatening. "I'm not sure I am."

"Do you want to—"

"No." Ben shook his head and grabbed him around the waist, pushing him down and pulling him closer in the same movement. "I don't want to stop."

"Good."

"Good," Ben said back. He adjusted his grip and directed the head of his cock, easing into Thomas's body at an agonizingly slow speed.

It stretched and it burned, and it felt better than almost anything Thomas could remember feeling before. He was very much aware that his body was molding itself to the shape of Ben's cockhead, barely making enough room to let him inside. But as the head of Ben's cock popped through his hole, the rest of the penetration was an easy slide home. Ben continued to move slow, until he was as deep as he could reach and his trembling thighs pressed against the backs of Thomas's legs.

Ben fought to breathe, gripping and letting go, readjusting the hold he had on Thomas's waist like it was a struggle to maintain composure. Thomas reached for him, grabbing his wrists with desperate fingers.

"Move," he pleaded, his voice sounding foreign to his own ears. "Benjamin, move please."

Ben's eyes flew open. "Say it again."

"Please."

"My name."

"Benja—"

The name left him as Ben pulled out, the flared rim of his cock testing the inside of Thomas's hole before the whole length of him surged back inside. The force of Ben's thrust took the breath out of him, his name as lost at Thomas's thought process.

"You feel so good, Thomas." The words sounded like praise, and he took them as such. Gooseflesh broke out from his stomach to his chest, tracking down his arms to the tips of his fingers. He wrapped his legs around Ben's waist and held him like that until Ben fell forward, bracing himself with one hand on either side of Thomas's head.

"Thank you for this," Ben whispered.

"Kiss me," he said and Ben lowered his head down, slowly enough that he was able to pump in and out, in and out, wringing pleasure out of Thomas before their lips even came close to touching. Frustrated, he raised off the bed enough to bring their mouths together.

Ben immediately opened for him, allowing Thomas to taste the musk on his lips and the salt from his sweat at the same time. He grabbed the back of Ben's head, holding him steady and kissing him, touching him, using his whole body to kiss and fuck and...

"Make yourself come," Ben muttered, breaking for air. The pace had turned frenetic, nearly frenzied, and Thomas relished watching him lose control that way.

"You," he demanded, expecting Ben to take him in hand.

Instead, Ben pulled away from him, raising up onto his knees and spreading Thomas's legs wider. It let him slide deeper, and Thomas grunted, the penetration still stretching and burning, just now in untouched parts of him. Ben shifted the angle and, with one sharp snap of his hips, forced the head of his cock against Thomas's prostate. Once he found it, his focus narrowed, and Thomas watched the way his muscles tightened. Ben's attention was concentrated on the short and rough thrusts required to milk the cum out of Thomas's balls.

It didn't take long, and Thomas came like that for the first time—with another man's cock in his body and his hands tangled in the mess they'd made of his bed. He cried out, and Ben rolled his head back, finally faltering as his own orgasm crashed into him. Ben buried himself and stilled, hot jets of his cum spurting as his cock jerked against Thomas's channel.

Ben cleared his throat with a low grunt and fell forward, body still seizing from the effects of his orgasm. He made a fist around Thomas's cock and milked the rest of his cum out and onto his stomach; then he gathered it on his fingers and smeared it over his lips. Thomas had never seen Ben like that before, dirty and debauched, and absolutely gone with want.

"Ben," he whispered.

Ben bit his cum-stained lip between his teeth and shook his head.

"Benjamin," he said, and Ben fell forward, their foreheads once again coming together.

"Thomas."

He wrapped a hand around the back of Ben's sweaty neck and closed the rest of the space between them, licking his cum from Ben's lips with a satisfied moan that had Ben's cock pulsing inside of him yet again.

"I love how it feels when you come," he said.

Ben shuddered, his entire body trembling as he reached down and ever so gently eased his dick out of Thomas's body. Again, his hole gaped and puckered, willing him to chase after the need to be filled again, but instead he tightened his hold on Ben and rolled them both onto their sides.

Ben raised his shaking hands up and traced the lines of Thomas's face, and Thomas wondered what Ben saw. When he looked in the mirror, Thomas saw an old man, a lonely man. He saw a man who had no right pursuing someone as young or handsome as Ben, but he also saw a man who didn't care.

"Thomas." Ben's brows knit together like there was something terrible he wanted to say. He braced himself, but Ben shook his head and instead gave him a gentle smile.

"What were you going to say?"

Ben continued to draw soft shapes and swirls up the angles of his jaw and cheekbones, moving and kissing all of the places his fingers touched.

"Thank you," Ben whispered. "I wanted to say thank you."

"That's not it."

"I'm not ready." Ben's cheeks burned red and Thomas moved his head so he could kiss the tips of Ben's shaking fingers. It was three words that might as well have been three other words, and Thomas understood the fear in Ben's eyes because he felt it too.

"I'm not ready either," he said, a confirmation and a promise for the future all in one.

"Okay." Ben nodded, his lashes fluttering as Thomas sucked one of his fingers into his mouth, his other hand dragging down between their cum-slick stomachs and reaching for Thomas's still hard cock. "Good. We're on the same page, then."

"We are, Benjamin." He sighed as Ben made a fist around his length. "We very much are."

CHAPTER 23
BEN

BEN SCRUNCHED HIS NOSE, watching Lara move around her ridiculous all white kitchen with a practiced ease. He'd come over because he needed help picking a birthday present for Thomas, but the birthday present needed to be more than a birthday present because it was also a divorce present and maybe it was also a little bit of him feeling closer to admitting—out loud—that he was in love with Thomas.

Time had passed quick, but it never felt fleeting. The moments he and Thomas spent together were solid and real, and each one more monumental than the last. They laughed together, and slept together, and learned more about each other. It had been an honor watching Thomas become more comfortable with the true version of himself, even if the intrusive voice in the back of Ben's head told him it would pass. Thomas would meet someone else someday, someone closer to his age, someone who shared more life experiences. Ben knew in his heart something would come between them, he just didn't know when.

"What things does he like?" Lara asked, putting a stack of white plates into one of her white cabinets.

"Plants." Ben shrugged. "Sex."

"Not together I hope."

"No." He blushed. "He's still learning a lot about himself. Like who he really is."

"What if you gave him an experience instead of a gift?"

"What?"

"An experience. Something that isn't tangible."

Ben sighed and drummed his fingers against her countertop. "That's a good idea, but it doesn't help. I don't know what experience I would want to give him."

"Why don't you take him on vacation?" she asked. "Let him cut loose a little in a place that's really far removed from here."

"He's not in the closet," Ben said.

"But he's not out-out, is he?"

He shook his head.

It didn't bother him that Thomas wasn't open with everyone in his life. He understood everyone had a different journey to acceptance and he wasn't going to judge Thomas for his. As it was, they went on dates and they held hands and kissed in public. Thomas didn't *hide* him, but Ben wondered if it would be nice to be away from home where they could just be with each other. Where Thomas could just be himself.

"What about the beach?" she asked.

"He's more of a nature guy."

"The beach is natural." Lara hung up her white dish towel. God, everything was white and it was uncomfortably sterile.

"Like plants and dirt natural."

"The mountains, then."

He slow clapped her, rolling his eyes. "Great second guess, Sherlock."

"You didn't have a single idea when you showed up here with your iced coffee bribe." She wagged a finger at him and leaned over the counter, snatching the aforementioned coffee.

"Fair, but now I have to find a good place to get away for the weekend that isn't too far of a drive, but is far enough away to provide the experience." He waved his fingers in the air like he was making magic, which in a way he was.

Lara came around the kitchen and sat down beside him on a stool at the island, sliding her laptop toward him. He flipped it open and started to type. Lara sipped her coffee while he browsed listings for campgrounds and hotels within a four hour radius of town.

"That one." She leaned across him and pointed at one of the listings.

He clicked it, bringing up a sleek website about a small campground nestled at the base of the Evergreen Mountains.

"That's a big tent," she said.

"It's a yurt."

"A what?"

"Yurt."

"How do you know what a yurt is?" Lara sucked the last of her coffee out of the cup, slurping the straw and rattling it around the ice.

"I saw it as a Jeopardy answer once and it's never left my head."

"As is the way of things."

Ben scrolled the website, reviewing the offerings and the amenities. "This looks really nice."

"Book it."

He pulled his wallet and his phone out of his pocket, dialing Thomas before he did anything. His ever presumptuous best friend opened his wallet and withdrew his credit card, tapping the corner of it against the metal of her laptop while he waited for Thomas to pick up the phone.

"Hey," Thomas greeted, sounding relaxed.

"You busy?"

"A bit, but I can spare a second for you."

Warmth flooded his chest and he felt the heat rise in his cheeks. Beside him, Lara laughed under her breath.

"I wanted to do something special for you birthday."

"Don't tell him." Lara elbowed him in the ribs, and on the other end of the line, Thomas laughed.

"Tell Lara I said hi."

"He says hi," Ben dutifully repeated.

Lara snatched the phone out of his hand. "Thomas. Hi."

Ben stole the phone back and put it on speaker, dropping it onto the counter beside the laptop.

"Is everything okay over there?" Thomas asked.

"Everything is fine," he promised.

"Ben wants to know if you have any plans for your birthday."

"I don't," Thomas said. "Besides celebrating with him, hopefully."

"That's honestly adorable," Lara said, holding Ben's stare. "If you don't have specific plans, don't make any. Ben has it all under control."

"Whatever you say, boss."

"I'll need you from Friday night after work to Sunday night," Ben said.

"You're taking a trip," Lara interjected. "And that's all you need to know."

"I can take a day off if you like," Thomas volunteered.

"You don't have to."

"I know," Thomas said slowly. "But I'm not against spending more time with you. Especially if it's away from here."

Something about the lilt of Thomas's voice made Ben wonder if he'd been wrong about Thomas being okay with being as out as he was, but he tamped it back down for another time. He was planning a birthday getaway, a divorce celebration, and he wanted it to be special.

"Monday then," he said. "So we can take our time."

"Monday it is." Thomas cleared his throat. "Will I be seeing you tonight?"

"If you wanted."

"I always want." Thomas's voice went low and raspy, and Ben grabbed the phone, flipping it off speaker before he could say any more.

"Mine or yours?" he asked.

"I'll come over when I'm off work," Thomas answered.

"Bring me food."

"So demanding."

"I think that's one of the things you loved first about me," he teased.

A short silence followed, and Thomas cleared his throat again. "I'll see you around seven."

"Okay. Bye." Ben quickly hung up the phone and turned away from Lara because he knew her well enough to know her eyes were rife with questions.

He'd done his best to pretend that they both hadn't been on the verge of confessing their love to each other on more than one occasion over the past few weeks, but he hadn't meant to slip up with his words just then. There were many nights when Ben had stayed up, either alone or long after Thomas had fallen asleep, wondering if it would be safe to admit just how strong his feelings for the other man were.

"One of the things," Lara said.

"Please don't." He grabbed the laptop and made quick work of booking a rental for the weekend of Thomas's birthday.

"One of the things," she said again.

Ben keyed in his credit card information, waited for the confirmation email to buzz on his phone, then slammed her laptop closed and shoved it back to her. "It was nothing."

"Are you in love with him?"

He licked his lips and tried not to look at her.

"That's answer enough," she said.

"It's a bad idea."

"Why?"

"Are you serious?" he scoffed. "A thousand reasons why. His

kids are my age, he's not even really all the way out, I'm the first guy he's ever been with. He's gonna get curious and want to try more, or he's going to decide he wants to be with women again."

"Oh, so you're just like a sampler menu for him?"

"No," he protested.

"Because that's what you just said."

"I'm not. It's not." He shoved the stool back and stood, turning away from the glaring and sterile white of Lara's kitchen. He found himself aching for the muted and dark colors of Thomas's apartment and the comfort and happiness it brought him. Maybe Thomas was a little farther along the path to knowing himself than Ben gave him credit for. Ben, a man with a basic apartment with box store furniture and white walls, having the audacity to worry about how well Thomas knew himself. Thomas with his plants and his dark paint and his soft white sheets.

All Ben had were curtains.

"Do you want to help me paint?" he asked.

"What?" Lara laughed, caught off-guard.

"I want to paint my apartment."

"Can you even? Aren't there rules."

"I don't get inspections, and I can paint it back before I move out," he said.

"What color?"

"Does it matter?" Hs put his wallet and his phone back into his pocket.

"No, because I love you, but I'm still not helping you. My arms are not cut out for that kind of work."

"You're the worst." He kissed the back of her head.

"I basically just planned your boyfriend's birthday weekend. You should be nicer to me," she teased.

"I'll see you later. I do love you even though you drive me mad."

She waved him off, cracking open her laptop and disregarding his entire existence.

Ben let himself out of Lara's house and practically jogged to his car. He had no idea what he wanted to paint or what color, but he was absolutely overcome with the desire to make his space his.

He drove to the paint store and spent far too long browsing the chips on the wall-mounted racks, finally settling on a rich and vibrant blue that looked like velvet in the paint can. Ben bought brushes, and trays, and a drop cloth, and everything else the associate told him he would need, then he drove home and stripped down, throwing on an old pair of basketball shorts and nothing else.

After twenty minutes of pacing between his living room and his bedroom, he decided the bedroom was the first to get painted. After all, the darkness of Thomas's bedroom had been what inspired him in the first place. With a little effort, he pulled his bed and dresser away from the wall. He opened the window, wrapped the curtains around the curtain rod so they wouldn't get messed up, and he set to work.

The painting was calming, soothing almost, as he laid intention into every roll of the brush up his wall.

This is me, he thought.

I am enough and I deserve the best.

Ben tried once and for all to clear any lingering doubts about the treatment from Cody and their short-lived relationship out of his mind, shifting his thoughts to Thomas and, for the first time ever, allowing himself to imagine what a future with him could look like. He wasn't sure he was ready to be a step-dad, or if something like that even mattered when the kids of your partner were adults.

His thoughts went down valleys and up mountains, entertaining so many scenarios and ideas that he lost track of time.

He'd just finished the last wall when a knock on his door startled him back into the present.

"Who is it?" he called out, finally seeing the room around him come together for the first time. It was like he'd been on autopilot the entire time he was painting, and he missed the way the color enveloped the room in warmth and safety.

"Me," Thomas's voice answered back.

"Shit." He checked the clock on his nightstand. It was seven already, and Ben had no idea where his entire afternoon had gone.

With the roller in hand, he went to let Thomas in, accepting a sultry kiss that sent what blood was left in his head straight between his legs.

"I brought Thai," Thomas said, stepping inside.

Ben closed the door and shook his head, still not quite back in the present. "I was painting."

"I see that." Thomas set the food down on the dining room table and undid the buttons on the cuffs of his pale pink dress shirt. "Did you need help?"

"I think I'm done."

Thomas shrugged out of his shirt, laying it over the back of one of the chairs. His belt followed suit, then his socks, which he tucked into his shoes near the door.

"Do you want to show me?" Thomas asked.

"Sorry. Yes." Ben smiled. "I just lost track of time and I know we agreed you'd come over, but I didn't realize how late it had gotten."

"It's okay. Show me what you've done, and then we can eat."

He tilted his head toward the hallway, and Thomas followed after him. The way the bedroom made him feel caught him unaware, and he stumbled, coming to a stop with a hand against a corner of dresser.

"It's gorgeous." Thomas came up behind him, resting his chin on Ben's shoulder. "It feels very sexy."

"It kind of does, doesn't it?"

"We can check for sure later."

Ben exhaled and leaned over to set the roller back in the tray. As he bent at the waist, Thomas grabbed him with firm hands and pressed his cock into Ben's ass. He was hard already, and Ben couldn't stop himself from groaning. He forced himself back into a standing position, twisting in Thomas's grip so they were face to face.

"Hi," he whispered, fingers pulling at the hem of Thomas's white undershirt.

"Hi." Thomas answered him with a smile. "What inspired the redecoration today?"

"Honestly, it was you." Heat flooded his cheeks, his forehead, the tips of his ears.

"Me?"

"I've been thinking a lot. I mean, I always think a lot. Especially about you."

"Not surprising," Thomas murmured, holding onto Ben and walking them out of the room, back toward the dining room and the delicious smell of coconut curry.

"I just wanted my space to feel more like mine," he said. "I wanted to be comfortable with it. With me."

Thomas shot him a speculative look, one eye narrowed and the brow arched, but he didn't speak to that. Instead, he tore open the bag and took out the containers of food and set them on the table.

"Did you want to get silverware?" Thomas asked.

He nodded, wanting a lot more than that. He returned with spoons and forks, joining Thomas at the table and digging into dinner.

"So, do I get any hints about this trip?"

"I don't want to ruin the surprise."

"You know that even if I know everything we're doing down to the second, it won't be ruined, right?" Thomas put the lid back on the empty soup container and tossed it into the empty bag.

"I know. I just want it to be special. It's kind of a big weekend."

"It's just a birthday."

"And your divorce is final," he said.

Thomas chewed the corner of his lip and nodded. "Are you done with that?"

Ben slid the mostly empty curry container toward him. "You seem less excited about the divorce than you do your birthday."

"I'm glad it'll be done with, but it's been a very long chapter. More than a chapter, if we're being honest. It's been a series, a volume. Like..." Thomas trailed off, jamming the rest of the containers into the trash bag. "I don't know how to put words to it."

"It's a big thing," he agreed.

"I don't want you to think that it's not important, because it is. And it's a good thing too." Thomas stood and took the trash into the kitchen. "It's just a lot."

"We don't have to go away." Ben stood and followed after Thomas into the kitchen, wrapping his arms around him and dropping a kiss against the space between his shoulder blades.

"I want to." Thomas turned in his arms and the tips of their noses brushed together. "It's just an old book closing, and there's this new one here with you and I'm ready to see what happens next."

"Curious where your own plot takes you?" He tilted his head to the side and Thomas leaned in quick, kissing the side of his neck.

Thomas's hands snaked up his back, fingers threading into his hair and pulling their faces back together. Ben could smell the curry against Thomas's mouth and he tried to lean in for a taste. He knew there were many more layers to the things

Thomas was feeling, but he also knew Thomas would talk when he was ready.

Things between them had turned serious, and Ben needed to trust in that. Trust in Thomas to know himself and what he wanted, even if it was different from what Ben expected of him.

"You could say that," Thomas teased, his breath hot against Ben's mouth.

He hummed a pleased noise in the back of his throat, looping his arms around Thomas's waist and taking a step backward. "I think the first stop is my bedroom."

Thomas chuckled and kissed the corner of his mouth, as confident in his movements and touches as he ever had been. "Then, by all means, lead the way."

CHAPTER 24
THOMAS

THE FRIDAY before Thomas's birthday came, and Ben showed up at his door with a backpack and a smile.

"Are you ready?" Ben asked.

Thomas was ready, surprisingly so. Not just for the weekend, but also for his divorce to be final. He was ready to be with Ben without the complications that lingered in the back of his mind over still being legally married.

"Are you going to tell me where we're going yet?" He picked up his bag from behind the couch and checked one last time to make sure his lights were turned off.

"I will if you want," Ben said. "But if you'll give me four hours, you can find out on your own."

Thomas tried to think about places that were four hours away and he drew an absolute blank. The vacations he'd taken when the kids were younger were always to national parks or places like Disney World. Once, Jennifer had wanted to take a cruise, so they'd done that when the kids were old enough to stay on their own. This trip with Ben…this was the first time someone had planned something for him to do. His entire life had been the other way around.

"I'll wait," he said, gesturing to the door. "You ready to get going?"

Ben smiled and kissed him, a quick and chaste peck against the corner of his mouth. Thomas offered to drive, but Ben told him no, so Thomas settled into the passenger seat with a gentle sigh. He didn't bother to ask for the aux cord, letting Ben play whatever he wanted to keep him awake for the drive. The miles passed with comfortable silence and easy conversation, and when they pulled onto a winding dirt road that led toward the base of the Evergreen Mountains, Thomas's heart began to race.

"Camping?" he asked, staring out the window as the car bumped down the gravelly road.

"Glamping," Ben corrected, pulling into a parking spot at the end of the road. There was a rock and wood-framed building tucked into the mountain with amber lights glowing out from the massive front windows. "You wait here. I'll be right back."

Ben jumped out of the car and ran inside. Through the glass, Thomas watched him chat with the host behind the check-in counter, then smile and head back toward the car. There was something in the moment, in the way the light caught Ben's hair when he stepped out of the building, and Thomas knew he was in love.

He swallowed the exhilarating and terrifying idea into the back of his throat just in time for Ben to get back to the car. He tossed an old-fashioned hotel keychain onto Thomas's lap and threw the car into reverse.

"You ready?"

"Yeah." He cleared his throat and grabbed the key.

Ben backed out of the parking spot and headed back toward the highway, making a sharp right off the dirt road and heading down a path thick with trees. It wasn't late, but the tree cover kept it cool and dark. Thomas unrolled the window and stuck his arm out, enjoying the dry air against his fingertips as Ben drove them closer to the mountains.

"Glamping?" he asked, watching the road get bumpier. "Are you sure?"

"That's what the flyer said." Ben laughed just as the tree line broke apart and revealed a massive beige tent that reminded him of a circus big top. "Holy shit."

"Is this what the flyer said?"

"I don't think pictures did it justice."

Ben parked and the two of them got out of the car. Thomas looked down at the key in his hand, realizing the tent didn't even have a door. The flaps were pulled open, revealing a massive bed against the far end, decked out with a dozen jewel-colored throw pillows and a thick white duvet that stood out against the natural browns and greens of the landscape around them.

"Why a key?" he asked.

"No idea."

Thomas followed Ben into the tent, taking note of the dark red Persian carpets that lay in a mismatched but intentional pattern across the floor. There was a small couch opposite the bed with a coffee table in front of it. On the other side of the tent there was a dorm size refrigerator hidden in a cabinet, but the real beauty of the space was the massive cut-out in the top of the tent that offered an uninterrupted view of the sky.

"This is amazing," he whispered, dropping his bag at the foot of the bed. He reached for Ben and pulled him close, turning him and pressing a gentle kiss against his lips. "Thank you."

"We just got here," Ben murmured, opening his mouth and making way for Thomas's tongue. Thomas kissed him deeply, bracketing his arm around the small of Ben's back to dip him down and bend over him to take all of his mouth.

"Three nights alone here with you?" he asked.

When he swallowed, his saliva lodged in his throat. The prospect of three uninterrupted nights and two full days with Ben alone in the middle of nowhere was overwhelming in a good way. Spending time with this man seemed like the best way to celebrate turning another year older and officially ending his marriage.

"Do you want to test out the bed?" Ben laughed and flopped onto his back. He kicked his shoes off and let them land on the rugs with two quiet thumps.

"Yes, but..." Thomas toed off his own shoes and climbed onto the bed, tucking himself in against Ben's side. "This is nice too."

"We can do this." Ben arranged himself so Thomas better fit alongside him and Thomas closed his eyes, relishing the now familiar scent of Ben's soap, his detergent, his skin.

He had assuredly not meant to fall in love with the first person he involved himself with after Jennifer, whether that person was a man or a woman. His intent had been to gather the experience and see what moving forward looked like, but he'd genuinely not stood a chance with Ben. Ben, who from the start had been so perfect for him. So unassuming and on the same page. So understanding and amenable. So...good. Thomas breathed in, resting his arm across the hard lines of Ben's stomach and relaxing further into him.

"When...when we get home—"

"I don't want to talk about there," Ben interrupted. "I want to be here with you now. Whatever is there and then can wait for us."

Thomas chewed at the inside of his cheek, torn between wanting to respect the separation Ben was trying to give him— trying to give them both—and wanting to speak the truth between them. In the end, the latter won out, and he sat up, crossing his legs and taking one of Ben's hands between both of his.

"You are here with me now," he said, dragging his lips across the smooth bumps of Ben's knuckles. "We're together here and it's the same as there."

"Is it?" Ben tucked his free arm behind him, pillowing himself on his hand.

"Not entirely, but I want it to be."

"What does that mean to you?" Ben asked.

"I don't have friends like you do, but I have my kids." He cleared his throat, doing his best to swallow back any trepidation. "When we get home, I'd like you to meet them. Or at least Kenzie."

Ben's fingers flexed in his and the corner of one of his eyes twitched. "If that's what you want."

"Is it not what you want?"

"I want to be with you," Ben answered quickly. "I don't know what that means for us or what it looks like. If it looks like meeting your kids, then that's what I want."

Thomas exhaled, turning his attention down to their joined hands. His skin looked old and battered compared to the smooth tan of Ben's and he tried to put the difference in their ages out of his mind.

"I want you to meet them," he said after collecting his thoughts. "But I worry..."

"That they'll hate me?"

"Impossible. But that's not where I was going. I worry that the things you say you want aren't really what you want."

Ben chortled, rolling his eyes and pushing himself to sit. Their knees pressed together and Ben grabbed his face, jerking him until they made eye contact.

"I've been worried about the same thing," Ben admitted, cheeks turning pink. "I've been concerned that because you're new to this, because I'm your first, that you don't really know yourself or know what you want. I've been trying to convince myself that because you've been with a woman your whole life, because you're barely divorced, that you don't know who you are or what you want."

"I promise you I do," he interrupted, but Ben pursed his lips, half a smile, and shook his head.

"I *know*," Ben said. "I know. I didn't at first and my head ran away with me a little bit, but I thought about it and now I think that you actually know yourself better than I know myself, which is honestly a bit terrifying."

"I'm older," he said automatically. "I've had more time."

"It's not that, though."

"No, I don't imagine it is."

"I lo...I really like you. I care about you," Ben said. The change in direction of his words wasn't lost on either of them, and Thomas studied Ben's face to catch any sign of back-tracking on the sentiment. Part of him hoped that Ben would, especially in light of his admission about feeling more uncertain than Thomas did, but he was met with silence.

The rebuff burned in his chest and Thomas's first instinct was to take his hands away, to look anywhere but in the depths of Ben's eyes, but something Ben was said stuck in his mind like a thorn.

I think you actually know yourself better than I know myself.

It was such a small statement, made on a rush of breath, but Thomas saw the truth in it. The worry and the fear radiated off of Ben in waves the longer they sat together on the bed, and Thomas understood the enormity of Ben's confession at the same time he understood the far reaches of his feelings. Ben wasn't wrong that Thomas was sure of himself, maybe more than he let on.

Thomas had lived his entire life for other people. He'd spent years silently and patiently cataloguing the things he'd given up for other people. From the decor choices, to the vacations, to the sex, to the lack of love and respect in his marriage. He'd spent decades forsaking anything that would bring himself happiness for the sake of others, and what had it gotten him? His silence had brought him nothing besides unhappiness and regret. Thomas was tired of living a life made of other people's demands and his would-have-beens. He wasn't going to let anything else pass him by.

"I love you."

"What?" Ben blinked so slowly that Thomas forgot to breathe.

"I don't know if I know myself as well as you think, but I do know that I'm in love with you."

"Thomas."

"It's okay if you don't feel the same," he said, even thought it was a little bit of a lie.

"I do love you," Ben whispered, fingers digging into Thomas's face, holding him steady. "Thomas, I…"

Before Ben could say it again, Thomas surged forward, roughly slanting their mouths together. Ben's lips parted with a low moan, and Thomas took him right down onto his back. He explored the depths of Ben's mouth, eager to see if he tasted different with the admission of his feelings fresh on his tongue. There was a hint of something new there, something curious and scared all at once, but something vibrant and ready. Something that was theirs for the taking, so Thomas did exactly that.

CHAPTER 25
BEN

ON THOMAS'S BIRTHDAY, Ben woke up rested and sore. Behind him, Thomas pressed his chest against Ben's back, his body naked and his cock hard between the split of Ben's ass cheeks. He closed his eyes and backed up, scooting closer to Thomas and twining their feet together. Above him, the sky was purple with a splattering of orange creeping into view and he knew the sun hadn't even risen yet.

"Are you awake?" Thomas groaned, tightening his arms around Ben's chest.

"I don't want to be yet."

"Mmmn." Thomas answered him with a sleepy and agreeable sound, burying his face against Ben's neck. "Then let's not be."

"It's your birthday. You make the rules." Ben yawned and fell back asleep with ease.

He didn't know how long he'd dozed back off for, but when he woke up later, the sun shone brightly through the top of the tent, casting them in a bright yellow glow and a wash of shadow. Thomas's hand had drifted lower at some point and now circled his morning erection, dragging slow and lazy pulls up his length before sliding back down.

"Wondered how long it would take you," Thomas murmured, kissing his shoulder.

Ben rolled onto his back, giving Thomas a better angle and allowing him to tighten his grip.

"How long have you been at it for?"

"You were soft when I started." Ben's cock could have cut a diamond for how hard he was. "I hope you don't mind me waking you up like this."

"You can always wake me up like this." He arched into Thomas's hand. "You could wake me up with your mouth if you wanted."

"Is that a request?"

"I know you like sucking my dick, Thomas." Ben groaned as Thomas began a slow slide down between his legs. "Consider it a birthday present."

"Maybe the straights do it different, but I was under the impression the birthday boy was the one who got a blow job." Thomas smirked up at him, the flat of his tongue out and ready to press against the slick head of Ben's cock.

"Would you rather I—" He lost his words when Thomas closed his mouth around the top of his dick with a low moan.

"No," Thomas answered, his mouth full. "I wouldn't."

Ben's eyes rolled back and he steadied himself with a tight hold in Thomas's hair. His mouth was wet and hot, and enveloped him nearly all the way down to the root. Ben clenched his jaw and bowed off the bed, gently easing himself the rest of the way into Thomas's mouth.

"Your mouth," he rasped, lowering himself down against the sheets. Thomas chased after him, face peppered with red patches and tears beading at the corners of his eyes. Thomas hollowed his cheeks and sucked, bobbing up and down his length like Ben was the one celebrating a birthday and not the other way around.

Damn, he'd gotten lucky with this man.

"I love you," he whispered, fucking his cock into the back of Thomas's throat until he made a quiet, choking sound that had Ben pulling back. His lashes fluttered closed and he murmured the three words again and again until they blurred into the soft whimper that announced the start of his orgasm.

Thomas doubled his efforts, widening his mouth and flattening his tongue. Hot saliva swirled around the tip of his cock, the tight eagerness of Thomas's mouth enough to drive him straight over the edge. His orgasm steamrolled him into the bed, a long and slow stretch of pleasure that drew wave after wave of cum out of his balls. Thomas took it all into his mouth with a chorus of muffled and greedy noises, sucking at his dick until Ben shoved him off.

Thomas was insistent, though, crawling up Ben's body and slanting their mouths together. Ben's cum sat in a pool on Thomas's tongue, and with slow and deliberate strokes, Thomas fed it back to him. Ben groaned and hauled Thomas on top of him, one leg on either side of his sated body. He kissed Thomas until he forgot where his own mouth stopped and Thomas's began, and he kissed him while Thomas humped the air above their bodies, searching for friction.

He only broke the kiss long enough to get the lube and hand it to Thomas, who generously poured it over his own cock and then pulled Ben onto his lap. Ben eased himself down, working his already sore hole open with the blunt tip of Thomas's solid cock. He held Thomas's stare as he sank down, his asshole swallowing inch after agonizing inch of Thomas's throbbing length.

"God." Thomas dropped his head back, baring his throat and Ben leaned in, sucking softly against his Adam's apple. Ben lifted his hips and sank back down, riding Thomas into the mattress. "God, Benjamin…"

"I love that," he whispered, smiling against Thomas's throat. "I love when you use my name."

"Benjamin," Thomas moaned again, fingers tightening around his hips, working him up and down faster.

The sound of their slapping skin filled the tent, overtaken only by the rough breaths that pushed out of Thomas's mouth and into his ear. Ben whimpered and moaned, his exhale turning into one long sigh as the head of Thomas's cock dragged its way against his prostate. His cock was fully hard again, and he reached between their stomachs to jack himself toward another orgasm.

Ben came with Thomas's name in his mouth and Thomas's fingers in his hair, and Thomas followed shortly after, fucking into Ben so deeply he lifted them both off the bed. They tumbled onto the floor, the tight pile of the rugs abrading against his spine while Thomas fucked the rest of the cum from his balls with a strangled—yet powerful—grunt. He fell forward, one hand on either side of Ben's head, sweat dripping from his temples onto the rug.

"I'm spent, birthday boy," Ben murmured, shoving Thomas's hair away from his forehead.

Thomas's chest heaved with a silent laugh and he slowly eased out of Ben's body, flopping down beside him on the rug with a forearm slung over his eyes.

"A nice way to wake up," Thomas said quietly.

Ben made a noise of agreement, his eyes closed. Absentmindedly, he reached for Thomas, his fingertips tracing slow circles over the angles of his hip and the slope of his stomach.

"Does it bother you I'm not as fit as you?" Thomas asked.

"I've never even noticed."

"Don't lie."

Ben snorted, turning onto his side to better reach Thomas's body. "I'm not interested in fucking myself. I'm interested in fucking you."

Thomas slid his arm down, letting one eye pop open, his

expression doubtful. "Then you're really missing out. You're a great lay."

He rolled his eyes. "Thanks for that. But seriously, you're really hot, Thomas. Gorgeous. Beautiful. Attractive. All of the words, they're yours."

Thomas covered his eyes again, face flushing darker than before. "I don't think anyone has called me beautiful before."

"That's why you're divorced."

"I am divorced, aren't I?"

"Happy divorce day?" He wasn't trying to make light of it, but Ben knew the day was something Thomas had been looking forward to and it deserved whatever kind of attention he wanted it to have.

"Happy divorce day," Thomas repeated, letting his arm fall down between them. Ben tangled their fingers together, studying Thomas's profile. He was all of the words Ben had used to describe him and more. So much of all of them, in fact, that if he stared too long, Thomas took his breath away. "Did you have any plans for us?"

"Just being with you. There's a hot tub down the path a little ways if you wanted to drink some champagne and soak in the bubbles."

"That sounds relaxing."

"That's the point."

"Are there other amenities?"

Ben chuckled and pushed himself up, resting his back against the side of the bed. "I think you've seen the best parts of what the campground has to offer."

"Is it you?" Thomas rolled onto his side and propped himself up on a bent arm.

"The main attraction," he confirmed.

"A weekend well spent." Thomas sat up and stretched his arms above his head. "This is already the best birthday I've had in years."

"That's kind of sad."

Thomas stood, rolling out his shoulders and his neck, leaving his red and half-hard cock at eye-level. Ben lightly touched his palms against Thomas's thighs, not in a sexual way, just a…search for connection. He felt better when Thomas was around and even more so when they were touching.

"It helps me to appreciate you more." Thomas held a hand down to him, and Ben used it to help stand. "I'm well aware how lucky I am to have you."

Ben made an appreciative noise in the back of his throat and flung his arms around Thomas's shoulders. "I'm lucky."

"Honestly, Ben." Thomas grabbed his face and held him, the eye contact sharp and focused. "I am lucky that it was you."

He swallowed, blinking back an unanticipated surge of emotion. Thomas wasn't the only lucky one, but there was no reason to talk it into the ground. He knew he'd taken a chance on Thomas, even though at first meeting he hadn't known just how inexperienced he was. He rarely let himself think about what would have been if Thomas had been upfront about that with him in the first place because a present that didn't involve them together wasn't one he was interested in.

The shrill chirp of a cellphone ringer interrupted his thoughts, and he raised an eyebrow in Thomas's direction.

"Do you seriously keep your ringer on?" he asked.

"How else would I know if someone was calling?"

"Oh, my God," he muttered, shaking his head and pushing Thomas away. "Go answer your phone. I have to pee."

There wasn't a bathroom in the yurt, but there was a door in the side that led into a stucco walled bathroom. He appreciated the space was separate, and it was simple enough to meet their needs. The bathroom had a shower with a bench, which while he would have enjoyed a bathtub, Ben supposed the hot tub down the trail would suffice. He took a quick piss and debated rinsing off in the shower, but decided to wait for Thomas to get off the phone. After washing his hands, he slipped back into the tent to find Thomas on the edge of the bed, wearing nothing more than his underwear. His cellphone sat on his knee, the screen lit up and the speaker on.

"I'm sorry that you and your mom fought," Thomas said, and a young female voice answered him back.

"It's not your fault she's a lying bitch."

"Kenzie."

"She is. I don't know what she expected to happen, just telling us lies about you the way she did."

Thomas looked up at him, the earlier relaxation gone from his face.

"My daughter," he mouthed.

Tight lines fanned out from the corners of Thomas's eyes, and Ben sat down beside him, resting his head on his shoulder.

"How did your brother take it?" Thomas asked.

"About as well as you'd expect. It was almost like he was looking for confirmation about his shitty behavior."

"Your brother is in the wrong for what he's done to Trent and he knows it. He's lashing out at anyone he can reach."

"I'm sorry again that you got the brunt of it," Kenzie said. "I wouldn't have invited him that day if I would have known."

"Water under the bridge, sweetheart." Thomas settled his hand on Ben's thigh, swirling his fingers over Ben's skin.

"I hope you're having fun out of town with Ben," Kenzie said, and Thomas reached to take the phone off speaker so fast he nearly fumbled it onto the floor. Ben rolled his eyes and lay back, giving Thomas as much space as he could muster to finish the conversation.

"It's our first day here," Thomas said, returning his hand to Ben's thigh. "But it's been really nice so far."

"So, you'll call me when you're back in town?"

"Of course."

"Alright, Dad. Love you," she said.

"Love you." Thomas ended the call and tossed his phone onto the pillow, lying back beside Ben.

"I told her about you before," he said.

"I remember."

"It was a relief that she didn't care you're a man."

Ben chortled. "You're telling me."

"I think it helps that her brother is gay."

"It's the 21st century. I'm sure he isn't the first gay man she's ever met," he teased. "Did something go sour with your ex?"

"Kind of. I mean, always, yes. But my son has been behaving badly and he was staying with Kenzie because his husband threw him out, but then Kenzie threw him out too. He was chasing after some approval about his behavior, thinking that Jennifer would coddle him the way she always has."

"I take it she didn't?"

"No, which is rich, considering she cheated on me too."

"The apple doesn't fall far from the tree, apparently," he said.

"I wish I had been a better parent to him." Thomas sighed. "He's twenty-four now and I don't know what to do with him."

"There's nothing for you to do. He's an adult and he's responsible for his own actions and the repercussions of those actions. You can't hold his hand forever, and it sounds like your ex can't either."

Thomas smacked his lips together and shrugged, turning his attention toward the hole in the tent above them. The sky was a pale blue and the sun was so bright he had to look away.

"Enough about them," Thomas said, clapping his hands. "I'm ready to get the rest of my present."

Ben laughed and stood, hauling Thomas with him, pressing their bodies together in every place they could touch. "Hot tub?"

"Champagne." Thomas kissed the corner of his mouth and walked them toward the fridge.

"Lube," he murmured, walking them back toward the bed. Their legs tangled together and Ben fell onto this back, Thomas landing on top of him and pushing the air out of his lungs. He laughed, and Thomas laughed, the sound mixing together like a rich symphony in his ears. The sound quieted and died down, leaving them together with heaving chests and the deep pools of Thomas's lust-filled eyes.

"Towels," Ben croaked, unable to look away.

"Towels," Thomas confirmed, pulling them both to their feet, but not letting go. They didn't make a move, eye contact still steady in a way that felt more serious than Ben would ever be able to find words for.

He cleared his throat and Thomas nodded, jerking away like he'd been burned, but he moved quickly, taking Ben's hand and pulling him toward the bathroom to get the towels. The moment was shattered, but it was far from gone. In the silence, something had moved between them and everything that happened from that moment forward would build on the foundation they'd made in that short, but knowing silence.

"I'm ready," Thomas said, and it wasn't a question.

"Me too."

CHAPTER 26
THOMAS

THOMAS WOKE early on Monday morning, the sky above their heads half purple and half blue. His body ached from use and his heart swelled with emotion. The weekend away with Ben was exactly what he'd needed—what he'd wanted—even though he hadn't known as much at the time. He found himself reinvigorated with a desire to return home, proud and open about the tentative life he and Ben were building. No, he wasn't so bold as to assume that things with Ben would last forever. He'd thought that once about Jennifer and been proven wrong. But he allowed himself space to enjoy the present, especially the heat of Ben's skin when they'd spent the night tangled together under high thread-count sheets.

"I don't want to go home," Ben muttered, rolling around and burying his face against Thomas's chest.

"I do," he said.

Ben looked up at him, eyebrows knit together in sleepy confusion. "Are you breaking up with me?"

"Not at all." He kissed the top of Ben's head. "I'm excited to go home and be with you there. Just like this."

"We have to work at home."

"You know what I mean."

"What *do* you mean?" Ben asked, hands trailing all over Thomas's bare skin and frying his brain.

"I want to get home because I want my kids to meet you, or at least my youngest. I want to get home because this is nice, but it's like a break. I want to have more breaks with you, but I want more than that too."

"You're really all in with me, aren't you?"

"I want to be. I don't want to scare you off and I'm not making promises or plans, but—"

Ben cut him off with two fingers against his lips. "I get it. I want that with you too."

Slowly, Ben dragged his fingers down, Thomas's lower lip popping free once Ben reached his chin. Thomas arched his head back, putting his throat on display for Ben to continue his slide. He didn't understand how Ben always made him so hard, how Ben knew the things to say, the ways to touch him. He wondered sometimes how his life might have been if he'd met Ben in high school instead of Jennifer. But he wasn't a fool. It was different then, and in his heart he knew he had Ben now because that's what he needed.

They got out of bed together, spending much more time than necessary in the shower to appreciate each other's bodies. Thomas dried Ben off, paying extra attention to his balls and spending some time to use his mouth and ensure they were properly emptied for the drive home. With the taste of Ben's release still fresh on his tongue, he packed up his bags and waited for the small coffee pot on the desk to brew him a cup for the road. Ben loaded up their things, and Thomas joined him around the back of the car, giving the tent one last look before climbing into the passenger seat.

"This was an amazing birthday," he said, leaning over the console and giving Ben a kiss. "And the best divorce day I could have asked for."

Ben huffed out a small laugh and turned the car on. "I'm glad you enjoyed it."

"You know…" He leaned back against the headrest as Ben started them on the long drive home. "I've never been big on vacations, but I think I'd like to be now."

"Oh? Is that so?"

"Yeah. I want to…even if things don't work out with us, I want to keep doing it," he said quietly.

"That's a little bleak."

"I'm trying to be realistic."

"Are you still expecting me to cut and run?" Ben asked.

"No. I just wouldn't blame you if you did."

"Please stop." Ben's fingers gripped the steering wheel and he frowned, looking over at Thomas. "I love you. I *love* you, and that's not a casual thing and it's not something I'm going to wake up one morning and have outgrown."

He exhaled, scrubbing a hand down his face and giving Ben an apologetic nod. "You're right. I know and I'm sorry. That wasn't fair of me to say."

"It wasn't."

"When we get home, would you be up for dinner with Kenzie tonight?" he asked.

Ben chuckled. "Horrible segue you made right there."

He shrugged helplessly.

"But yes," Ben said, "I'd love to meet your daughter."

They settled in, with Thomas picking the music this time. The four hour drive went by faster on the way home, and for as excited as he was to introduce Ben fully into his day-to-day life, he immediately missed the seclusion—and fantasy—the vacation had allowed them.

Ben dropped him off at home with a lingering kiss and the promise to return at five, and Thomas texted Kenzie with dinner reservations and an address. She sent him back four different kinds of smiling emojis, so he took that as a win. He used the downtime to catch a distraction-free shower, then he watered his plants and putzed around the apartment until it was time to get ready. Thomas found he was lonely, not in the conventional sense, but in the...he wanted to be able to tell someone about Ben. He wanted someone who could share in his excitement over his new relationship, over his new understanding of himself.

He collapsed onto the couch with a beer, scrolling through the long abandoned contact list in his phone, trying to think about which husband of Jennifer's friends would be the best for him to reach out to again. Every name gave him a dead end, and with a sigh, he gave up. Instead, he texted Ben and said he could come over whenever he was ready.

Ben landed on his doormat ten minutes later, face flushed like he'd run the blocks between their apartments and a nervous tension in his shoulders. He looked great, more dressed up than Thomas had ever seen him, in a pair of navy slacks and a short-sleeved, white button-up. He wore a brown belt and brown shoes, and the whole outfit put together only served to emphasize Ben's lanky swimmer's body. Thomas grabbed him by the biceps, stroking down to his elbows and back up again, relishing the feel of his skin.

"There's nothing to worry about," he promised unprompted.

"What if she doesn't like me?" A rare burst of insecurity shone out from Ben's eyes, and Thomas hated to see it.

"What's not to like?"

"My age, for one," Ben offered, and Thomas cut him off with a rough and demanding kiss that had them tumbling out of the apartment and against the far wall.

"None of that," he begged against Ben's delicious and willing mouth. "Your age isn't her problem."

"If you say so." Ben nipped his lower lip, smiling and relaxing.

"She's sharp, like her mother, but she's not cruel," he said.

"I trust you."

Thomas kissed Ben's knuckles. "And I love you. Let me lock up and we can head over."

He grabbed his wallet and phone from the apartment and locked the deadbolt, checking the knob before joining Ben back in the hallway. With ease, he threaded their fingers together and headed down to his car. Driving was the least he could do, considering how much Ben had put in for the weekend. The restaurant was the place he and Kenzie often met at for brunch, which wasn't terribly far from the apartment. Ben's nerves radiated off of him for the entire drive, and no matter how tight Thomas held his hand, they didn't waver.

In the parking lot, he stopped Ben and grabbed him by the face, forcing his stare and hoping that he could get through to the man he loved. "I promise that this will be okay."

"I know."

"If you want to back out, you can take my car home and I'll meet up with you later. No hard feelings," he said with absolute sincerity.

"I can't just go home."

"You can."

"I want to meet her," Ben said, covering Thomas's hands with his own. "But you were nervous when you met Lara, right? It's just like that."

"I need you to know that I won't stand for either of my children treating you poorly," he said, pressing his fingers into Ben's cheeks with the promise. "You're part of my life and they'll treat you the same as they would treat me."

"That's…" Ben swallowed back whatever he wanted to say. "I can't ask that of you."

"You're not asking. I'm telling."

"I know things have been touchy with them for years, and I don't want to make it worse," Ben worried aloud.

"Impossible." He leaned close and pressed their mouths

together. "I love you and so will they. Besides, Dakota isn't even here. It's just Kenzie."

Ben snorted an unamused sound in his throat. "The sharp one."

"She's the best parts of me." That seemed to do the trick and some of the fight fell from Ben's shoulders. "Are you ready?"

"As I'll ever be." Ben tried to shake out of his hold, but Thomas refused, instead taking Ben's hand and meshing their fingers together. He led Ben into the restaurant, relieved enough to find that Kenzie hadn't gotten there yet. It gave them time to get in and get settled, and after Thomas ordered them both drinks, Ben excused himself to the bathroom.

In his absence, their drinks arrived, and so did Kenzie, with an unexpected guest in tow.

"Dakota." Thomas stood from the table to hug Kenzie, but he wasn't sure how to greet his son. Kenzie chuffed at the confusion and slid into one of the empty chairs, ignoring the awkward greeting Thomas was trapped in. "It's good to see you again."

"Kenzie said I should come," Dakota said, sounding as petulant as a five year-old.

Thomas sighed and sat back down, glad his drink had already arrived and well aware that he would need it. Maybe he should have sent Ben home anyway. Even though he hadn't anticipated Dakota showing up, the table was already fraught with tension at their arrival and he knew it would only get worse once Ben returned.

"I told him I was meeting your boyfriend and he said he wanted to tag along," Kenzie said.

"Meeting my boyfriend?" He arched a brow at her, smirking as she reached for the bread and immediately began to de-crust it. "I thought this was to celebrate my birthday."

"Do you think if I tell the host we're celebrating, dessert will be free?" she teased.

"The sheer number of candles required would burn the place down."

"Maybe your boyfriend can help blow…them out," she said.

"Watch your mouth." He wagged a finger across the table at his youngest child, attention slowly drifting to his oldest.

He wasn't stupid enough to think that Dakota had any interest in actually meeting Ben, and he worried that he'd only shown up to try and get money or, worse, a place to stay out of him. Neither of those things would be happening, though, and that knowledge helped him rest a little easier.

"Where is this boyfriend?" Dakota asked, glancing at the second drink on the table before looking over his shoulder.

"He went to use the restroom. I'm sure he'll be right back."

"Did you and Ben have a nice trip?" Kenzie asked, tossing her crust at him.

"Ben?" Dakota asked. "Is that his name?"

"Ben," he confirmed, looking toward the bathroom, worried Ben had bolted for the parking lot after all. "And, yes, it was a really nice trip. I'm glad we went."

Movement from the corner of his eye caught his attention, the knot in his chest relaxing when he caught sight of Ben weaving his way back from the bathroom. He smiled, and it must have given him away because Kenzie and Dakota both immediately turned to follow his line of sight.

"Ben," Dakota murmured, standing up so quickly his chair almost fell over.

Ben smiled at Kenzie, the commotion with Dakota's chair stealing his gaze, and when he saw Dakota, Ben drew to an immediate stop.

"What are you doing here?" Ben asked.

"These are my kids," Thomas explained, standing up. "My daughter Kenzie, and my son, Dakota."

Ben's jaw went tight, the muscles tighter through his shoulders than they had been in the parking lot. It was instantly clear to Thomas that Ben and Dakota knew each other, but he had no idea how.

"You told me your son is married," Ben said, voice jerky as he refocused his attention on Thomas's face.

"He is."

"Cody," Ben sighed, using a diminutive of Dakota's name that he'd never heard before. It sounded familiar, and then *everything* clicked into place.

"This is your Cody?" Thomas balked. "My son is your ex-boyfriend?"

"I didn't know he was married." Ben took a step backward, face white as the china on the table. "I wouldn't have gotten involved if I knew he was married."

"What?" he sputtered, unsure of what that had to do with anything. If what Ben said was true, it meant that Dakota had cheated on Trent with Ben—and lord knew who else—but it also meant that his son was abusive, and that made him sick to his stomach in a way he'd never have words for. "Dakota, is this true?"

"I'll go," Ben said quickly, raising his hands and taking a step backward. "Can I still have your keys or... you know what, I'll just call a car."

"Don't go," he said, almost a plea. "Please. I..."

"You're sleeping with..." Dakota looked between them, expression laced with horror. "*My dad?*"

"Oh." A soft gasp from Kenzie, balled-up sourdough slice between her fingers. "I see."

"I'm in love with your dad," Ben corrected, taking another step toward the door and color returning to his face. "But I'm not sure that matters."

"It does," Thomas promised, holding up one finger, begging Ben for a minute to get his head around what was going on. He turned a sharp glare toward his son, jaw tight. "Can I have a word with you? Outside?"

Dakota sighed loudly, righting the fallen chair and snaking his way through the restaurant to the front door. Ben didn't move, rooted to the spot a few feet away from Kenzie, and Thomas hoped he'd be there when he got back. With one last look, he turned away from Ben and followed his son out of the restaurant, hoping he was strong enough to be the kind of parent he'd always imagined himself to be, when it was what his son clearly needed the most.

CHAPTER 27

BEN

BEN DIDN'T WAIT.

He apologized to Kenzie, called for a car on his phone, and ran out the back door of the restaurant before Thomas could come after him. He knew it was only a matter of time before Thomas showed up on his doorstep, but he hoped it was long enough to get his thoughts together.

What were the odds that his manipulative and cheating ex-boyfriend would be the son of the first man he ever truly loved?

Clearly, high ones.

It took less time than he expected for Thomas to show up, and since he'd been anticipating the showdown, he hadn't even bothered to close the front door all the way after he got home. Thomas burst through it in a rush, breathing loudly and searching for him with wide and frantic eyes.

"You left." Thomas righted himself and straightened his clothes, putting his scratched and abraded knuckles on display. That was when Ben realized two of the buttons on Thomas's shirt had popped off...or been torn off.

"What happened to you?" He fought his instinct to go to Thomas, instead hesitating a few feet from the front door.

"You left." Thomas stepped inside and closed the door

behind him. Ben took a step back, holding up his hands. Thomas's face blanched and he retreated, pressing his back against the door. He looked like Ben had slapped him.

"Of course, I left."

"Why?"

Ben scoffed. "Why? Are you serious?"

"Very."

"I ruined your son's marriage," he muttered, embarrassed to admit the truth of the matter. "After everything you told me you went through with your ex-wife, I went and put your son's husband through the same thing."

He turned away from Thomas, unable to face him.

"Are..." Thomas sounded confused, and his footsteps slowly approached. "Are you serious right now?"

Ben whirred back around, finding Thomas much closer than he'd expected. He was far worse for wear than Ben's initial inspection had led him to believe, and it was reflex alone that had him trying to pull Thomas's shirt back together where the buttons had gone missing.

"He cheated with me." Ben rolled his eyes. "I remember thinking that he was cheating *on* me, but it had been the other way around all along."

"And you think that's somehow your fault?" Thomas balked, grabbing Ben's hands and holding them against his chest. "My son lied to you."

"I should have known."

"How would you have known?" Thomas asked.

Ben shook his head, turning Thomas's hand over in his and examining the wounds on his knuckles. "What happened to you?"

"I would have put Dakota through the wall of that restaurant if it wasn't built so well."

"What?"

"Ben." Thomas's mouth hung half open and his eyes scanned

his face, his expression marred with confusion. "Do you really think that it's your fault?"

He did think it was his fault, even though the thought of explaining why made him feel childish and silly. Of course, it was his fault. Whose fault would it be if not?

"Dakota thinks it's your fault," Thomas went on, drawing out Ben's biggest fears. "He told me that you never asked if he was married."

"I didn't," he confirmed.

"It's not a standard getting-to-know-you question."

"Can I clean this?" He tapped his finger softly against Thomas's bruised knuckles.

"You don't have to."

"Right. But can I?"

Thomas swallowed and nodded, following Ben into the bathroom. Ben closed the lid of the toilet and Thomas sat down, shoulders sagging like the weight of the night had just caught up to him. He slumped forward, forearms resting on his thighs. Ben grabbed the first aid kit from under the sink and arranged himself on the floor between Thomas's feet.

"If it's anyone's fault, it's mine," Thomas said.

He squirted peroxide onto Thomas's hand, drawing a grunt out of him. "How is it your fault and not mine?"

"Because you aren't his father. Because it wasn't your place to teach him better. It was mine. Or Jennifer's."

"Seems like he watched her more than you," Ben murmured, patting at the scrapes on Thomas's hand with some gauze.

"Her fault then." Thomas sighed. "Hers and mine. Not yours."

"You know that doesn't make any sense, right?" He tossed the gauze into the trash can and laid a couple band aids across Thomas's knuckles. The scrapes weren't deep, more like road rash, but he was sure they ached. "How did you hurt your hand? Did you punch the wall because you couldn't put Cody into it?"

Thomas's head hung low and, with his good hand, he rubbed

at the bridge of his nose. "I grabbed him outside, I was so mad. I shouldn't have done it, but the look on your face when you saw him…when you realized…"

"Thomas."

"When *I* realized." Thomas looked up, eyes red. "When I realized my son was your ex. That my son was the one who'd done that shit to you. That he was the one who'd made you doubt your worth."

Ben fell onto his ass, back against the wall. He mirrored Thomas's posture, with his forearms on his knees. Dinner had taken a turn for the worst and he was starving, but nauseous at the idea of eating all at the same time. His stomach grumbled, and he wasn't sure if he was from hunger or the need to throw up.

"What else happened?" he asked.

"I grabbed him, but then I realized…" Thomas shook his head and stared at the floor. "I let him go and he shoved me, saying it wasn't his fault, spewing some nonsense about Trent and about you. Blaming it on me and his mother. My shirt tore…"

Thomas trailed off, flicking at the ruined placket of his shirt. Ben didn't know what to do—or what to say—so he raised back onto his knees, reaching for Thomas and working to undo the remaining buttons on his shirt and helping him shrug out of it.

"Come on," he said, pulling Thomas off the toilet.

He led him into the bedroom and pulled an old band t-shirt out of his dresser for Thomas to put on. The shirt was too long and a little too tight around the shoulders, but Thomas filled it out in a way that had Ben's chest expanding in uncomfortable ways. It was the first, and likely the last, time he'd ever see Thomas in his clothes and a small part of him couldn't help but mourn that.

"Then what?" he asked, sitting on the edge of his bed.

"Then Kenzie came out, chastised us both for making a

scene. I backed down and Dakota didn't, because he never does."

"Yeah, I noticed that about him," Ben murmured.

"I told him I didn't have time to deal with him. That he was an adult and that I was disappointed in him."

"Then what?"

"Then I came here." Thomas fell to his knees at Ben's feet, the opposite of the positioning they'd had in the bathroom. "I came to you."

"Why?"

"At the risk of sounding like a broken record, are you serious?" Thomas grabbed his knees, and Ben stared down at the tension in his knuckles, the raw scratches that peeked out from beneath the strips of bandage.

"I wouldn't ask if I wasn't."

"Because you're my boyfriend?" Thomas said it like a question. "Because I love you. Because you were ambushed by your abuser and then you ran away."

"He wasn't my…" Ben bit back the rest of the sentence because he wasn't sure if it was the truth or not. He'd never had a problem giving a name to the things Cody had done to him, but it felt different in this moment. Like calling Cody what he was, acknowledging what transpired between them, would affect more than just the two of them now. The pain was clearly etched across Thomas's face, and Ben hated to be responsible for any of it.

He sighed, changing course. "Have you talked with his husband?"

"Trent? No." Thomas shook his head. "Why?"

"He probably needs checking on, all things considered."

"Shit." Thomas fell back onto his ass and he looked up at the ceiling like there were answers to be found. Ben followed his stare in case it were true. "I'll call him in the morning."

Ben's stomach growled again and since he still didn't know

what to do or say, he stood up and held his hand down for Thomas. "Are you hungry?"

"No, but I should eat."

Ben nodded and pulled Thomas to his feet. Together in the kitchen, they pulled vegetables out of the fridge. It was all Ben could manage. Thomas helped slice bell peppers and cucumbers, and Ben scooped hummus onto a plate. He carried it into the living room while Thomas washed the cutting board and the knives before joining him. He sat down as close as he normally did, and Ben wanted it to be a comfort, but the doubt lingered around him like a cloud.

"This doesn't change anything between us," Thomas finally said, casting a sideways glance at him.

"No? I thought it would change everything."

"It changes things for him and me. Not for us."

Ben dragged a strip of bell pepper through the hummus and shoved it into his mouth, chewing slowly so he'd have more time to respond.

"How can you look at me the same?" he asked.

"I look at you and all I see is the man I love. The man who took a chance on me when I had no idea what I wanted from him. I look at you and see a far better man than I could ever deserve."

Ben snorted, rolling his eyes, but Thomas grabbed his chin, jerking him and forcing eye contact.

"I look at him differently," Thomas said. "I look at him with shame and disappointment, and embarrassment. Everything you think should land on you is on him, Ben."

"I really want to believe you."

"Ben." Thomas pursed his lips, a half-grimace. "I don't know how to make you see that this isn't your fault and everything I told you this morning, this weekend, the past few months—it hasn't changed because of this."

"There's nothing you *can* say," he admitted, a tear slicking out of the corner of his eye. It burned his cheek, and he angrily swiped it away. "This is…"

He couldn't say it. He couldn't admit to Thomas that all of the doubt he felt had been instilled in him by Cody…by his son. He didn't see a way out, and he sure as hell didn't see a way forward. All of the words he wanted to say caught in his throat and the ones that would have done nothing besides hurt them both bubbled to the surface. It was a wonder he swallowed them back, leaving silence between them.

"It hurts me to see you like this," Thomas whispered, thumb stroking over his chin. "To know that I had a part in this."

Ben wanted to protest, but nothing came. The bell peppers rolled violently in his stomach, threatening to make him sick after all.

"This is…this is exactly what we didn't want, Thomas."

"No." Thomas shook his head. "Please don't."

He pushed Thomas's hand away from his face, frown angled sharply on his lips. "This is what we didn't want then and I don't want it now. The mess and the complication. That's not…"

As he said it, the words burned his throat as intensely as the tears that now flowed freely down his cheeks.

"I want you, but it's a mess in my heart, in my head. I don't know how to be with you right now," he admitted.

Thomas worked his jaw, and Ben watched his eyes fill with tears. Thomas was better at reining it in, though, and with a few blinks, they were gone.

"My feelings for you haven't changed," Thomas said again.

"Neither have mine." He grabbed Thomas's hands, forgetting to be careful of the bandages, of the physical reminder that everything between them *had* changed. "But everything else has, and I can tell you don't think it should have, but it feels different for me now. And I'm sorry if that's a me thing."

"It can be an us thing," Thomas offered. "I want to be with you. You aren't something I want to walk away from."

"But what if I asked you to?"

He closed his eyes as the question fell out of his mouth, lashes clumped and sticky from the tears he'd shed. There was no point in trying to stop them, so he didn't. His heart was breaking in his chest, but he didn't see another way out. He didn't want to rebuild himself on Thomas's back, and he knew —he fucking *knew*—that there was a part of Thomas that understood that.

"I'd ask that you please don't," Thomas answered.

"Maybe not forever," he whispered.

"Ben, please."

"Just…I need some time."

Thomas dragged his tongue across the front of his teeth and looked toward the door like his body knew what to do even if his heart was fighting him. And Ben hoped his heart was fighting him because his own wanted to stage a rebellion in his chest.

"This isn't what I want. I hope you know that," he said, like it mattered. He knew it didn't. "But it's what I need and I want to come back to you. I want to be better and stronger for you."

"None of this is your fault," Thomas said, voice raising louder than it had been the whole conversation. "This is him and his shortcomings and my fuck-ups as a parent. You don't have work to do here, Ben. I do."

"I really want to believe that, but the fact that I can't is proof that I have work to do too."

Thomas's expression fell with his posture, and he turned to look at him once again. "Not forever?"

"I hope not."

"I don't like this."

"Me neither," he agreed, digging his nails into the palms of his hands to ground him in the present, to stop his heart from taking over when it needed to take a back seat.

Thomas stood and Ben followed suit, more out of habit than

intention. It felt like a spear in his side, and he squeezed his eyes closed, hating himself as much as he hated Cody.

"Can I..." Thomas trailed off with a strangled noise and Ben opened his eyes in time to watch Thomas's hands flex and ball into fists.

"Can you what?"

"A kiss," Thomas said quickly, taking a step away like he knew the answer would be no. "Just one more kiss before I go. Until I see you again."

It was the optimism that did Ben in, and he'd barely finished nodding his consent before Thomas was on him. Thomas grabbed his face, yanking him forward and bringing their mouths together in a kiss far fiercer and more passionate than Ben had expected. He whimpered, curling his fingers around Thomas's wrists so he didn't fall over and he returned the kiss with all of the desperation and apology he could muster. Neither of them got hard, and the kiss ended sooner than he wanted, but he knew it was for the best. His body would fight his brain on this one; he knew himself well enough to know that much.

Finally, Thomas released him, taking another step backward. He looked down at the bandage on his hand, tracing it with the tip of his finger like it was Ben's skin. Ben grabbed his own hand, like he could feel the touch if he concentrated hard enough. He couldn't, though.

"Until I see you again," Thomas repeated, reaching the door.

"I love you."

"I'm a patient man," Thomas said.

"I love you," he repeated.

Thomas opened the door, still in Ben's old t-shirt, both of their tears smeared across his lips. "I love you too."

CHAPTER 28
THOMAS

AFTER TWO WEEKS of radio silence from Ben, and from Dakota, it took Thomas half a bottle of wine and all of his weight to work up the courage to call Trent. As a general rule, he hated to walk into unpredictable situations, and the call to his adulterous and abusive son's husband was the textbook definition of unpredictable. But he swallowed the last of his third class of wine, scrolled through his contacts, hit call, then sat on his hands, resigned to not move until he either spoke with Trent or left a message.

"Hello?" Trent answered before Thomas even had a real chance to figure out what he wanted to say.

"Trent."

"Mr. Fullier."

"You know I hate that."

"What did you need, Thomas?" There was an unmistakable edge to Trent's voice. "I don't know where Dakota is, if that's why you're calling."

"It's not," he said quickly, clearing his throat. "Well, I'm calling about him, but I don't care where he is."

"I filed for divorce. I don't know if he told you."

"He didn't, but he deserves it."

On the other end of the line, Trent laughed quietly. "That he does."

"I found out recently that he'd…not been faithful."

"Yeah. That's a thing that happened. Hence the divorce."

"Are you okay?" he asked.

"I'm basically undoing the past few years of my life because my entire marriage was a lie," Trent snapped. "Okay isn't a word I'd use, but it's what I'm working toward."

"My wife cheated on me," he said. "It's not the only reason we divorced, but it was the catalyst for things breaking down."

"Shit," Trent muttered. "I didn't know, Mr. Fullier. I'm sorry."

"Don't you dare." Thomas didn't feel as uncomfortable with the conversation as he'd feared, so he eased off his hands and refilled his wine, settling more comfortably into the couch. He studied the wall in front of him, the vines of the pothos plant snaking their way down the wall and around the entertainment center. He wanted to get another pothos for his room. The way the plant grew, and twined, and stretched spoke to something deep inside of him that he wanted to embrace more fully.

"I didn't call you to talk about the disaster that is my life. I'm calling because some things about Dakota have recently come to light and…"

"Oh." Trent's voice fell, and Thomas knew that Ben wasn't the only one to experience the brunt of his son's attitude.

"We don't need to have a discussion about it. I just wanted to apologize. For him or for me, or maybe both. If I would have known—"

"You wouldn't have known," Trent interrupted, "because I haven't told anyone. I don't know how you know."

"I…I've recently met someone else that he's mistreated." Thomas didn't think it important to go into the nature of his relationship with Ben. That wasn't the point of the call.

Trent answered that with a doubtful noise that quickly turned into a tired sigh. Thomas could picture Trent sitting at his and Dakota's dining room table, rubbing the bridge of his nose in the way he always did when he'd spent too many hours thinking about work.

"You don't have to apologize because you haven't done anything wrong. And Dakota won't ever apologize because he doesn't think he has. Or, rather, he'll apologize to manipulate, not because he means it."

"I'm sorry all the same," he said.

"Well, I appreciate that."

"Is there anything I can do to help you through the divorce?"

Trent exhaled a long breath. "Your son leaving me alone is all I can ask for at this point. I don't want to deal with getting a restraining order. It…it wasn't ever that bad, but it's best he stays away. So if you see him, just remind him of that."

"I will," he promised.

"I'm moving back to Florida," Trent continued. "I'm going to stay here until things are finalized because it'll be easier, but I talked with my sister and she's going to let me stay with her until I get everything sorted out again."

Starting life over had been easy for Thomas. Sure, it had been an adjustment after an entire life lived, but in hindsight, it wasn't so bad. He'd been able to see the good in the changes that life brought him, and he hoped Trent could do the same.

"That'll be nice," he said, but it didn't feel like enough. He realized how Ben felt, apologizing for something that wasn't his mistake. Thomas was near desperate for Trent to accept his apology or to let him shoulder some of the blame for what Dakota had done, much how Ben had acted the last time they'd seen each other. He recognized the root of the emotion, and his entire body ached again to hold Ben and console him. To help him. To love him.

"I'm looking forward to it," Trent confirmed. "Was there anything else, Mr. Fullier?"

"No. No, Trent. That's all." He finished off the wine in his glass and debated the merits of finishing the bottle.

"If I do think of anything I need, I will call, though," Trent said, quickly following up with, "Bye, Mr. Fullier."

The phone beeped loudly in his ear before he was able to say goodbye and he let out a long breath, sinking back into the couch with his phone in his hand. He wasn't delirious enough to think that his phone call had changed anything, but Trent's unacceptance of Thomas's responsibility had cast Ben's reaction to the event in a new light.

He'd been trying his best to give Ben the space he asked for, even if the silence chipped away at him in almost unbearable ways. He'd sent himself a message whenever he wanted to reach out to Ben. He'd talked to himself in the mirror whenever he wanted to call. When he couldn't sleep at night, he buried his face in the pillow that still smelled like Ben's shampoo, and embarrassingly enough, he'd slept in Ben's shirt every night for the past two weeks.

With Trent fresh on his mind, Thomas scrolled to the chat logs with Ben, fingers itching to send a text even though he knew better than to reach out. He wished he had Lara's number, at the least, so he could check up on the side, so he could *know* Ben was okay without him there. That was what really ate at him—the not knowing of everything. When they saw each other last, he'd been the one asking for it to not be goodbye. Ben was the one asking for space, asking for him to leave. He found himself faced with the very real possibility Ben would never come back to him.

It was with that miserable thought at the forefront of his mind that Thomas decided he wanted gelato. He wasn't above moping and he had every intention of sulking his way to the gelato shop and getting mint chocolate because it was the one Ben had gotten the first time they went. He corked the wine and shoved the last of the bottle into the fridge, then put on a pair of pants that didn't have stains on them and headed down the street.

He walked the long way, as to avoid Ben's building, so when he walked up and found Ben and Lara at one of the cafe tables on the sidewalk, he almost turned around and went home.

"Are you stalking me, Thomas?" Lara asked, a little louder than necessary to get his attention. He stopped and shoved his hair back out of his face, the mirth and tease in Lara's eyes bright under the neon signage of the gelato shop.

At her greeting, Ben turned around, his head snapping on his neck like a rubber band. He looked like hell, tired with more scruff on his face than Thomas had ever seen. He didn't hate it, but it didn't feel like it suited Ben in the least.

"Just came for dessert," he said, trying to not let his stare linger on Ben, but it was just so good to see him. He jammed his hands into his pockets. "Ben."

"Hi," Ben rasped.

"Are you well?"

Ben licked his lips, pulling them between his teeth and nodding.

"Good. I…" Thomas bit the inside of his cheek. "I won't keep you. Good seeing you, Lara."

He moved past them quickly, slipping inside and ordering his gelato. Thomas didn't even want it anymore, his entire body tense from seeing Ben and soured from not being able to grab him and kiss him silly. But he took it anyway and snuck out of the shop without paying Ben and Lara any more mind than a quick nod of his head. He wasn't trying to be mean or rude. He was only trying to respect Ben's wishes.

Even if he hated them.

Thomas got back to his apartment and collapsed inside his door, not even closing it before his knees gave out. He slid down the wall, his legs straightening in front of him, his already melting cup of gelato in his hand. He let his arms fall to his sides and he closed his eyes, trying to catch his breath, trying to still his heart, trying to face the prospect of saying goodbye to the first man he'd ever loved.

"You walk fast."

Ben's voice startled him and he flailed in what was most certainly an inelegant way, the cup of gelato falling onto his thigh and then leaking down onto the floor.

He lurched forward, scooping what he could back into the cup so it didn't stain the carpet.

"I was trying to give you space," he muttered. Thomas went into the kitchen to get a sponge and towel, returning to find his gelato still on the floor and Ben still in the doorway. He cleaned what he could, making note of the nervous way Ben shifted his weight from foot to foot in silence.

"Did you want to come in?" he finally asked, gathering his mess and taking it back to the kitchen.

Ben didn't answer; he just stepped inside and closed the door behind him. Thomas dumped everything in the sink and wiped his hands on the front of his shorts.

"Did you want a drink or something?"

Ben chuckled, giving him a tired smile. "That's what I asked you the night we met."

"And I said no."

"I won't," Ben said, taking a step toward the kitchen before stopping. Thomas closed his eyes, one hand braced against the edge of the countertop for support.

"Everything's where you remember," he said, gesturing toward the fridge. "It's not like I rearranged everything after we…"

Ben winced, but nodded. He joined Thomas in the kitchen, pulling the almost empty bottle of wine from the fridge and getting a glass from the cupboard. He emptied the bottle and took a tentative sip, eyes locked on Thomas's wavering form.

"How have things been?" Ben asked.

Thomas snorted, so uninterested in pleasantries, but not sure what else to say or do in the moment. "Not great."

"Did you want to talk about it?"

"I don't know what you want me to say, Ben. I don't know what you want from me." He brushed past Ben and out of the kitchen. He caught a whiff of Ben's natural musk and he had half a mind to ask him to go lay down on the bed, just so the sheets would smell like him again.

"I just...are you okay? Have you talked to..."

"No, I haven't talked to Dakota," he said, returning to the couch because he didn't know where else to go. "I haven't talked to Kenzie. I left Jennifer a scathing voicemail calling every decision she's ever made into question, but for some reason she didn't call me back. The only person I've talked to is Trent."

"His husband." Ben sat on the other end of the couch, far enough away someone would have assumed they were strangers.

"I wanted to make sure he was okay. I wanted to apologize to him."

"For what? You didn't do anything."

He shot Ben a sharp look, and Ben's cheeks flushed.

"Neither did you."

"Yeah," Ben said quietly. "I know."

"Oh?" This was news. This was a change. This was...

This was hope.

"I needed to work through it, and don't take this the wrong way, but your kid really did a number on me," Ben said with a half-laugh.

"I know."

"So much of the reason I didn't want anything serious with you in the first place was because of the way he made me feel. But after a while, I realized that I was thinking about it all wrong. That I deserved to be with you if that was what I wanted," Ben said.

Thomas fisted his hands together in his lap and dared a glance up at Ben, who was staring at the pothos on the opposite wall.

"It's silly that he's fucked me up the way he has."

"It's not silly," Thomas said. He looked down at his knuckles. The scrapes from the brick wall of the restaurant had long since faded, their marks superficial compared to the wound Ben's absence had left on his heart.

Ben didn't say anything for a while, and Thomas could barely manage a breath. The couch creaked, and Ben shifted, turning his knees inward toward Thomas's legs.

"I missed you," Ben whispered. "I *miss* you."

"I'm right here."

"Are you?"

Thomas blinked quickly and caught Ben's stare, which was now fixed solely on him. Thomas's own focus narrowed down to nothing more than the tired loneliness in Ben's eyes. There was more to the question and he could see the depths of the meaning in Ben's eyes.

"It's not too late," he said. "You didn't take too long. You haven't said the wrong thing. I would keep waiting—"

Ben cut him off with a kiss, throwing himself across the couch and tackling Thomas onto his back. He brought their mouths together in a tangle of chapped lips and teeth that had him gasping for breath beneath the onslaught of Ben's long-missed attention. He dropped one foot onto the floor, spreading his legs and making more room for Ben's body to slot against his, and he arched upward, wrapping his arms around Ben's back, desperate to not let him go again.

He didn't know which answer was the one Ben needed to hear, but he was thankful he'd found it.

"How long would you have waited for me?" Ben asked, kissing the corner of his mouth, his chin, his throat.

Thomas dropped his head against the arm of the couch,

giving Ben room to explore his body again. Stars danced against his ceiling and, for the first time in weeks, his cock came to life, eager for attention. It pulsed, pressing insistently against Ben's stomach as he continued to trace his tongue along the curving slope of his neck.

"However long you asked," he answered.

"Good." Ben still looked tired, but something familiar sparked behind his eyes. "I need a little bit more time, though, Thomas."

He did everything he could to school his expression, giving Ben a slow nod in answer. "How much longer?"

Ben looked over his shoulder toward the hallway that led to the bedroom. "I'm thinking about twenty seconds. That's how long it'll take to get into bed, right?"

CHAPTER 29

BEN

BEN KNEW AS SOON as he saw Thomas's tired and miserable face lit by the hot pink neon gelato sign that he was going to go after him. Lara essentially told him to fuck off and leave, but Thomas was quick. Ben didn't catch up to him before reaching his apartment, but he also hadn't run. He didn't want to look as desperate as he felt, and when he found Thomas's door open and his ass on the floor, something tightened in his chest that had him fearing he might be ready to throw up all over the floor. His first instinct was to reach for Thomas—it was always that. To touch him, to console him, to make things better, but that wasn't where they were at. That wasn't how they'd left things.

Kissing Thomas again was the biggest relief of his life, feeling Thomas's hands and his body heat, and the hard press of his erection. He shouldn't have assumed that Thomas would take him to bed, but he had to try. Ben was now the desperate one. Desperate to recoup the lost time and salvage things between them.

He was still looking toward the hallway when Thomas's arms wrapped around him and, with a very ungraceful grunt, lifted him. Ben wrapped his legs around Thomas's waist until Thomas was off the couch, well aware of how much he weighed, then he let his feet fall onto the carpet.

"You'll hurt yourself carrying me," he teased, grabbing Thomas's head in his hands and kissing him again. Thomas kept his arms around his body, leaning in with a needy groan. The press of knees encouraged Ben backward, and they stumbled down the hallway like that, arms and tongues entwined.

He fell back onto Thomas's bed, the familiar touch and smell of the bedding enough to make his cock leak against his underwear.

"Are we doing this?" he murmured, neck arched back as Thomas peppered kisses up his throat.

"I hope so," Thomas answered.

He grabbed the hem of Thomas's shirt and tugged it up, giving him a shove at the same time so there was space between them. "Please get naked, then."

Thomas huffed out a laugh and climbed backward off the bed, tossing his shirt onto the floor and making quick work of his gym shorts. On the bed, Ben wiggled out of his jeans and underwear, then finally his socks and his shirt. He grabbed his cock, the heat of his hand paired with the intent focus of Thomas's eyes, a welcome feeling after what felt like years without.

"What now?" Thomas fisted his own cock and raised a brow.

Memories of their first times together flashed through his mind and he glanced toward the nightstand. "Now you get your cock wet and you put it inside of me."

Thomas's breath hitched, but he reached for the lube, drizzling a generous amount down the length of his cock. With slick fingers, Thomas lay back over him, sliding between the cheeks of his ass and prodding insistently.

"The last man I was with told me I had a thick cock,"

Thomas whispered, easing his fingers into Ben's hole. "I should get you ready."

Ben let go of his cock, instead giving his balls a rough tug away from his body so he didn't come from something as simple as a good fingering, but Thomas had gotten better than good, the pads of his fingers dragging over Ben's prostate like that was exactly the thing he wanted to happen.

"I've been ready," he promised.

Ready in more ways than one.

With an almost practiced ease, Thomas pulled his fingers out and lined up the head of his cock. "Spread your legs, Benjamin. Make room for me."

Ben spread his legs wider, feet firmly planted in the sheets, and in the same breath, Thomas pressed inside of him. He didn't lie. He'd been ready for the penetration, but taking Thomas's cock into his ass after weeks without was more shocking than he expected. If not for Thomas's weight on top of him, Ben would have flown into orbit. He threaded his fingers into Thomas's hair and pressed their mouths together, licking and sucking moans and promises from between both of their lips.

Thomas seated himself fully, pushing the breath from his mouth with a sharp snap of his hips.

"I'm sorry," he apologized, Thomas's hands working fervently to brush his hair out of his eyes.

"No."

"I'm sorry," he said again, as Thomas started to move inside of him, turning the apology into a breathy moan.

"It's the past. I don't care about it. You're here now."

"And I'll be here. I want to be here."

Thomas's pace faltered, and with a flushed face and a tremble that wracked through his entire body, Thomas came. Heat pulsed inside of Ben's body and he shivered, muscles clenching to milk everything he could from Thomas's cock.

"Shit," Thomas mumbled, dropping his forehead against Ben's.

"I love you." He flipped Thomas onto his back and snatched the lube from the pillow, slicking up his painfully hard shaft. For good measure, because he liked how it felt when Thomas was inside of him, he circled his hips, making sure his channel had sucked every drop of cum from Thomas's cock, then he rose up, separating their bodies.

Thomas groaned his disapproval, and Ben made a quiet tutting sound with his tongue.

"Just wait," he cooed, reaching down with slick fingers and drawing light circles around Thomas's asshole. "Is this okay?"

"More than," Thomas rasped.

Ben eased a finger inside, then quickly added another. Even if things didn't work out between them, a thought he hated to entertain, he'd never for the rest of his life forget the way Thomas's eyes rolled back in his head when Ben teased his prostate. It must be tender after his orgasm, and beneath Ben's body, Thomas shuddered, thrashing to get away and humping his hand at the same time.

"There you go," he praised, testing a third finger against Thomas's pucker. "Get yourself open for me now that you've gotten off before me."

"Don't stop talking," Thomas begged, eyes flying wide when Ben got another finger into him. Heat flared up Ben's spine, and Thomas's body tightened around him.

"I'm going to come so deep inside of you," he whispered, spreading Thomas's body as much as he could manage with an unsteady hand and a desperate ache between his legs. He prepped him and readied the head of his cock against Thomas's now gaping hole, and then he slowly pressed in.

This was still something new to them, new to Thomas, and in that moment it was maybe more important than it had been the first time they did it. In Thomas's eyes, the promise and the love were clear as day. How had Ben ever walked away from him? He traced his finger over the place where their bodies joined, drawing another shiver out of Thomas's already unsteady form.

Ben's lashes fluttered when he bottomed out, cock pulsing with the need to thrust. He started to move, slow at first and then faster, fucking into Thomas until the cum inside of his own ass leaked out, slicking down his balls and his thighs. He grunted, hips snapping forward, hands roaming freely over Thomas's body.

"I'm sorry I left," he murmured, climbing onto the bed and forcing himself deeper into Thomas's body. Thomas shook his head, and Ben arranged himself against the headboard, hauling Thomas into a seated position on his lap. Thomas lowered himself around Ben's dick, head lolling back as he took the whole length of him at the new angle.

"Don't do it again," Thomas whispered.

"I won't." He gripped Thomas's waist and encouraged him up, then down, until he figured out the rhythm. He moved his hands again, tweaking Thomas's nipples and feeling his pulse strum like wildfire against his throat.

"Benjamin."

"I won't."

Thomas finally found a pace, and Ben grunted, not ready to come, not ready for it to be over. But Thomas's body wouldn't allow him more, the tight heat of his hole clamped down, forcing him over the edge. Ben came with a strangled groan, fingers fisting into Thomas's hair and scrabbling at his sweaty shoulders, trying to bring himself deeper, feeling Thomas in every way he could manage.

His head fell forward and he held Thomas tight, his cock spurting and emptying with furious pulses that left him feeling empty and boneless. Ben's vision went white, and then he felt Thomas's hands on him, his mouth, his sweat. The hot slide of Thomas's tongue against the seam of his lips, begging for him to open up and let him in.

Ben took them both down to the sheets, now wrecked with sweat and cum, and he kissed Thomas until his cock went soft and slipped free of the other man's body. He kissed him until they were both hard again, deep and languid swipes of the tongue that turned to spit-soaked mouths and clashing teeth, and then back to peppered pecks across his face again.

"What happens now?" Thomas asked, lying beside him long after Ben's mouth had turned sore from the kissing. Outside the window, the sky was pitch black, and Ben kicked the blankets off the bed so they were on the clean fitted sheet.

"You mean we can't pretend your son isn't my ex?" As much as he wished that future could be possible, he'd known even when he chased after Thomas earlier in the night that it wasn't. And that had been a huge part of what kept him away over the past two weeks too. Sometimes, it felt like it was too much for them both to reconcile. That Thomas raised the man who had done so much damage to Ben's mental health, and, at the end of the day, that Ben had slept with both father *and* son. Never mind it wasn't intentional, and if he'd known Thomas was Cody's dad, he would have sent him away the first night he'd shown up on his doormat.

Life had dealt them a messy hand, and it was up to them now how to rebound from the harm it had caused them both.

"I don't think so." Thomas gave him a soft laugh that sent gooseflesh up his arms. He rolled onto his side and wrapped his arm over Thomas's waist. His skin had turned cold from the sweat and he moaned, pressing back into Ben's hand.

"I think the guilt is going to be here awhile," he said. "I hate that. For both of us. But I love you and the guilt isn't enough to keep me away from you any longer."

Things with Thomas felt more solid and less certain simultaneously. But maybe that was what his other relationships had been lacking. It wasn't to say Ben wasn't bright-eyed about what the future could look like, but his eyes were open for what felt like the first time. He wasn't looking at the road ahead of him with rose-colored glasses. He saw the world for what it was, saw Thomas for *who* he was. And he'd never wanted anyone more. The self-assured way Thomas handled himself in all things, in and out of the bedroom, was one of the things that had first drawn Ben to him, and now in the aftermath of the hottest sex he'd ever had, it was what brought him back around.

He trailed his hands up Thomas's sides, counting his ribs before swooping down around his pecs and up his sternum. Thomas craned his head back, letting Ben's hand collar his throat, the length of his fingers pressing up on the underside of Thomas's chin. He dragged his thumb across Thomas's kiss-swollen mouth, wincing with a surprised groan of pleasure when Thomas took his thumb between his teeth and bit down. He dug his fingers in, pulling his thumb free and continuing along, twisting his hand up and over, feeling the sharp cut of Thomas's cheekbones and the swell of his brow. He traced his fingertips over the dark hair before leaning in and leaving the gentlest kiss as the corner of his mouth.

"Never let me leave you again," he said. "Unless it's the last time."

Thomas shook his head, eyes falling closed so his lashes fanned out across the cheeks Ben had just caressed. "I don't want to talk about that."

"Promise me," he pleaded, voice quiet as the night.

"I'm too old to make you promises of a long future." Thomas's mouth tightened into a sad kind of half-smile, but he opened his eyes and held Ben's stare with a gaze full of hope and honestly. "But I can promise you today. I can promise you right now. And I promise I won't let you leave me today, if that's enough for you."

Ben's heart twisted in his chest, tight and soft and too big all at the same time.

"Is it enough for you?" he asked.

"For today."

Ben nodded, and Thomas kissed him one more time.

CHAPTER 30
THOMAS

THE FRESHLY CUT key to his apartment had been burning a hole in his pocket for six days. He had every intention to give it to Ben, to try and be casual about it, but whenever *he* felt ready, the *time* felt wrong. So he kept it with him, every day things between the two of them growing stronger, their connection going deeper. But both of them needed to go back to work, forcing a new routine to develop. With phone calls and sleepovers and intimacy that lasted late into the night, Thomas was afforded the opportunity to truly get to know Ben, and to show himself in return.

The weekend rolled around, and Thomas woke early on Saturday morning, burying his face against the back of Ben's neck and dropping kisses against his hairline until Ben woke up.

"You can't be serious," Ben murmured, reaching behind him and pushing Thomas's face harder against him.

"I couldn't fuck you again even if I wanted to." He smiled against Ben's neck, rearranging himself when Ben rolled so they were chest to chest.

"Too old?"

"If three times in one night makes me old, then yes."

Ben laughed softly and kissed the spot on his chest above his heart.

"Do you have plans today?" Ben murmured, kissing him again.

"You."

"I thought you were spent." Ben reached down and palmed Thomas's tender and soft cock.

"I am," he whispered, even as the sensation of Ben's fingers caused him to groan and lean into the touch. "But when you came over for dinner, you said you wanted to go home shopping."

"Hmmn." Ben made a thoughtful sound that bordered on a pout, fist still loose around Thomas's dick. "How do you remember that?"

"Because I listen when you talk."

"Refreshing."

"You won't make me hard," he sighed, hips pumping against Ben's hand. "No matter how much I want that to happen."

"I'm not a quitter."

"You quit swimming," he teased.

"I quit swimming seriously." Ben squeezed him, then let his cock fall limp against his leg. "Now I do it for fun."

With that, Ben rolled him onto his back, straddling him and grinding his ass down against Thomas's cock. His eyes rolled back and he grunted, grabbing Ben's waist to still him.

"You wanted sheets," he murmured, Ben moving again under his hands. Even though he knew it wouldn't make him hard, the heat and the feel of Ben's body against his made him feel like anything was possible. "A new duvet."

"I like yours."

"We can get you mine."

"I like *yours*," Ben said again, taking his dick into his hand.

"Are you trying to put me into an early grave?" He tightened his hold on Ben's waist to still him again.

"So dramatic," Ben grumbled, crawling off of him and standing beside the bed, his cock still in his fist. Thomas rolled onto his side and propped himself up on his hand, elbow bent. He licked his lips, watching Ben work his length, although he didn't get much harder than Thomas had earlier.

"Sheets and what else?" he asked.

"I don't know." Ben leaned against the dresser, letting his cock land against his leg. He folded his arms in front of his chest and sighed. "I painted before, like I was just really inspired by how *you* this place is and I wanted my place to be *me*."

"We can browse." He sat up and turned, setting his feet onto the floor and stretching toward the ceiling. "Get what suits you."

"After a shower?"

"And coffee." He stood and stepped forward, landing a soft kiss against Ben's mouth. "And breakfast."

"I like all of those things." Ben smiled against his lips and kissed him back. "Are you sure you can't go again?"

"I'm positive that I need at least half a day to recover, on either side."

Ben chuckled and sidestepped away from him, starting toward the bathroom like it was his own place. The happiness that now permanently lived inside of Thomas's chest expanded and twisted, growing into a bigger and messier—and better— thing. He didn't have a name for it, but he followed Ben into the bathroom, pulling two clean towels out of the cabinet and dropping them on the counter.

"You know, if you didn't have such a thick dick, I could probably go again."

He arched a brow. "Is that really what you'd prefer?"

"Absolutely not." Ben bent over, swaying his ass in Thomas's face, and turned the shower on. Ben checked the temperature and stepped under the spray, gesturing for Thomas to join him.

The shower went easy enough, with roaming hands that

distracted without derailing, and then they were clean and rinsed, dry and dressed. Thomas made them both coffee and Ben fried a couple eggs. The ease with which Ben already moved around his space did something else to the feeling in his chest and he reached into his pocket, fingers tracing over the sharp edges of the key.

"Ben." He switched off the coffee pot and turned, key cutting dangerously into his palm.

"Yeah?" Ben glanced quickly at him, offering him a double take when he caught Thomas's apparently serious expression. "Oh, no. What's wrong?"

"Nothing," he said quickly, fist tightening around the key. "Nothing. I promise."

"Okay…"

"I fully…I just…I'm happy you want to make your space yours." He cleared his throat and pulled his hand out of his pocket, spinning the key so it became apparent what he held. "But I wouldn't mind if you also wanted to make part of my space yours too."

"Thomas."

"I'm not asking you to move it, so don't…" He groaned and inhaled, trying to get himself back on track. "I want you to be here whenever you want to be here. I want you to be comfortable here."

Ben held out his hand, palm up, and he dropped the key. They both looked at it, like it was magical or unexpected, and then Ben closed his fist around it so tightly his knuckles turned white.

"Thank you," Ben whispered.

Behind him, the pan popped and sizzled, shaking Thomas out of the moment.

"The eggs are burning," he said.

"Eggs don't burn." Ben shoved the pan onto the back burner

and turned off the stove, eyes still on his closed fist. "You really want me to have a key?"

"I'll even clean out a dresser drawer for you. Some space in the closet."

"Are you sure?" Ben opened his fist, one finger at a time, staring down at the key in his hand and the lines it had cut into his palm.

"Very."

"I love you." Ben closed the space between them and smashed their lips together, his hand and the key pressed between their bodies.

"I love you."

"I'll get you a key too," Ben said. "To my place."

"You don't have to."

"I want things to be equal between us."

Thomas closed Ben's fingers back around the key and kissed his knuckles. "I know you do. But I'm comfortable in my space and, because of that, I'm ready to share it. You...you're still learning how to lean into that. It's important to me that you have the opportunity to make your space yours before we make it ours."

Ben exhaled loudly, enough of a protestation without any words to follow.

"You can give me a key if you want me to have it," he added with a lopsided grin. "But I'm not going to use it until you're ready."

"You're stubborn."

"I know." He stepped back, reaching for his forgotten coffee and taking a drink while he eyed Ben over the brim of the mug. "So what color scheme are you thinking?"

"I like the darks you have here." Ben placed the key into his pocket and then reached around him for the second mug of coffee. He cleared his throat and plated the eggs, which had long gone cold. Thomas carried the plates to the table anyway, sitting down and waiting for Ben to join him.

"For my space, yes. But yours?"

Ben forked some egg into his mouth, a rough expression flashing across his face as he chewed. "I honestly love gold. As an accent."

"Gold is a good color."

"With something dark." Ben rolled his eyes. "Like navy or green."

"Sounds like a good start to things."

Ben gave him a shy smile and Thomas forced himself through ingesting the cold eggs and coffee. They washed up together, and while Ben was freshening up in the bathroom, Thomas went into the bedroom and rearranged his drawers. Ben found him in there, the top right drawer in the dresser now open and empty.

"That one mine?" Ben asked, hip checking him.

"All yours."

"Do I get the other nightstand too?"

"Only if you promise to keep the lube well stocked," he said with a laugh.

"What if I wanted to fill this whole drawer with dildos?"

"Is that what you want?"

"I'm just asking."

"It's yours," he said. "Do whatever you want with it."

Ben went to Thomas's underwear drawer and pulled it open, rifling around in the back until he found the small prostate massager. Thomas wanted to say he'd forgotten about the little thing, but he hadn't. He just hadn't had an occasion to use it, with Ben being as good with his hands as he was. Ben dropped the massager into the empty drawer and swiped his hands back and forth, like he'd just finished a task.

"You're a fan of that one?" he asked.

"I'm a fan of using it on you." Ben pushed the drawer closed. "Ready to go?"

"Very. I'll drive."

Thomas drove to the home store where he'd bought his sheets. It wasn't a name brand, top-of-the-line place, but it wasn't cheap either. Ben grabbed his hand as soon as they were out of the car, but he let Thomas lead the way into the bed section. He pointed out the sheets that he'd bought, and Ben threw them in the cart, taking control and steering them toward the small furniture section in the back corner.

"What do you think about this?" Ben asked him, coming to stop at a pair of side tables with white tops and sharp gold bars making up the sides.

"What do you think about them?" he asked.

Ben huffed. "If I didn't like them, I wouldn't ask your opinion."

"It's your apartment. I have no opinion."

Thomas didn't like the tables. They were awkwardly shaped and would look horrible with Ben's couch, but that was for Ben to learn—or not—and not for him to say.

"I wish the gold parts were a little thinner and like..." Ben drew an angular shape from the bottom of the table to the top.

"Then wait and see if you find something you like more." He rested his chin on Ben's shoulder and kissed his ear. "Don't settle."

"You're right." Ben smiled and headed further down the aisle. Thomas took the cart and followed behind him, seeing plenty of things he himself liked that Ben brushed by without a second look.

Good.

"This one is nice." Ben reached out and dragged his finger across another white table, this one wrapped with thin metal rods twisted into triangles and hexagons. It was complicated and messy, but simple at the same time. Thomas didn't hate it, but he kept his face neutral. Ben flicked his stare from the table to Thomas and back again.

"They have a coffee table that matches it," he offered, pointing a little farther down the aisle.

"Then I think it's perfect."

Ben didn't hesitate, doing his best to stack the two side tables in the oversized cart and jogging down the aisle to pick up the coffee table.

"Let's go drop these off at the register and get another cart," he suggested. "I assume you want to shop more."

Ben peered at him from over the edge of the coffee table, his eyes excited and eager, sending a thrill up Thomas's spine.

"Right," Ben agreed. "We're just getting started."

CHAPTER 31
BEN

AFTER BEN FINISHED SPENDING FAR TOO much money at the store, they'd both gone back to his apartment. Together. Thomas had hovered while he washed the new sheets and put them on the bed, and he'd remained silent while Ben fought with arranging his new furniture in a way that felt right. He liked the company, and he appreciated the space. At first, he'd been put off by Thomas's lack of input, but the longer he rolled the idea of it around in his head, the more sense it made. Thomas was only trying to do him a service. Finally settled, he opened a bottle of water from the fridge and leaned against the corner of his dining room table, giving the newly furnished living room a onceover.

"What do you think?" Thomas asked, standing beside him.

"I like it." He didn't bother to ask if Thomas liked it because he knew Thomas wouldn't answer.

"Did you want to get dinner?"

"Honestly, yes." He twisted the cap back onto the bottle and set it down behind him. "But Lara has been pushy about how long it's been since I've seen her."

"I can take off."

"I...I'd like to see her, but I'd like you to come. If that's something you're okay with."

"I like your friend, Ben. I don't mind coming; I just don't want to intrude."

Ben sighed. "I've never heard you talk about any friends."

"I don't really have any," Thomas admitted, his throat turning a dark red just above the collar of his shirt. "Casualty of the divorce, I suppose."

"Who do you talk to when you're sad?"

Thomas scoffed, rolling his eyes and pushing away from the table. "My plants."

"That's..."

"It's pathetic, I know." Thomas cleared his throat and pasted on a smile. "I'd love to come with you and Lara as long as she's okay with it."

"Our friend Owen too."

"The more, the merrier."

Ben pulled his phone out of his pocket to text his best friend. He snapped a picture of the living room and sent it to her, then asked what she and Owen had decided to do. She answered him quickly with a text.

Lara: *We're coming over to eat takeout on your new coffee table.*
Ben: *Bring enough for 4. Thomas is here.*
Lara: *Of course he is.*
Ben: *Is that okay?*
Lara: *Of course it is.*
Ben: *You're as bad as he is with texting. Can you give me a freaking emoji or something so I can gauge your tone????*

Lara sent him a middle finger emoji.

He dropped his phone onto the table with a loud clatter and turned to Thomas.

"They want to come over," he said. "So they'll get here when they get here."

"Do we have enough time to…" Thomas tilted his head to the side, one eyebrow arched.

"I thought you needed a period to convalesce?" he teased.

"I've had all day."

Ben stepped toward him, reaching down in the same breath and flipping open the button on Thomas's jeans. He unzipped him and slid his hand behind the waistband of Thomas's underwear, taking hold of his half-hard cock.

"Are you asking me to come?" He tightened his grasp, giving Thomas a long and slow stroke.

Thomas's breath shuddered out of him like thunder, and he bent forward, bracing himself on the back of one of the dining chairs. Ben continued to tease his length, not giving him enough to get him there, but not so little he could forget it.

"Benjamin."

He rumbled a low groan, picking up the pace. "You know I love when you say my name like that during sex."

"I do want to come," Thomas panted, hips bucking into his hand.

"Should I let you come?"

"Please."

"Should I *make* you come?" he asked, taking a step closer and adjusting the angle of his fist so he could get a better grip on Thomas's now hard cock.

Thomas shuddered again, working his jaw and bracing himself against the chair. Ben smirked, appreciating the tension that unraveled through Thomas's body as he fought to not come in his pants.

"Keep talking," Thomas rasped.

"You love my mouth, don't you?"

Thomas answered with a jerky nod.

"You like when I tell you what I'm doing?" he asked. "When I tell you what I want you to do?"

"Benjamin." His name came out of Thomas's mouth like a feral growl.

They both liked to talk during sex, but this felt like a new layer. This was a little more demanding, a little more controlling. It wasn't something he'd played around with before, but based off the way Thomas's body responded to it, he definitely wanted to.

"Is that a yes, Thomas?"

"Yes."

A loud bang on the door startled them both, and Thomas's expression immediately fell.

"Who is it?" Ben shouted, not letting go of Thomas's dick.

"You know it's me," Lara called back.

Thomas shook his head, a silent plea for Ben to not stop.

"One second," he yelled back.

"I don't want you to come yet," Ben whispered, not stopping.

"I'm close."

"I want you to save it for later." He pressed a kiss against the base of Thomas's throat, tasting sweat. "So you can put it inside me."

Thomas's body shook, his cock leaking a stream of precum against Ben's fingers. His orgasm was dangerously close, and for as much as Ben wanted him to come, he wanted to tease Thomas too. He wanted to drive Thomas mad and then be on the receiving end when he finally cut loose. It was the moment their entire relationship had been building toward anyway. From their first time together with Thomas's quiet confidence that he knew what to do—even though he never had before—to the way he let Ben take the lead to help him explore. Over the months they'd been together, Thomas had gotten more comfortable with himself, with Ben, and that was great. But Ben wanted to see what it was like when his control snapped. He wanted Thomas so delirious with want for him that he wasn't worried about prep or tenderness.

Ben already knew Thomas loved him.

He wanted Thomas to *fuck him*.

"I want you so much," Thomas whispered, fingers tangling into Ben's hair and holding him against the crook of his neck.

"Ben!" Lara shouted, banging against the door.

"I want you," Thomas said again.

"You can have me." He tightened his fingers around the head of Thomas's slippery cock, then tucked him back behind the waistband of his underwear and zipped his pants back up.

"Benjamin," Thomas growled.

"You can *take* me," he corrected, smoothing his hand over the ridge of Thomas's erection. "Later tonight."

"You're cruel." Thomas cleared his throat, expression pained, but approval and interest sparkled in the dark pools of his eyes.

"Are you okay?" he asked. "Honestly. With…"

"Yes. I just…it hurts. But it's good."

Ben smiled, pressing his lips against Thomas's, rewarding him with a chaste and far too quick kiss.

"As soon as they're gone," he promised.

"If you don't open this door, I'm using my key," Lara called out.

"Do you need a minute?" he asked.

"I'll be fine."

Thomas shifted his weight and adjusted himself, finally giving Ben a quick nod. Ben went to the door and pulled it open, coming face to face with Lara's narrowed eyes and Owen's amused smirk.

"Sorry," he said by way of greeting. "Thomas needed help with something."

"I bet." Lara looked around him, giving Thomas a onceover. "Good to see you again, Thomas."

"Lara."

Ben stepped to the side so Lara and Owen could come in. Owen gave Thomas a questioning look, his brow furrowed.

"Owen, this is my boyfriend, Thomas. Thomas, this is my friend Owen," Ben said.

"Nice to meet you." Thomas held out his hand and Owen took it, features still pinched in confusion. "Everything okay?"

"You just look familiar."

The muscles in Thomas's shoulders tightened, and Ben knew without him saying anything he wasn't worried about being outed, but from being recognized by someone who'd known him during his life with Jennifer.

"Do I?"

"Do you work downtown at the Greeley building?" Owen asked.

"Yeah."

"That must be it." The tension left Owen's face and he smiled. "I work there too. Or, rather, at the sandwich cart out front."

"I love that place," Thomas said, the tightness from his own body visibly unwinding. Ben also let out a breath, and Lara dumped all of the takeout onto the coffee table.

"So, what do you do there?" Owen asked, and Ben left them to the conversation, instead joining Lara by the couch.

"Do you like it?" he asked.

"It's nice. It's unexpected."

"I feel like a lot of shit has been unexpected lately," he said.

She snorted, rolling her eyes. "Tell me about it."

When he'd found out Cody was Thomas's son, Lara was the first person he called and the only person he'd confided in. She thought him walking away from Thomas was stupid, but he didn't expect her to understand the complicated web that Cody had wrapped around his brain during their relationship. Even though he was mostly better and back with Thomas, even though things were better than they'd been before, there were still dark memories that lingered in the corners of his mind that he hadn't been able to fully clear out yet.

"But things are better now," he said.

Lara threw a quick look toward Thomas and Owen, who were laughing and leaning in close while they talked.

"Good." Lara flipped her wrist dismissively toward the dining room. "Come eat."

"There's a table?" Owen pointed beside him to the dining room table.

"Coffee table is new," Thomas told him.

"So don't spill," Lara said.

Ben slid down onto his ass, sticking his legs beneath the table and resting his back against the couch. Thomas joined him, making a pained noise in the back of his throat while he situated himself and crossed his legs.

"You good?" he asked.

"I'll survive," Thomas said, leaning close and lowering his voice. "But you night not."

"That's what I was hoping to hear."

That answer drew a sharp turn of Thomas's head, his eyes locking on Ben's and searching his face for the answer to a question that neither of them had actually asked. It was a new thing—again—and a big thing, and something they would have to talk more about when they were alone. And hopefully after Ben had been fucked through the mattress.

"Enough sex eyes," Lara admonished.

Thomas's cheeks turned pink, but he hesitated before looking away. "What's for dinner?"

"Chinese," she answered. "Because you can't go wrong with four kinds of protein."

From the far side of the table, Owen snorted and Lara rolled her eyes again, flinging a pair of chopsticks at his face. He smacked them away with a laugh, and Thomas finally looked elsewhere.

Lara said something that he didn't hear and Owen laughed again. Containers of food were opened and they ate together on the floor of Ben's apartment, his life still coming together, but feeling authentically his for the first time in years. Beside him, Thomas ate, chopsticks in one hand, the other resting firmly and possessively on Ben's thigh. The heat burned through his jeans, and while he was happy to have his friends around, he wanted them gone in the same breath. He wanted the things he and Thomas had begun to build, not just earlier that night, but in the weeks and months they'd been together too.

It blew his mind to think that the first time Thomas stepped through the door, Ben had told him no feelings. That he'd treated this man, this handsome and giving and tolerant and brave man, as nothing more than a rebound fuck. Even then, Thomas had deserved more from him.

"Excuse me." Ben jumped up, Thomas's hand falling onto the carpet. He ran into the bedroom and pulled open the top drawer of the nightstand on the side of the bed that Thomas favored. He knew exactly what he was looking for and it was right there on top as he'd left it. A brand new key beside a well-used bottle of lube. He'd put it there on purpose, for Thomas to discover on his own, but there was no way Ben could wait another minute longer to give it to him.

"Everything okay?" Thomas's figure appeared in the doorway, his body silhouetted by the hall light behind him.

"Yes." Ben came around the foot of the bed, key in his hand. "Yes. Everything is good."

He went to Thomas and grabbed his hand, pressing the key against his palm with a nod.

"This is for you."

"I meant what I said before," Thomas told him.

"I know. And you can mean it all you want, but I was thinking while we were eating and I wanted you to have it now.

Because I'm ready for you to have it now. Use it whenever *you* want, but it's important to me that you have it."

"Ben." Thomas put they key into his pocket without looking at it, purely trusting what Ben had given him to be real. Thomas's hands moved to his face, cradling him like that as he stroked his thumbs across Ben's cheeks. "Thank you."

"I love you," Ben answered back, leaning into Thomas's hand.

"I love you too. But what brought this on? I mean, right now?"

"I was reminiscing in my head," he admitted with a small frown. "Thinking about how things were when we first met."

"It wasn't that long ago."

"And we're in such a different place now. A better place."

"We are," Thomas agreed.

"So, I wanted you to have it. Because we're in that place together. Even if we learn some things on our own and grow separately in the ways we need, I want to do it *with* you."

Thomas let out a huff of breath and smiled, eyes crinkling around the edges.

"I want that too."

Ben surged forward, throwing his arms around Thomas's neck and kissing him. Thomas moaned and leaned against the door frame, mouth opening without question or thought for Ben's tongue. Immediately, his brain and his body went back to before, with his hand around Thomas's cock on the couch. The words they'd said, the things he'd promised.

"I can't," Thomas muttered against him, hips bucking forward even as his hands pushed Ben away. "Not until we're alone."

"I know," he groaned, cock throbbing against his leg. "I know."

"Later," Thomas promised. "Later, I'll bring you back into this room, Benjamin. I'll take your clothes off and I'll put my tongue up that tight hole of yours until you're writhing against those brand new sheets for how bad you want me."

"God."

"And when I think you're good and ready for my cock, I'll give it to you."

Ben's lashes fluttered and something twisted in his gut that made his balls heavy and hot. "How do you do that?"

"Hmn?" Thomas reached forward and smoothed Ben's hair away from his face and then straightened his clothes.

"How do you turn the tables on me like that?"

"Everything is give and take," Thomas said, adjusting his own cock, his own clothes. "But for now, your friends are waiting for us."

"Can I throw them out?" He glanced longingly toward the bed.

Thomas chuckled and shook his head. "The longer you entertain, the more worth your while I'll make it when they're gone."

"But it hurts," he whined.

Thomas took a step backward down the hallway, crooking a finger for Ben to follow after him.

"But like all good things, it's worth it, yes?" Thomas asked. "*I'm* worth it?"

"You're worth it, Thomas," he agreed. "Very."

CHAPTER 32
THOMAS

THOMAS HAD BEEN on edge all day.

Literally.

Ben had woken him up an hour before his alarm, hot mouth wrapped around his cock and slick fingers teasing against his hole. Ben brought him to the edge three times, then leaned back, wiped his fingers on his thighs, and offered to make him coffee to go. Thomas had intended to jack off in the shower, but the touch of his own hand felt like sandpaper against his dick, so he ignored his half-hard cock and busied himself with getting clean and then ready for work.

In the kitchen, Ben had met him with swollen lips and a smirk, handed him his coffee, and promised to see him later. Ben had no idea about the world of hurt he would be in for when Thomas got home from work, or maybe he did. This was a game they'd started to play as they eased into new routines together, learning and testing limits and boundaries in all of the best ways.

When Ben got like that, it was his torturous way of asking to get fucked though the wall, and Thomas was more than willing to oblige him. He'd gotten more accustomed to taking Ben's cock up his own ass, but there was something to be said for the way he could take Ben apart from the top too.

But he'd struggled through the day and come out the other end. He'd grabbed a late lunch with Owen, who'd become more of a friend than he'd expected, and he talked to Kenzie on the phone while he drove home. They rarely talked about Jennifer—or Dakota—but sometimes she had important news to share. Today brought the update that Jennifer and Jarrod had broken up, which didn't surprise him, and Dakota had moved in with his mother, which did. Trent had apparently made good on his promise to leave, and instead of being the adult he was, Dakota had retreated back to the safety of Jennifer's consolation. It felt fitting that the two of them ended up under the same roof, left to think about the repercussions of their miserable and selfish actions.

Before saying goodbye, he promised Kenzie brunch on Saturday with her girlfriend and Ben, then he put his phone on do not disturb and took the stairs to Ben's apartment. He let himself in with the key Ben had given him, as he often did these days, catching Ben off-guard in the bathroom. He'd just showered, but the smell of chlorine permeated the apartment, and Thomas knew he'd been for a swim.

"You're off early," Ben said, using his hand to shake the water out of his hair. The bath towel hung low around his hips, the sharp V of muscle pointing right where Thomas wanted to go the most.

"I had a hard day," he said.

Ben's mouth twitched into a smirk and he adjusted his hold on the towel. He hadn't even had time to knot it. "Did you now?"

He made an affirmative noise in the back of his throat while he worked loose the knot on his tie. Ben's eyes flickered toward the navy blue and pink floral strip of fabric, and he dropped the towel at his feet.

"Very hard," he confirmed, dragging his tongue across the front of his teeth. He draped his tie over his shoulder, then removed his belt. He dropped it on the floor and they both watched it land, half on the tile, half on the towel.

"Was that my fault?" Ben asked.

"Very much."

"Are you going to take it out on me?"

He chuckled, shaking his head even though the answer was yes. This was exactly what he wanted and exactly what Ben had been angling for in the morning when he'd worked Thomas into an absolute uncontrolled frenzy.

"Do you think I should?" he asked.

"Probably best," Ben rasped.

"Give me your hands, then."

This was a new thing for them, newer than the rest, but Ben produced his wrists, underside turned up and arms extended. Thomas made quick work, leaving enough space between the silk and Ben's skin that it could breathe before he knotted the tie twice. The knots were sturdy and he knew he'd need scissors to get the material separated, but he had no qualms about losing a tie to the cause.

He wrapped the loose end of the material around his fingers and led Ben through the apartment and into the bedroom. Ben's arms fell, the silk lying over his already hard cock, and Thomas licked his lips while he worked open the buttons of his dress shirt.

"Leave it on," Ben whispered, chewing his bottom lip between his teeth. His pupils were shot, dark black pools of want that implored Thomas to debauch him.

"Hmn?"

"Leave your clothes on," Ben said. "Fuck me with your clothes on."

"You think I'm fucking you?" He undid his fly and pulled his cock out from his underwear, staying dressed. He could touch himself finally, but he knew once he buried himself inside of Ben's body, he would burst.

"I can't very well fuck you," Ben rasped, raising his bound hands in the air.

"Oh." He tutted his tongue against the roof of his mouth. "I bet you could. But that's not in your cards today, Benjamin."

Thomas moved quickly, grabbing the lube with one hand and bending Ben over the bed with the other. Ben arched his ass up, and Thomas pressed the small of his back, holding him down against the sheets. He flipped open the lube with his other hand and poured it down his cock. The slippery liquid ran down his length, coating his cock, his balls, and his slacks. Nothing a little dry cleaning couldn't fix. He made sure the whole of his erection shone with lube, and he pushed the head of his cock against Ben's hole and snapped his hips forward.

The tip of his dick breached that tight ring of muscle, and Thomas growled, easing in deeper and spreading Ben wider.

"Shit," Ben cursed, hips wriggling as Thomas gave him half an inch at a time. It was cruel, half an inch in, half an inch out, an inch in, an inch out, over and over until the water from the shower mixed with the sweat that had beaded up against Ben's spine and Thomas was seated so fully the rough wool of his slacks pressed against the backs of Ben's thighs.

"Is this what you wanted?" he asked, easing back slowly and sliding in. He knew it wasn't what Ben wanted, and it wasn't what he wanted either. Ben wanted him to lose control, but after the day he'd had, he wasn't going to make it easy.

"More," Ben grunted, trying to fuck himself back and get some friction.

Thomas had to steady himself because he wanted more too.

He wanted everything.

"Thomas," Ben whined, turning his head to the side with one cheek flat against the sheets. "Please. More."

Ben didn't need to ask again.

Thomas's control snapped as fast as his hips, and he buried himself into Ben's tight and slick hole with a low grunt.

His movement was rewarded with Ben's mouth twisting open into a silent cry, and he fucked so hard the sound of their skin slapping together was quick to drown out the sound of his heartbeat in his ears. His fingers scrabbled along Ben's sweaty back, finally finding purchase—and leverage—around Ben's muscular shoulders. He fucked him hard and deep, pulling Ben back and off the bed, bending his knees so he could get him at a different angle.

Thomas reached around, bending Ben's arms at the elbow so they sat below his chin, and with his finger hooked through the tie that kept him restrained, Thomas buried himself balls deep, his orgasm crashing into him like a tsunami. He fucked through it, the imbalance of being fully clothed against Ben's nakedness a heady power trip on top of his already desperate need to come. Thomas didn't falter, body still moving with short and deep thrusts as cum sprayed from the tip of his dick.

The orgasm was messy—he could tell by the way it took him apart. By the gooseflesh that covered him, to the cold sweat, and the frenzied heartbeat. Against him, Ben cried out, the strangled sound of a painful orgasm that Thomas had become familiar with in the past weeks. He finally slowed himself down to a stop, waiting for his cock to soften and come out of Ben's body on its own before turning Ben around and sitting him down on the bed.

Ben grimaced, joined hands falling onto his thighs, his cock red and soft beneath his cum-covered stomach.

Thomas fell to his knees at Ben's feet and picked at the knot, surprised at how steady his hands were and how freely the material gave way. He would have cut it if he had to, but now he could save it as a memento. He unwrapped the tie from Ben's wrist and cast it aside, rubbing his skin and bending low to drop kisses against Ben's wrist bones and the tops of his hands.

When he felt he'd paid enough attention, he slid down lower, resting his head on Ben's thigh with a quiet sigh. Ben moved his hands, making circles with his wrists before settling his fingers into Thomas's sweaty hair.

"Hard day, then?" Ben asked, voice scratchy from how loudly he'd cried out while Thomas fucked him. This moment, this man...these were all things Thomas never used to think he'd be able to have. Meeting Ben had been a fluke, falling in love with him had been an accident, and the rest of it...

Maybe that had been fate.

He knew it felt that way sometimes, like he'd never had a chance, never had a choice. Everything he'd done, every decision he'd made had led him to this life, this future, with Ben by his side. For as hard as things had been before, he'd live the same life over again a thousand times if it would bring him back to Ben's life when all was said and done.

"Worth it," he murmured. "It's always worth it with you."

Ben made a pleased sound, fingers still working gently through Thomas's hair, and then he spoke so soft, Thomas barely heard the words, "So are you."

ACKNOWLEDGMENTS

Thank you to all my readers who HAD SO MUCH FAITH that I would be able to write a standalone. I really couldn't have done this without the intense and petty desire to prove you all wrong.

ALSO BY KATE HAWTHORNE

Not Ready for Love

Not Allowed

To Love You

Until Now

Room for Love

Reckless

Heartless

Faultless

Fearless

Limitless

A Very Messy Motel Brothers Wedding

Giving Consent

Worth the Risk

Worth the Wait

Worth the Fight

Worth the Chance

Secrets in Edgewood

A Taste of Sin

The Cost of Desire

A Love Made Whole

Secrets in Edgewood: The Complete Series

Two Truths and a Lie

A Real Good Lie

A Cold Hard Truth

A Matter of Fact

Duality

Dual Destruction

Dual Surrender

Dual Defiance

The Lonely Hearts Stories

His Kind of Love

The Colors Between Us

Love Comes After

Until You Say Otherwise

Standalones

Daybreak - Vino & Veritas

Unfettered

Dreams

A Thousand Lifetimes

COLLABORATIONS

With E.M. Denning

Irreplaceable

Future Fake Husband

Future Gay Boyfriend

Future Ex Enemy

With J.R. Gray

May the Best Man Win

ABOUT KATE HAWTHORNE

With over two dozen published romances to her name, Kate Hawthorne has built a recognizable brand around telling emotional stories that pack a figurative (and sometimes literal) punch.

Existing on a steady diet of wine and coffee, Kate spends her days dreaming up angsty stories full of heat, kink, and heart. Kate now lives in Louisville, where she writes romance, reads romance, and hides her curly hair from the humidity.

Visit her website
http://www.katehawthornebooks.com

Sign up for Kate's newsletter
http://www.katehawthornebooks.com/extra

facebook.com/authorkatehawthorne
twitter.com/katewriteswords
instagram.com/kate.hawthorne
patreon.com/katehawthorne